Praise for

# THE VINTAGE TEACUP CLUB

"This heartwarming story of finding new friends is a lovely debut."
—Carole Matthews, bestselling author of *The Christmas Party*

"A delicious brew of love and friendship."
—Trisha Ashley, bestselling author of *Every Woman for Herself*

"As charming and cozy as the English village of its setting, *The Vintage Teacup Club* celebrates the transformative power of female friendship. Readers who enjoy a blend of drama, romance and humor will be smitten!"
—Andrea Lochen, author of *The Repeat Year*

"A heartwarming, quintessentially British tale."      —*Stylist*

"A stylish, upmarket bit of chick lit."      —*The Bookseller*

"Greene crafts an endearing tale of three women who form a friendship after finding a vintage tea set that they then agree to share . . . The perfect book to escape everyday reality and enjoy curled up, sipping a cup of tea."      —*RT Book Reviews*

ALSO BY VANESSA GREENE

*The Vintage Teacup Club*

# THE SEAFRONT TEAROOM

## Vanessa Greene

BERKLEY BOOKS, NEW YORK

**BERKLEY**

**An imprint of Penguin Random House LLC**
**375 Hudson Street, New York, New York 10014**

Copyright © 2014 by Vanessa Greene.
Penguin supports copyright. Copyright fuels creativity, encourages diverse voices,
promotes free speech, and creates a vibrant culture. Thank you for buying an authorized
edition of this book and for complying with copyright laws by not reproducing, scanning, or
distributing any part of it in any form without permission. You are supporting writers and
allowing Penguin to continue to publish books for every reader.

BERKLEY® and the "B" design are registered trademarks of Penguin Random House LLC.
For more information, visit penguin.com.

Library of Congress Cataloging-in-Publication Data

Greene, Vanessa.
The seafront tearoom / Vanessa Greene.
pages cm
ISBN 978-0-425-28126-0 (paperback)
1. Female friendship—Fiction.  I.  Title.
PR6107.R4443S43 2015
823'.92—dc23
2015025758

PUBLISHING HISTORY
Sphere paperback edition / October 2014
Berkley trade paperback edition / December 2015

PRINTED IN THE UNITED STATES OF AMERICA

10  9  8  7  6  5  4  3  2  1

Cover photo by Sanja Kulusic/Trevillion Images.
Cover design by Lesley Worrell.
Interior text design by Laura K. Corless.

Penguin
Random
House

*For Susan*

# Acknowledgments

Thanks to Manpreet Grewal, my brilliant editor, for her ideas, inspiration and attention to detail at every stage. Also to my agents, Caroline Hardman and Joanna Swainson, for their invaluable advice and support.

I'm grateful to the team at Sphere for working with such determination and creativity to get this book out to readers. In particular, Thalia Proctor, Sian Wilson, Sarah Shea, Stephie Melrose and all the folk in Sales. Thanks also to all the staff at Berkley Books across the pond, who publish my books so beautifully.

I couldn't have written this without my mum, Sheelagh, who gave me space to write by looking after my son, and gave me useful feedback on the first draft. Thanks also to Susan, his other grandmother, for her friendship, and her kindness in sharing my novels in Chestnut Avenue and beyond.

To Caroline and Emma, fellow friends of books—and to Katharine, Lisa and all the girls. Thanks also to Miki, Elaine, Paula and Bee—for the laughter, no-holds-barred conversation and plentiful cake while we all got used to being mums.

Thanks to James for always being by my side. And finally to Finn, who, as I finished writing this book, learned how to turn a page. I'm sorry this one doesn't have flaps or squeakers.

In a tranquil location overlooking the sandy cove, this tearoom is a place caught in time. Once inside, with a cup of expertly selected tea warming your hands, you'll rediscover something that, in the hurry of life, is too easily forgotten. A hidden gem, a place you'll want to whisper about to only the closest of friends.

—*INDULGE* MAGAZINE FEATURE
ON "BRITAIN'S SECRET TEAROOMS"

# The Seafront Tearoom, est. 1913

## LETTY'S CLASSIC AFTERNOON TEA
Served on a tiered cake stand.

### SAVORY:

A selection of finger sandwiches—
cucumber, smoked salmon
and egg mayonnaise

### SWEET:

Raisin and apple scones warm from the oven,
with clotted cream

Victoria sponge

Rose and pistachio cake

Profiteroles

Strawberries dipped in chocolate

## A SELECTION OF LOOSE-LEAF TEAS:

English Breakfast, Assam, Darjeeling,
Earl Grey, Jasmine, Spiced Orange

# PART ONE

Love and scandal
are the best sweeteners of tea.

—HENRY FIELDING

# 1

Thursday, August 14
*Scarborough*

Kat Murray and her three-year-old son, Leo, walked together along the beach in flip-flops, his small hand in hers. The rock shops and arcades of the South Bay were busy with holiday-makers and weekenders, making the most of the rare burst of warm sunshine on the British coast. As the two of them neared the harbor, the familiar smell of fresh-caught fish from the pier reminded Kat that they were almost home.

Leo dropped his mother's hand and ran toward the shop underneath their flat, with its neon-pink sign and a doughnut model that was bigger than him. She ran after him, laughing. "I'm the winner!" he called out, touching the doughnut.

"Not again," Kat said, sighing in defeat, then smiling at him. "One day. One day I'll beat you." She got her keys out of her bag.

She unlocked the front door and Leo climbed the hallway stairs ahead of her. She and Jake had moved into the flat four years before, when she was twenty-two, in love and carefree. A lot had changed while they'd been living there.

"What's for tea today, Mummy?" Leo called over his shoulder.

Kat tried to recall what was left in the kitchen cupboards and fridge.

"Dinosaurs," she replied. "On the menu tonight, sir, are

Tyrannosaurus rexes and diplodocuses. I hope you're not veg-etarian."

"No way," Leo said joyfully. "I love eating T. rexes."

Upstairs, Kat took a slice of rye bread and a sharp knife and cut carefully around the paper template she'd made—a dino-saur's body shape. She cooked some long-stemmed broccoli and placed it around the dinosaur to make trees, then formed the earth with a homemade vegetable chili.

She'd decided to stay on in the flat after she and Jake broke up in order to keep a constant in Leo's life. Anyway, there was something about the place—the sea view, the cheap rent, even the bent-clawed seagull that tapped with its beak at their window each day—that she thought she would miss.

She took the food through to Leo in the living room, and he smiled when he saw it.

"I like him," he said, looking at the plate. "I'm going to bite his head off first."

"You go for it," Kat laughed. "Before he does it to you."

Leo chuckled, picking up his fork.

"Can you bring my stegosaurus to watch?"

"Sure." Kat went into Leo's room and found the stuffed toy on top of his red chest of drawers. Above the chest, on the wall, was the Gruffalo mural Jake had painted. She paused for a moment to look at it. Things had been good, when they were good.

She put Leo's stegosaurus down on the table, so that he could see it while he ate.

"Mummy, you know where I'd like to go soon?" he said, chewing on a piece of broccoli.

"Where's that?"

"The Sealife Centre!" he pronounced, slamming his fork down in glee.

Kat nodded, smiling. He had been asking almost daily through the summer. But it wasn't cheap, and each time she set money aside, a bill would come. Hopefully, tomorrow things would change—her friend Cally, receptionist at the South Cliff Hotel, had put her forward for a job there. Apparently the manager had all but confirmed that it was Kat's if she wanted it. A few hours a week would mean enough money for the extra things Leo needed, plus the occasional treat, and with the hotel within walking distance of his nursery, she'd still be able to pick him up easily.

"Billy says it's fun. There are jellyfish. And sharks."

"I'm sure it is. We'll go soon," she said, kissing her son's head. "I promise."

Leo looked up at her. When she saw his dark brown eyes it was impossible not to think of Jake.

She'd get the money together.

The next day, Mr. Peterson, the hotel manager, ticked Kat's name off on the list of interviewees. She turned her silver and turquoise ring around on her finger, waiting for him to say something.

Kat must have passed the South Cliff Hotel a hundred times, on days when she'd taken the funicular up from the beach—but today was the first time she'd been inside the grand white building. She'd arrived at the same time as a coachload of Italian tourists, and from the back room she could still hear them talking out in reception.

For the interview, she'd concealed the tattoo on her wrist—a bold circle, identical to Jake's—underneath the long sleeves of a black blazer, and blow-dried her dark cropped hair so that it lay smooth. It was warm in the room though, and she longed to take the blazer off. It wasn't the kind of thing she'd normally wear.

"So, Kathryn. What is it that attracts you to the South Cliff?" Mr. Peterson asked.

She tried to remember what she'd practiced in front of the mirror the night before, and took a breath.

"I'm very interested in working in hospitality, and the South Cliff is internationally renowned. I'd be proud to be part of the team and I feel I could contribute a lot in terms of . . ."

Mr. Peterson looked down at her résumé, then took off his glasses and laid them down on the table. His expression seemed to soften.

"This is primarily a cleaning job, you know that, don't you?"

"Yes, Cally told me," Kat said, feeling a little flat.

"Right . . ." Mr. Peterson nodded slowly. "Well, Cally is quite insistent you would be perfect."

"I work hard," she said. "Whatever I do, I work hard."

"Yes," the manager said, putting one hand on her résumé. "It certainly looks like it."

The tension in Kat's shoulders eased a little.

Mr. Peterson sat back in his chair. "I hope you'll take this the right way. A degree in Hospitality and Culinary Arts, courses in tea-tasting, patisserie . . ."

"I know what you're going to say, but I'm happy to do—"

"You're overqualified."

The words rang out and Kat tried to think of a reply to counter them.

"I should have looked through your details more carefully, but you know Cally. She can be very persuasive. Look, Kathryn—you're young. You're only, what . . ." He glanced back at her details. ". . . twenty-six? You've still got time to build a career for yourself. I don't think I'd be doing the right thing employing you as a cleaner, not for either of us."

"Is it that you think I'd leave? Because I wouldn't. I need something steady."

Mr. Peterson shook his head. "I'm sorry if I've wasted your time."

"OK," Kat said numbly. She got to her feet. "Well, thanks for seeing me all the same," she said. "Could you—"

"Of course. We'll keep your résumé on file."

Outside, Kat took off her jacket, the sea breeze cool against her skin. She crossed the road to the rose garden on the cliffside, sat down on a bench and texted Cally a quick message to update her. Putting it down in writing made it more real. She felt as if she'd let Leo down.

At times like these, she wondered if things would have been easier if she and Jake had stayed together, if they could somehow have worked things out. Now he was back home in Scotland, his work was no longer steady, and it was Leo who would have to go without.

She walked down through the park, until the view opened up to reveal the full expanse of the sea. In front of her a little farther down the hill was the place she was heading to: the Seafront Tearoom.

A couple of people were sitting at tables outside, but inside the café looked quiet. She pushed the stained-glass front door, a bell signaling her arrival. As she stepped inside, she breathed in the unmistakable aroma of freshly baked scones. It enveloped her, as comforting as a duvet on a chilly winter's day. The interior of the Seafront was reassuringly familiar—the wooden tables neatly laid with pressed white tablecloths, the delicate china teacups lining the shelves, and the 1920s table lamps.

"Kat." Letty, the owner, smiled and tucked a strand of her silver-gray bob back behind her ear. "Come in. I was hoping we might see you today."

Kat closed the door behind her. "Hi there," she said, leaning in to kiss her hello. Letty was in her usual pressed black slacks, and an apron with a dusting of flour on it. Her son, Euan, was sitting up at the bar, dressed in a suit, looking at something on his iPad.

"Thought I'd pop by and say hello."

"Everything OK?" Letty asked, her pale blue eyes inquiring gently.

"Yes," Kat said as lightheartedly as she could, sitting down at her usual chair by the window. "I had a job interview. It didn't work out."

"I'm sorry to hear that." She put an arm around Kat sympathetically. "Well, it's their loss."

"It probably wasn't right for me anyway." Kat shrugged.

"That's the spirit. There'll be something better out there for you, I'm sure."

"I could seriously do with the money, though."

Letty's brow furrowed. "Are you OK to cover the basics? I can always help you out, you know."

"Don't worry," Kat said. "We'll be fine. Leo can really eat, though . . . and he's outgrowing his clothes so quickly."

"Oh yes," Letty said. "I remember how it was. Euan was the same," she said, nodding over at her son, who was devouring one of her scones. "Thirty and he's still over here eating my profits on his tea breaks."

"I can hear you talking about me, you know," he called over, a glint in his blue eyes.

Letty rolled her eyes indulgently. "Cheeky monkey!" She turned back to Kat. "Can you have a word with Jake?"

"He's still getting the business set up in Scotland and it's taking time."

"Right. I suppose that's not something that happens overnight. He'll get there. Until then, what can I get you? An Earl Grey? I've got a Victoria sponge fresh out the oven. Cake's on me today."

Kat looked over at the counter. She could see the scones that were scenting the air so irresistibly, a Victoria sponge cake and a tray of brownies.

"Oh, go on then," Kat said, a smile creeping back onto her face. "Thank you."

Letty disappeared off into the kitchen and returned to the table a few minutes later with a pink-and-green-patterned teapot, a matching teacup and a slice of cake layered with jam and cream.

"Here you go," she said, putting the things down.

Kat thanked her and took a bite of Victoria sponge cake. "Wow, this is delicious, Letty."

Letty smiled. "Thank you. I consider that high praise—I know what your standards are like."

Kat laughed.

Euan got to his feet, pulled his suit jacket back on and came over to them.

"How are you doing, Kat? It's been a while."

"Good, thanks." It was comforting to see Euan. They'd grown up on the same street and while they'd moved in different social circles, with four years between them, he'd always been kind to her.

"And Leo?"

"Growing fast. I can barely catch up with him these days." She smiled.

"You'll have to bring him in next time."

"I will do. He loves this place."

"See you later, Mum." Euan gave Letty a hug. "I need to head back to site."

"Bye, love," Letty said, putting her hand gently on his arm.

"Bye, Kat." Euan gave Kat a nod good-bye and walked out, starting up a conversation on his mobile.

"What's Euan working on at the moment?"

"The old cinema—they're turning it into a restaurant. He's done some of the designs for the project. It's a shame they couldn't keep it open—but this is better than it sitting empty."

"Yes."

"I'll ask him to keep his ear to the ground for you," Letty said. "It might be that some work comes up."

"Thanks, that would be good."

No use being sentimental. Her old job at the cinema ticket office hadn't been perfect, even though she'd enjoyed working there, especially the matinees full of friendly pensioners and new mums. Kat sipped her tea slowly, gazing out of the window. Life moved on, and places changed. She'd find a way to move forward too.

An hour later, Kat was waiting by the door to Leo's nursery, holding a jumper for him. She was glad she'd put it in her bag—the warm day had cooled a little and Leo had only been wearing a T-shirt when she'd dropped him off before her interview that morning.

She'd browsed on her phone at the tearooms and found one new job that might be suitable—as an admin assistant at an estate agents. It was outside town, so would mean a long journey there and back, but she could manage that if she had to.

A meter or so away two mothers were chatting—Amelia,

a redhead with a pregnancy bump, and Emma, a dark-haired woman carrying a pink scooter. She knew the women from pickups and drop-offs, and had chatted to them occasionally. Today she kept her eye on the nursery door, waiting to see Leo come out.

"How about this Sunday? Are you and Sam free for lunch?" Amelia asked her friend. "Work has been crazy, so I could do with something to look forward to."

"Sounds great," Emma replied enthusiastically.

"Sam and I are taking Lily to soft play in the morning, so some adult company after that would be wonderful. Can't count on my husband for that!"

Amelia laughed. "It's a date, then. Do you like rhubarb crumble? We've got some rhubarb fresh from the garden and—"

A tickle in Kat's throat made her cough. Amelia turned, noticed her and looked faintly embarrassed. "Hi, Kat, didn't see you there."

"Hello," Kat said with a smile.

"I was just saying—" Amelia seemed to stop herself. "You know, we must have Leo round for a playdate one of these days. He and Lily get on so well."

"He'd enjoy that," Kat said.

They stood quietly for a couple of minutes that stretched out. Finally, the nursery door opened.

Kat looked out eagerly for her son. He was still at the back of the room, taking his time as he walked over. Amelia and Emma greeted their toddlers.

"Well, best be off," Amelia said, with a smile at Kat. The two women set off with their children, who were squealing with excitement, in the direction of the shops.

Kat clutched Leo's jumper to her chest. He caught sight of

her and, waving a quick good-bye to his friend, dashed over to her with a huge smile. As soon as he reached her he gave her a bear hug, encircling her legs.

"Hello, sweetheart," Kat said, ruffling his dark-blond hair. "Here, put this on." She passed him his red jumper and he slipped it over his head quickly.

He looked at her suit skirt and wrinkled his nose. "Why are you wearing those funny clothes?"

"Oh," she said, looking down and touching the synthetic material. "I had to be smart for something."

"Boring. I like your green dress better."

"I'll put that on when we get home," she said, smiling. "OK?"

That night, after she'd put Leo to bed, Kat opened the antique wooden cabinet in her kitchen. Inside were glass jars filled with different types of tea—from fragrant Indian blends to refreshing herbals, each one with a handwritten luggage tag attached. She chose a jasmine bud that expanded in the water into a flower, put it in a delicate china teacup and carried it over to the sofa. She picked up the quilt she'd been working on for Leo, made from scraps of old duvet covers, and pushed the needle into the fabric, bringing together colorful sections of material. Each fresh new stitch of white cotton soothed her.

Tomorrow morning she'd apply for the admin job she'd spotted, tailoring her résumé more carefully this time. Yes, it had been two months of unreturned applications, and interviews ending in apologetic shakes of the head, but this could be the one.

She was distracted by a buzzing sound.

Her phone was vibrating on the coffee table, the screen lit up. She reached for it.

*JAKE.*

The name that used to be half of her world. Now it was a few letters, nothing more.

"Hi, Jake," she said, picking up.

"Hey," he said. "How're things?" His Scottish accent sounded stronger now.

"I'm fine," she said. "What's up?"

"Nothing. Listen, Kat, I'm here. Downstairs. The bell's not working."

She got up and went over to the kitchen window, peering out. Jake looked up at her from the street and smiled, still talking into his phone.

"Can you let me in?"

# 2

Thursday, August 14
*A village near Bordeaux, France*

"No more for me, thank you," Séraphine Moreau said. Her father, Patrick, offered her the slice of raspberry tart again, ready for her to change her mind, but she put her hand over her plate. "Honestly, Papa, I've had enough."

Patrick drew his dark eyebrows together and set the tart down reluctantly, then shook his head. "Just like her mother," he said in English to their guests, Ravi and Anna. "They do all the hard work in the kitchen and then let everyone else do the eating."

A warm laugh went up around the table. Séraphine's mother, Hélène, nudged her gently in the ribs and whispered behind her hand in French, "They don't see what actually goes on when we're baking, of course." She smiled, toying with the gold pendant on her necklace.

Since Séraphine was a young girl, she and her mother had baked together, the two of them feasting on the freshly picked berries, flaked almonds and pieces of chocolate that never made it as far as the oven.

Today, sunshine warmed Séraphine's shoulders, bare in a strappy red sundress, and glinted off her wineglass. A few baguette crumbs and an olive stone were all that were left on her plate, remnants of the long afternoon's dining under the apple tree in the garden of her family's chateau. The twins, her brother and sister, both eight years old—splashed contentedly in the swimming pool nearby.

"I'm glad you could make it down," Anna, one of her parents' guests, said to Séraphine over the narrow table, with its red-and-white gingham tablecloth. "Your mother said you weren't feeling well earlier."

"I'm much better now, thank you," she replied politely. She twisted her wavy dark-blond hair up and secured it with a clip. The late-afternoon breeze was cool on the back of her neck. "It was only a headache."

Séraphine had been tempted to stay in bed that morning, her mind still buzzing from the events of the past weeks, but in the end distraction had been welcome. Conversation with Ravi and Anna, an English couple who'd recently bought the neighboring chateau, had been relaxed and unhurried, as if she'd always known them. It had been good to practice her English with them, too—over the summer, since finishing her exams, she'd barely spoken a word.

"Mathilde, Benjamin," Hélène called out to the twins, who were splashing water over the side of the pool as they threw a beach ball to each other. "It's time to come out now." She turned back to her elder daughter. "Séraphine, have you seen their towels?"

She picked up the fluffy beach towels on the grass next to her and passed them to her mother. "Here you go."

Hélène went over to the twins as they clambered out of the pool, shivering slightly.

"Your mother said you like to read. Do you read in English?" Anna asked Séraphine. "I have a few books you might enjoy."

"Thank you, yes. My favorites are mysteries and crime novels—Agatha Christie, that kind of thing. Classics too. I'm reading *Rebecca* at the moment—I'm enjoying it."

"A wonderful book," Anna agreed.

"I love the part where she describes the laying out of afternoon tea, the performance of it—the silver tray, the kettle, the cloth."

"Yes. Quite an important part of the day—or at least it was back then," Anna said. "Most people don't have the time, or take the time, now. I have to admit I was more in the habit of grabbing a latte than stopping to sip Earl Grey."

"Séraphine's always been keen on English culture," Patrick said to Anna and her husband. "And of course she's the linguist in the family. My English, well, as you can hear, it's terrible. Luckily, it comes naturally to her."

Séraphine felt a flush creep onto her cheeks. "Dad, shhh," she said, laughing. She looked at Ravi and Anna and rolled her eyes playfully in her father's direction. "I'm pretty rusty. I've finished my teacher training course, but want to improve my English before I start looking for a job."

"That's good. Such an exciting time in life—preparing to fly the nest," Anna said.

Séraphine's confusion must have shown.

"Sorry—flying the nest, leaving home," Anna explained.

"Oh," Séraphine laughed. "That's a nice phrase. Yes, I suppose so. Though I won't be going too far—I'll be looking for work in Bordeaux, private classes to start off with, then a permanent job next autumn."

"And before that—wouldn't you like to go to England?" Ravi chipped in. "Now's the time in life for big adventures. How old are you now?"

"Twenty-three," she said.

Age didn't mean much, Séraphine thought. What mattered was how you felt inside. She remembered the sensation of grass beneath her bare feet, by the river the day before.

Laughing. Feeling free. The butterfly touch of a kiss on her neck. She felt complete in a way she never had before.

"That's the way to perfect a language, too," Ravi continued. "Total immersion."

"Hang on, Ravi." Anna nudged her husband. "That's what we said about coming here, isn't it? And look—we're still so incompetent we've got these lovely people talking to us in English." She laughed. "But you'd be more disciplined about it, Séraphine, I'm sure. And you're already quite fluent."

"I wish we could invite you to be our guest," Ravi said. "But now we've sold up and there's definitely no going back."

"You prefer it here?" Séraphine asked. She was more comfortable talking about them than herself.

"We adore it," Anna said. "Who wouldn't? Good food, wine, company . . . We were ready for a change after the kids left home."

Instinctively, Séraphine glanced at her parents. A look passed between them. Her brother Guillaume had left home the year before, in difficult circumstances, and they hadn't been at all ready for the change.

". . . But England's a wonderful place for a young person, you'd enjoy it."

"You thought about living there, didn't you, sweetheart?" Patrick prompted his daughter gently. "Earlier this year you were saying . . ."

Séraphine tensed. "It's very expensive though, isn't it? A friend of mine went to London and—"

Anna laughed and wrinkled her nose. "There's more to England than London, you know."

"She's right, Yorkshire's the place to visit," Ravi said. "Would you consider going up north?"

"Maybe," Séraphine said. "I don't know. Where were the two of you living?"

"In Scarborough. It's a lovely town. You're right by the sea, and while—granted—we can't guarantee the glamour, or the weather, of Antibes or Nice, it's fun in the summer. The people are friendly, and it's affordable."

Séraphine sensed that the others were waiting for her to respond. "It sounds nice. I don't expect there'd be many jobs, though. Summer's nearly over."

"Bet you'll find some au pair work going," Anna said confidently. "Hang on, what about Adam, Ravi? Is he still looking for someone?"

Ravi nodded. "I think he is, actually." He turned to Séraphine. "Lovely guy. He was our neighbor for years—has a ten-year-old daughter."

"His wife was from here," Anna said. "They married very young, and lived in France until she passed away in an accident four or five years ago. I don't know what happened, but it must have been terrible for them. I remember him saying he's keen for his daughter to speak French, to keep the connection—so he's looking for someone to live with them and teach her."

"You'd make a wonderful au pair," Hélène said, wrapping a squirming Mathilde in one of the warm towels. "Would you like that, darling?"

"Maybe," Séraphine said, slowly.

Anna was already reaching into her handbag for a pen and paper. She checked her phone and wrote something down. "Here's Adam's e-mail. Think about it?"

Séraphine took the piece of paper and smiled politely. "Thank you."

Evening fell, and while Hélène put the twins to bed, Séraphine and her father carried the dishes inside to the kitchen.

"Are you sure you won't join us for a drink in the library?" he asked.

"No, it's fine. I'm a little tired." She said good-bye to the guests and went upstairs.

In her bedroom, she walked over to the window to close the wooden shutters, pausing for a moment to look out. The well-tended garden and the vineyards beyond were warmly tinted by the gray-pink sky at dusk. Out to the east was the village square, a cobbled area with shops around it, where a market was held once a fortnight. A few meters away was the school she'd gone to, and the church the whole family, including her grandparents, attended every Sunday. The landscape, streets and buildings were as familiar to her as her own fingerprint.

And yet every stone, branch and street corner looked different to her now. Meeting someone who understood her made her realize how much of her real self she'd kept hidden. She drew the shutters and lowered the catch to secure them.

From the room next door came the sound of giggling. She stepped into the corridor and put her head around the twins' bedroom door. In her sternest voice, she demanded, "Mathilde? Benjamin? Why are you two still awake?"

In tandem, without a word, they ducked under the covers, rolling onto their sides. Séraphine quietly closed the door and glanced along the corridor toward her brother's room. Even though he'd moved out, the room still had his football posters on the walls, a rack of his old shoes by the wardrobe. With only two years separating them, Guillaume and Séraphine had been close. She used to sit on the chair in his room and he'd strum his guitar, playing her the new songs he had written, while incense burned in the corner.

Back in her own room, Séraphine turned on a lamp and lay back on her bed. When Guillaume left, a crack formed in their home. In truth, the hairline fracture had appeared earlier and only deepened when he walked out; he had been slipping away from them for over a year—spending most of his time with his band in Bordeaux, rarely bothering to come home at night. As his band grew more successful and started touring in Europe, he'd seemed less happy, somehow. On the rare occasions when he was home he'd appeared disconnected, listless.

Her parents chose not to see the change in him, the deadness Séraphine noticed behind his eyes. He'd finally left before Christmas, saying good-bye but not leaving an address. "A commune," he'd said to Séraphine in an offhand way. "You can be yourself there, not like in this place, this prison. If you want to find me, come to Bordeaux. Ask and they'll show you." He'd walked out with a sports bag in his hand, nothing else.

Séraphine looked up at the shadows on her ceiling. She had always wondered if, when the right person came along, she would know if it was love. If you could be sure, instinctively, that was what you were feeling. She'd had boyfriends before, of course, but she'd never lain awake at night thinking about them. Now she knew: love was an absence of questions, of doubt. It was a certainty that you had found what it was you'd been looking for and there was no reason to go on searching.

She knew how her parents would react, and that was why they must never find out. If she followed her heart, she'd be straying from the good upbringing they'd strived to give their children. She'd be like Guillaume. As bad as Guillaume. Her love—pure and kind and honest as it felt—to them would represent nothing more than defiance.

She couldn't be the one to hurt them all over again. At the same time, she couldn't undo what had happened in the last couple of weeks, unknow that part of herself, forget how she felt.

Her actions, however, were another matter—she could still do the right thing.

England. Until her father brought it up, she'd forgotten how—before that first kiss had knocked the sense out of her—she'd dreamed of moving to England.

Perhaps going away would make her stronger. Perhaps when she came back, she'd be strong enough to resist.

She switched her iPad on and typed a word into the search bar: Scarbrah.

Did you mean Scarborough? the search engine pinged back in response.

"Yes, I did," she whispered, frustrated with herself. "Thank you."

A photo of a white lighthouse came up on her screen, in front of it the stone statue of a woman poised to dive into the water. Other pictures appeared: one of a harbor, with boats glinting in the sun, another of a miniature railway. She swiped her finger through more images—sandy bays, a castle on top of a hill, shops and cafés. She tried to imagine herself in the seaside town. It looked like a different world. Could she even cope living in someone else's home?

The ping of an instant message interrupted her thoughts.

Salut, ma belle

She saw the name, and her heart thudded. A smile came to her lips even as she tried to fight the feeling.

She took a deep breath and closed the chat window. Today

would be her new start. Her finger hovered over the icon for a second. No. She wouldn't.

She leaned over to her bedside table to get the note that Anna had given her that afternoon. She unfolded it, read the e-mail address and typed it into a new message.

Dear Adam . . .

# 3

Thursday, August 14
*Brooklyn, New York*

Charlie Harrison leaned against the metal bar at the edge of the rooftop restaurant, looking out at the view, salsa music blaring from the raised speakers around her. The balmy night had brought New Yorkers outside to dine in their droves, and the tables at La Mesita were almost all full. Charlie had been daydreaming about her trip to see her friend Sarah for weeks, her morning commute on the Piccadilly line drifting away as she read a *Time Out* guide to the city. At last, she was finally here.

Sarah appeared at her side with two ice-cold margaritas. "Here you go," she said, handing one to Charlie before joining her friend in admiring the view. "Beautiful, isn't it?"

The lights of Brooklyn Bridge dotted the horizon, reflected in the still waters of the river, and skyscrapers were silhouetted beyond. But it was more than the way the place looked—the city had an energy to it that no postcard or film could ever hope to convey.

"Yes. Incredible," Charlie said. She took a sip of her cocktail, relishing the sharp taste of the lime and tequila as it settled on her taste buds, layers of flavor coming through the citrus. Could have been shaken for a little longer—but it was pretty good.

Sarah glanced down at Charlie's hand, which was trembling on her glass. "What's with the shakes?"

"Is it that obvious?" she said, putting the glass down and cradling her hand. "Caffeine overdose." She laughed. "We're featuring Brooklyn coffee shops in the October edition of the magazine, and with only a couple of days here I had to cram in the cappuccinos today. Good job I'm in the city that never sleeps."

"Well, I'm up for an all-nighter if you are," Sarah said with a smile. She was elegant in a green halter-neck dress, her red hair clipped up at the side. "The two of us have some serious catching up to do, and anyway, I've put our names down at a club later."

"Great." Charlie brightened at the thought. "I haven't been out dancing in ages. I knew I could rely on you."

"Yep. Might be past it professionally, but I'll always be a dancer. It'd take more than a couple of failed auditions to knock that passion out of me."

A young Latino waiter appeared by their side. "Señoritas, allow me to see you to your table."

He led them to a nearby table and motioned for them to sit down, then placed two menus in front of them. "I'll be back in a moment to take your order."

"Wow!" Charlie said, running her eyes down the menu, her mouth starting to water. "Fish tacos, Oaxacan cheese quesadillas . . . God, I could eat everything on this."

Sarah called the waiter over.

"We'll have a selection of your starters, a chicken burrito and spicy beef tacos to share," she said swiftly. "With plenty of guacamole."

He looked from Sarah to Charlie, seeking confirmation that she had nothing to add.

"If we wait for her to decide, we'll be here all evening," Sarah told him.

"Hey, that's not fair!" Charlie protested.

"Tell me I haven't got a point."

"OK, OK." Charlie held her hands in the air, conceding.

"You're off duty tonight, remember?" Sarah passed the menus back to the waiter with a smile. "Two cosmopolitans as well. Thanks."

"Have you always been this bossy?" Charlie said. She took out her phone and checked it for new messages.

"Yes, I have. Anyone interesting?" Sarah raised a quizzical eyebrow.

"Oh, it's nothing like that." Charlie smiled and shook her head. "I should be so lucky. My sister's pregnant again. Due any day."

"Again?"

"Yep. This'll make three. Another girl this time."

"That's fairly prolific. Are you and Pippa getting on any better these days?"

"Not really," Charlie said, with a shrug. "But living in different cities helps. Anyway, let's not talk about that. Not tonight." She put her phone away.

"No family chat. OK. I can do that. So, work's going well? I hear you're making quite a name for yourself. 'The female Jay Rayner'—saw that on Twitter."

"Hardly," Charlie said, wrinkling her nose, but flattered all the same. "But yes, it's going all right. The canalside dining feature I did brought *Indulge* a lot of new readers—and the restaurants I featured have been packed out all summer."

"That's fantastic."

"Thanks. I've been there eight years now. Can you believe it?"

"That long? I can still remember when you got that editorial assistant job after your internship. You were over the moon. Who'd have thought, you'd soon be Features Editor and reviewing the best restaurants all over the world."

"It's not all glamour." Charlie smiled. "In spite of the perks, I've been feeling a bit stuck in a rut lately. Jess, the editor, has very strong ideas about how she wants the magazine to be, and so I always have to work to her brief."

"So what's next? Are you thinking of moving on?"

"Hopefully I'll be able to move up. Jess is leaving in the new year and she's hinted I'm in with a good chance of taking over as editor. I'll be guest-editing the winter edition as a trial."

"That sounds like a perfect opportunity," Sarah said. "You're bound to get it."

"I hope so," Charlie said, excited at the thought. "I'll need to come up with a strong concept for the issue, but putting it together should be straightforward. I do a lot of the writing and commissioning these days."

"I can picture it," Sarah said. "You were always destined to get to the top."

"I don't know about that," Charlie laughed. "What about you anyway, how's the personal training going?"

"I'm enjoying it," Sarah said. "A few high-maintenance clients, but most of them are lovely. It pays the bills, and even keeps me in banana pancakes and lattes."

"It must be wonderful, living here," Charlie said enviously. "And it certainly seems to suit you."

Sarah, who'd been a complete tomboy throughout their teenage years, was sleek and glamorous now—her hair color deepened with lowlights, and her summer dress showing off perfectly toned arms. Charlie, in indigo jeans and a strapless black top, felt less polished—but she was comfortable, and the jeans were a wardrobe essential, stretching forgivingly when she put on weight. Her straight blonde hair was loose tonight, brushing her shoulders, and she'd dressed the jeans up with gold wedges.

"Thank you," Sarah responded. "It's my kind of town, that's for sure. Impossible to get bored."

"Do you miss *anything* about home?"

"What, like the King's Head?" Sarah said, recalling their South London local. "Nope, I don't miss that leg-humping pub dog one little bit."

Charlie laughed. "OK, perhaps not that. But surely there must be something?"

"People, obviously. Family. Living with you."

"*That's* the answer I was looking for," Charlie said, smiling. "And one other thing . . ."

"Yes?"

"A good cup of tea. I mean a seriously good cup of tea. And a proper scone with cream. The food here is incredible, don't get me wrong—but a good old-fashioned tearoom? They don't exist."

"Do you remember that teashop hidden away behind the train station?"

"The Rosebud?" Sarah smiled at the memory. "Yes, of course I do. Almost made getting dumped worth it, that cake."

*In Guerrilla Coffee, the aroma of freshly ground Arabica beans fills the air. While the service is brisk to the point of being offhand, the feisty espressos more than make up for it. A mix of early-to-rise city workers, freelance writers and morning-after clubbers congregate around oak banquettes and sip from steaming hot cups . . .*

Charlie rubbed her eyes as she wrote, her MacBook balanced on the tray table in front of her. She would have given anything to have a hot macchiato about now. She checked the corner of her computer screen, still on UK time—four hours till they touched down, and six more reviews to go. She'd finished writing up her notes on two venues—the boutique dog café and the underground iced-coffee bar—typing as the plane flew over the Atlantic.

She and Sarah hadn't got back till the early hours of the morning. They'd gone out in Greenwich Village with a group of Sarah's friends, partying like old times, dancing on the bar and laughing until their sides hurt. She'd crashed for a couple of hours on the sofa bed in her friend's loft apartment, then caught a cab directly to the airport. Saying good-bye to Sarah had been bittersweet; they both knew that it would probably be a year or more until they saw each other again. The trip away had been energizing but all too brief, and Charlie was in no hurry to get back. Home meant being reminded of her breakup with Ben.

Hopefully next year would be better than this one. She thought of the old copy of *Say I Do* magazine that was on the coffee table in her flat. Planning her wedding to Ben earlier that year, she'd turned the corners of certain pages—a backless dress, a tree-house venue, an arrangement of roses and baby's breath. She needed to throw that out. Ben was out of her life for good, and she was a different person now. She recalled the day that they'd met, two years ago.

"You got time to show a new boy the ropes?" Ben had asked in the office canteen.

"OK," she answered with a smile. "Can't have you sitting on your own on your first day, I suppose."

"Thank you," he said, with a mock sigh of relief. "It's like something out of *Mean Girls* round here. Look at that lot," he said, indicating a cluster of immaculately made-up women, and men in dapper clothing, all leaning in toward each other conspiratorially.

"*Cutting Edge Style* magazine," Charlie said. "You should probably steer clear of them."

Ben looked down at his outfit—pressed chinos and a blue shirt—and raised an eyebrow. "What are you saying?"

"No offense, but they'd eat you for breakfast." She laughed. "You'd be better off sticking to the foodies." She nodded across the room. "That's the *Savor* publicity and marketing team; they're pretty friendly . . . And *Indulge* are the best of the lot. The only downside is, there's no such thing as a quick lunch break: every dish has to be dissected and discussed in minute detail."

"God. Pass," he said. "I know hardly anything about food—apart from that I enjoy it."

"How did you end up working here, then?"

"Shameless nepotism. My brother happens to be married to the sales manager. That and I've got a sales background. I've never worked for a food magazine before though."

"OK, well, seeing as you can't hold your own yet, I'll ease you in gently. We can sit next to the girls at *Brides* magazine— they're usually too wrapped up in flower concepts to give anyone the third degree."

"Not bad-looking either," he commented, glancing over.

A stab of jealousy surprised her, and she narrowed her eyes.

"I'm joking," he said.

"Hmmm. Now, be nice to Carol-Anne," Charlie said, indicating the eldest of the women serving, "and she'll sort you out with the biggest portions for your whole time here."

"Note taken. Let's get in line, I'm starving."

They'd chatted easily that day, and before long they were exchanging e-mails and IMs across the crowded office floor.

Ben's warm humor made even the days leading up to a deadline pleasurable, punctuating her day with laughter and a delicious frisson.

At the office summer party, they'd ended up kissing in the middle of the dance floor, only to be shamed the following day by an Instagrammed shot of the event circulating around the office. But soon they'd become the darlings of the *Indulge* office, as close as the magazine got to a power couple. When Ben proposed, Charlie said yes, as everyone expected her to.

In the weeks that followed, Ben had looked over at the pages of *Say I Do* magazine as she showed them to him, but always with a noncommittal "hmm" or "yeah, nice." She should have realized earlier that his heart wasn't in getting married. But they were Charlie and Ben—the couple everyone wanted to invite to their dinner parties—they were meant to be together. Until one day, they weren't. And it still stung.

She had thought she'd be getting married next spring. Now, with the wedding off, she needed to move on in a different way. To prove to herself she was better alone. And of course it wouldn't hurt if Ben—still working in the same office as her— realized it too.

"Tea or coffee?" The stewardess's voice cut into her thoughts.

She opened her mouth to order the coffee she'd been craving, then—recalling what Sarah had said—changed her mind. "A tea, please."

She remembered the Sunday afternoons she and Sarah had spent at the Rosebud, catching up over cups of English breakfast and carrot cake. Everyone treasured a unique café, didn't they? Somewhere special they could call their own.

Getting out her notebook, she jotted down some ideas.

*Teacups . . . history . . . chat . . . afternoon tea . . . tearooms.*

An edition of the magazine that readers could cozy up with, just right for November, when the nights were drawing in. She chewed on her pen, mulling the idea over. Perhaps there was something in it.

Sorry, miss, you're going to have to raise your tray table. We're coming in to land."

"Sure," Charlie said, closing her laptop.

She put her computer away and watched as the clouds thinned, allowing glimpses of land as they approached London.

*We will shortly be arriving at London Heathrow. It's a pretty gray day down there, a chilly fourteen degrees . . ."*

Charlie looked down at her denim skirt and flip-flops. Back to British summertime, then, she thought gloomily. At least she'd remembered to put a jacket in her hand luggage.

Later, in the taxi rank outside the airport, she switched on her mobile phone again. Missed call: *MUM*. She pressed the button to return it.

"Charlie!"

"Hello, Mum. Just got back. You called, has anything happened?"

"Yes. Wonderful news: Pippa's had a healthy baby girl."

"That's great," Charlie said, relieved. "Have they picked a name yet?"

"Gracie."

A kind, friendly face came into Charlie's mind and she smiled. "Granny's name."

"Yes. It was a lovely thought. They're all doing fine. Jacob and Flo are enjoying meeting their new sister, she says. Your dad and I are going up this weekend."

"That's good. How is Dad?"

"Oh, you know your father . . ." She lowered her voice to a whisper. "Never easy."

"I'm sure he'll be cheered up by seeing the baby."

"Exactly."

Charlie, now at the front of the queue, maneuvered her luggage trolley into position as a black cab drew up.

"Listen, I can't chat," Charlie said. "I'm still at the airport."

"OK. But, Charlie—"

"Mmm-hmm," she said, cradling the phone between shoulder and ear as she loaded her bags into the taxi.

"I know you and your sister don't always see eye to eye, but you will visit her sooner this time, won't you?"

Charlie thought of her work schedule—packed solid until January. Then came a flashback of how she and Pippa had argued last time she'd gone to stay in Scarborough. She chewed her lip. Somehow she'd have to find a way to fit in the visit. And this time she'd be more patient.

"Of course, Mum. I'll talk to my boss about taking some time off next month."

# 4

Friday, August 15

Jake leaned in toward Kat and kissed her gently on the cheek, in the hallway of what had once been his flat. The bristle of his stubble against her skin, the smell of his shampoo—it was the tiny things that brought memories back.

"Bit out of the blue I know, but a friend was driving down from Edinburgh and asked if I wanted a lift . . ."

"It's OK," she said, with a smile. "I'm used to surprises." They walked up the stairs together.

"Those are new." He pointed at the black-and-white photos Kat had taken of the seafront ice-cream shops and put in handmade driftwood frames. "Nice."

"Thanks. Leo found some of the wood for them. A few things have changed since last time."

"Two months is way too long." He shook his head. "I've missed Leo loads and he must've grown up so much. Where is he?" He peered down the corridor toward Leo's room. "Can I say hello? I got him something." He held up a plastic bag with a wrapped box inside.

"Sorry, he's in bed."

Jake hit his palm gently against his forehead. "Oh yeah. Of course."

"Come through. I'll put the kettle on."

Jake sat down on the sofa, running one hand distractedly over the corduroy material on the arm. "So, how've you been?"

"Good," Kat said, stepping into the kitchen and getting a mug out of the cupboard, flicking the kettle on. "Busy." She made Jake's tea on autopilot: milky with two spoonfuls of white sugar.

Back in the living room she put Jake's drink down in front of him and joined him on the sofa. "Leo talks about you all the time, you know."

"Really? He does?" Jake glowed. He took a sip of tea, not waiting for it to cool. "Look, I'm sorry I couldn't send any money over this month . . ." He ran a hand through his hair and looked down at his feet. "I'm doing everything I can, but I'm starting from scratch in Edinburgh and there's a ton of other painting-and-decorating companies. I'm slowly picking up jobs by word of mouth, but—"

"I understand," Kat said. "I'm not going to lie, though—it's hard covering the bills when I'm not working either."

"You haven't found anything?"

"Not yet. I've been interviewing."

"You'll get something. You've always been the brains of the operation."

"Ha," she said, and smiled. "Well, hopefully it'll be soon. You know how it gets here in winter."

"Yep," he said, his eyes meeting hers. "Absolutely freezing. Don't worry, I'll make sure I send money next month."

Kat nodded. "OK."

"In the meantime, I've got a proposition for you."

"Hmm?"

"I've barely seen Leo these past few months, and Mum and Dad are desperate to spend some time with him. They haven't set eyes on him since their last visit down here, and that was . . ." His words trailed off.

"When we were still together."

"Yes."

She remembered the visit clearly. It had been a sunny spring weekend last year. The four of them had taken Leo to the beach, with his kite, and they'd had a picnic on the sand. From the outside it must have looked like the perfect outing.

"Could I take him back to Edinburgh with me for a couple of weeks—three maybe? Mum and Dad can look after him if and when I get work."

"Three weeks?" she said, feeling winded. She hadn't been apart from Leo for that long since he was born. "But . . . what about nursery, Jake? His routine . . ."

"Come on, Kat. I'm his dad—these are his grandparents. Isn't it more important that we spend some proper time with him? We'll make sure we keep things as normal as possible."

She tried to imagine the flat without Leo; his room, empty. The quiet. "I don't know—"

"You need to look for a job, to send out résumés—that's what you keep saying. Don't tell me you did all that work at uni for nothing. If I had Leo for a few weeks you'd be able to focus on your career."

A cough came from Leo's room, and Kat turned toward the sound. Was it selfish to want to keep him with her? The flat fell silent again.

Jake spoke up. "We did say we would share looking after him."

"You're right."

Jake finished his tea. "Listen, I should be going. I'm staying at a friend's tonight. I'll come back in the morning to see him. Think it over?"

"OK," Kat said, hoping that in the morning the idea of parting with her son would seem easier. "Let's talk then."

# 5

Friday, September 5
*Scarborough, Peasholm Park*

The taxi slowed as it approached the semi-detached house. Over the road, exactly as Adam had described, was a park with a Japanese pagoda, still and mystical in the early evening light.

"This is it," Séraphine said to the driver.

That morning she'd kissed good-bye to her parents and the twins at Bordeaux airport. It felt a world away now.

She could see a girl in the window—brown hair in a ponytail, her nose pressed up against the glass. Séraphine waved at her. Adam opened the door. "Hi," he said warmly. She recognized him instantly from their chat on Skype—about thirty, with dark hair, a little scruffy at the front, and brown eyes, dressed in a gray jumper and jeans. He stepped forward and held out his hand for her to shake.

"I'm Adam." He shook his head and laughed shyly. "But you already know that. Here, let me take your bag for you."

As he took her suitcase from her, she returned his smile. "Thank you."

She followed him in. Compared to the entrance hall in her family's chateau, the house seemed cramped and untidy—coats were piled one on top of another and muddy shoes and Wellingtons dirtied the carpet by the door. Two empty cat baskets and a hamster cage formed a precarious pile beside them.

"Excuse the chaos," Adam said. "You'll get used to it, I hope."

"It's fine, don't worry," Séraphine assured him. "You have pets?" she asked, peering at the cages.

"Not at the moment," he replied with a smile. "But we do have the occasional short-stay guest. I'm a vet—with a weakness for taking in waifs and strays. I probably should have warned you."

"That's OK, I'm fond of animals."

She looked past Adam to the doorway of the living room, where his daughter was standing. She was wearing jeans and a top with a silver star on it, her gaze fixed on Séraphine.

"This is Zoe," Adam said, putting his arm around the girl and bringing her out into the hallway. He seemed young to have a daughter of ten. "Zoe, this is Séraphine, who we talked about. She's going to be staying with us and teaching you some French."

"Hi," Zoe said.

"Hello," Séraphine said kindly, bending to her level. "Here, I brought you something," she said, handing her a present. A notebook with a lock she'd picked out in a market back home.

"Thanks." Zoe took hold of it.

"I have a sister a little younger than you. You look quite alike, actually."

"Oh yeah?"

"Zoe, how about we show Séraphine up to her room?"

They climbed the carpeted stairs together. On the walls were photos of Adam, Zoe and a woman who must have been her mother—she had a kind smile, glasses and long dark hair. They reached a small attic room.

"This is where you'll be sleeping," Adam said.

In the center of the room was a single bed with a worn red rug next to it. A dormer window, with a chair next to it, offered a view of the park. In the corner of the room was a sewing table and a machine that looked as if it hadn't been touched in years.

"It's not much," Adam said, apologetically.

"It's perfect," Séraphine replied.

"Take your time unpacking, and then I hope you'll join us for dinner at about seven?"

"That would be great."

"It's cottage pie—an English classic."

"Sounds delicious. And tomorrow it's my turn. Something authentically French."

"Excellent," he said. "Do you enjoy cooking?"

Séraphine felt instantly at ease. "Yes, I love it. Especially baking—pastries and cakes are my specialty."

"Did you hear that, Zoe?" Adam said, squeezing his daughter's shoulder gently. "If we're nice to Séraphine, perhaps she'll bake something for us one day."

He smiled and turned to head back downstairs.

Zoe lingered in the doorway of the small room, toying with the bronze door handle.

"Have you got a picture of your sister?" she asked.

Séraphine brought up a photo of Mathilde on her phone and showed it to Zoe. "Here she is. Pretty like you. She's a twin. I have two brothers also."

"She doesn't look much like me," Zoe said. "Not at all."


Séraphine showered, called her parents to let them know she'd arrived safely, and then pinned a couple of photos up on the wall by her bedside table. She dressed in jeans and a cream top, and checked her watch: six thirty—still half an hour till dinner.

She sat down at the chair by the window. She'd done the

hardest thing in leaving, but at the same time she knew she'd been a coward, and it nagged at her. On her phone she scrolled down her contacts and started a new message.

I'm sorry I left without saying good-bye . . .

She bit her lip, trying to fight back the tears. It pained her to think of what she'd lost.

. . . This is difficult for me.

A moment later, a reply beeped through and her heart leaped.

I know. I was there once too.

# 6

Saturday, September 6
*South Cliff, Scarborough*

"Auntie Charlie's here," Pippa called out into the hallway behind her. Her pale blond hair was up in a ponytail, and Gracie, the newest addition to the family, was strapped to her chest snugly in a sling.

"Hi, Luke," Charlie said, kissing her brother-in-law on the cheek and stepping into the Edwardian house, putting her small suitcase down in the hall. She'd packed light for the week's stay. Thankfully, her boss, keen on Charlie's tearooms feature idea for the next issue of the magazine, had agreed that she could use the days for research. Charlie had Googled possible places the previous night, some on the coast and others in York and Leeds.

Pippa's house was exactly as Charlie remembered it: spotless and tidy, with immaculate cream walls and carpets.

"Good journey?" Luke asked.

"Not bad, thanks." She looked him up and down. "What's with the suit? It's Saturday."

"I've got a big project on. Sorry I can't stick around but I'm needed in the office today."

"Luke works most weekends," Pippa said. "I'm used to being on my own on Saturdays."

"Pip, that's not tr—" Luke started, shaking his head.

"Auntie Charrrlie!" The cry was followed by a stampede

as Flo and Jacob rushed down the stairs to greet their aunt with hugs and kisses. She bent down to embrace them back.

"Wow, you two have got so big," Charlie said, crouching to take them in. Six-year-old Flo was taller, with long legs in stripy tights and a pinafore dress, and Jacob, who'd recently turned two, was now running around the place rather than tentatively cruising along the furniture as he had been the last time she saw him.

"They've been so looking forward to your visit," Pippa said. "We made a cake this morning. Didn't we, you two?"

"Yes," Flo said proudly. "A chocolate one."

"Sorry, I have to dash," Luke said, giving his wife and kids a hurried kiss good-bye. "Have a good day. I'll be back late, so don't worry about dinner."

"OK, sure," Pippa said. Charlie thought she saw a flicker of frustration on her sister's face.

"I'll see you tomorrow, Charlie," Luke added with a polite smile before heading toward the front door. As the door closed, Pippa's smile returned.

"Charlie, do you want to come through the kitchen for some cake?"

"How could I refuse an offer like that?"

Venus, a sleek Prussian blue cat, snaked her way around Pippa's legs as she walked, leading them all through to the open-plan kitchen. The room was airy and light, with French doors opening onto tidy grass and a weeping willow. On the fridge and walls were pictures the children had drawn, and the bookshelves were filled with the latest cookery books.

"Take a seat," Pippa called over her shoulder while she busied herself taking the cake out the fridge—all without a peep from the baby, who had dropped off in the sling.

"I got a little something for Gracie," Charlie said, as the

kids buzzed around the cake adding extra decorations. She passed her sister a turquoise gift bag.

"Thank you." Pippa took the bag and opened the tissue wrapping inside. "You shouldn't have." She pulled out a babygro with a picture of the Cat in the Hat on the front, and matching bootees. Charlie had found the clothes in a boutique in Greenwich Village and immediately fallen in love with them.

"Mum used to read us the books, do you remember?" she said. "Hopefully Gracie will like them too."

"How nice," Pippa said. She inspected the label. "It's organic cotton, right?"

"Oh, I'm not sure," Charlie said, reading over her shoulder.

"No, it's not," Pippa said flatly. "A lovely thought though. Thank you." She put the babygro back in the bag and to one side on the counter. "Now, kids, shall we sit down?"

They crowded around the oak dining table and Pippa poured juice for the children and cut the cake, dishing it out onto plates.

"How's it been with Gracie?" Charlie asked.

"Oh, fine," Pippa said. "She's an easy baby, same as the other two. Flo and Jacob are usually off at their music lessons and activities, so I've had lots of time with Gracie, the two of us. Mum and baby bonding." She smiled lovingly at Gracie's sleeping face.

"That's good."

"I'm enjoying it. It's a very pure kind of happiness," Pippa said. "The one upside to Luke not being around that much." There was a hint of sadness in her voice, but she brightened quickly and continued:

"Of course it's fascinating to see the change in these two now they have a little sister."

Jacob was pulling pink decorations off the cake and scooping off icing with his finger. Pippa seemed not to notice.

"So, Mum mentioned you're in line for a promotion."

"Hopefully," Charlie replied. "I'm not the only one they're considering, but my boss thinks I'm in with a good chance."

"That's wonderful," Pippa said. "You certainly live for your work, don't you?"

"I enjoy it, if that's what you mean."

"Yes, of course," Pippa said innocently. "And you're so good at it, aren't you?"

Charlie waited for it. The inevitable dig. She knew how her sister operated.

"But don't forget that other things are important too," Pippa said, tenderly brushing a hair away from Flo's face. "Life can pass you by when all you're thinking about is your job."

"I do have a life too, Pip."

"No need to get touchy," Pippa replied.

"I'm not being touchy."

"All I'm saying is, after all that business with Ben . . . I'd have thought maybe you'd want to reassess . . ."

Flo looked up from her cake, suddenly interested. "Ben?"

Charlie seethed inside but reminded herself of her vow to be patient. Somehow she managed to reply coolly and calmly:

"No, Pippa. There is absolutely nothing I want to reassess."

The next day, a Sunday, Charlie left Pippa and Luke's house and walked into town in bright autumn sunshine, looking for the café her sister had recommended as perfect for her tearoom feature.

In the middle of the High Street, Katie's Kitchen was impossible to miss—pink-and-white polka-dot curtains were draped in the front window, with a row of teapots on the sill. Charlie stepped inside. The room buzzed with chatter, and oversized canvases with pictures of teacups adorned the walls. The counter, covered in a plastic tablecloth with a flowered print, was laden with cupcakes and muffins. Next to them was a large birthday cake with a princess on it.

Charlie spotted an empty table in the corner, and stepped carefully over other customers' shopping bags to reach it. She picked up the laminated menu and read through the items on offer.

Eventually a teenage girl with her hair in a high ponytail came over to her table. "What can I get you?" she asked, getting out her notebook and not meeting Charlie's eyes.

"I'll have a blueberry muffin, a slice of gingerbread and . . ." She looked back at the menu. "What flavor are your pink cupcakes?"

"They're pink flavor," the girl said. "Nice, lots of icing."

"Oh," Charlie replied hesitantly. "A chocolate one, please."

"That's a lot of cakes. Are you expecting someone else?" the girl asked, glancing at the empty chair.

"No," Charlie said, forcing a smile. "It's all for me. And a cup of English breakfast tea too. Thank you."

As the waitress walked away, Charlie got out her phone and dialed her boss's number. She had woken up to two voice mail messages asking her to call Jess urgently, something that wasn't unusual even on the weekend.

"Hi, Jess, I just got your messages—"

"Charlie—thanks for calling back. So, the October edition's just gone to press, and your Big Apple coffee feature looks amazing."

"Great," Charlie said, relieved. She looked up and nodded in acknowledgment as the waitress set down the things she'd ordered on her table.

Charlie eyed the chocolate cupcake suspiciously. She poked

at it with her fork and dry bits of icing flaked off. The cupcake then crumbled into pieces.

"The tearoom research is going well, I hope?" Jess asked.

"Oh, fine," Charlie lied. "Plenty of good places to choose from up here."

She picked up the blueberry muffin and took a tentative bite—it was doughy and flavorless, and she had to resist the temptation to spit it out. A swig of overbrewed tea did nothing to help.

"I'm glad to hear it," Jess said, "because there are a couple of changes I need to update you on."

"Changes?" Charlie put her cup of tea to one side.

"As you know, sales loved the tearoom concept, so much so that they don't just want an article—they want a twelve-page pull-out section of reviews. The idea is to tie the release in with the tea exhibition at Earls Court, and distribute the edition early there. So we'll need more content, and we're working to a new print deadline."

"OK, that's great," Charlie said, excited but feeling slightly panicky at the same time. "What dates will we be working to?"

"We'll need copies for the exhibition at the end of October, so all the content from you will have to be delivered, ready for editing, by early October."

Charlie bit her lip. She relished a challenge, but this was pushing it.

"That gives me just over three weeks." Her mind raced. It was twice as much content as she normally put together for the magazine. "Could I have Nicky to help me out with the research?"

"Sorry, she's busy helping Marcus at the moment." The line went quiet. "You can still deliver this though—right? This is a real opportunity to prove yourself, Charlie. Don't let me down."

"I won't," she said confidently. "I can do it."

Charlie hung up and looked at her diary. Three weeks! She would have to pull out all the stops on the research, compiling a list of tearooms and then visiting them all. And one thing was for sure, she thought, eyeing the sorrowful cakes in front of her. They'd have to be a lot better than Katie's Kitchen.

A re you OK with lentil casserole?" Pippa asked her sister in the kitchen that evening, clicking the oven on to preheat.

After a day walking around the town, trying and failing to find a tearoom worth reviewing, Charlie was looking forward to eating something heartier than a cupcake. She'd already planned that night's dinner, though—stopping by a supermarket on the way home and buying ingredients for a lasagna.

"Pip, I thought we agreed I'd cook tonight? You can put your feet up for once."

"Oh, it's no trouble, honestly." Pippa batted away her words with a French-manicured hand. "I whipped it up this morning, it only needs warming up." She removed a dish from the fridge and set it on the counter.

"OK, well . . . thank you." There was no point arguing about it. "I'll pour the wine, in that case." She took two glasses out of the kitchen cabinet. Most things can be improved with a glass of Rioja—it was the closest thing Charlie had to a motto.

"Say when," she said as she poured the wine.

"Oh, none for me, I'm breastfeeding," Pippa replied. She tilted her head slightly. "Did you forget?"

"Oh, sorry. I thought you could still have a little bit?"

"I suppose some people do." Pippa shrugged. "If I wanted

to put my own pleasure ahead of the future well-being of my child, I guess I would too." She laughed hollowly.

Charlie silently returned the second glass to the cupboard, and filled her own. "Is Luke going to be in tonight?"

"No. He's finishing something at work. He'll be home late again."

"That's a shame. Hopefully I'll get a chance to catch up with him soon."

Pippa merely nodded in reply. Charlie noticed a distant look in her sister's eye.

They sat down at the kitchen table, and Pippa took a sip from her glass of water. "I spoke to Mum and Dad earlier."

"Oh? How are they?"

"Mum's had a hard time with her back, but it's getting better."

Charlie tried to recall a mention of it.

"She pulled a muscle gardening," Pippa continued. "But you knew about that, right?"

"No, I don't remember her saying anything. Is it bad?"

"It's causing her a fair bit of pain, yes."

"Poor Mum. I don't expect Dad's much help with that."

"You don't speak to them very often, do you?" Pippa said curtly.

"I'll call. I didn't realize . . ."

Charlie felt a niggle of guilt. Ringing her parents had a tendency to slip down her to-do list, even though she thought of them quite often. She was sure it hadn't been *that* long since she'd phoned them for a proper chat.

"Look," Pippa continued, taking a deep breath, "I probably shouldn't interfere. I told her I wouldn't say anything." She bit her lip. "Mum got upset the other day, saying that you hardly ever ring anymore."

The words stung. "OK," Charlie said. She sat back in her chair, her hand on the stem of her wineglass. "Well . . . perhaps she's right. Yes, I suppose I should call them more. From now on, I'll make sure I do."

"I mean, I know it's hard sometimes . . ." Pippa smoothed back her pale blond hair and glanced out of the French windows toward the garden. "And Mum and Dad understand that you're busy, but the thing is, Charlie, even with three kids I still find time—"

"Point made," Charlie interrupted her sister gently.

"I was only saying." Pippa looked wounded.

"I'll make more of an effort. What else can I say?"

"God, Charlie, you are so sensitive at the moment."

"Am I?"

"Yes. You were snappy with me last night, too, remember?"

"Oh, come on. You were implying that my attitude to work was affecting my personal life."

"Now you're being silly. That's not at all what I was saying," Pippa said, with a weary laugh. "I was merely making a general comment. How was I to know mentioning Ben was out of bounds?"

"It's not," Charlie said. "But I didn't particularly like the direction the conversation was taking. Besides, there's a time and a place, and that's not in front of Flo. You know how she was looking forward to being a flower girl."

"She felt very let down when you called off the wedding, that's true."

"Look, I realize this is hard for you to understand, Pip. But I'm actually happier now."

Pippa leaned back in her chair. "*Now*, maybe."

"Meaning?" Charlie tried to suppress her growing irritation.

"I'm only trying to protect you."

"Protect me from what?"

"From disappointment," Pippa said softly and slowly. "I don't want you to miss the boat, Charlie. Having children is such a wonderful thing—and you're in your thirties already. I'm not the only one who's concerned."

"So what, you and Mum have been discussing me behind my back?" Charlie's cheeks grew hot.

"We're worried about you, that's all. Ben seemed nice enough, a few things aside. If it hadn't been for you working all the time . . . Don't you agree there's a chance that might have pushed him away?"

The last shred of calm inside Charlie disappeared. "Have you forgotten what happened?"

"He backed off from the relationship, from the sounds of things."

"Backed off? Is that what you'd call it? I remember it slightly differently," Charlie said, struggling to keep her cool as she recalled the humiliation.

"Classic cry-for-help behavior," Pippa said quietly.

Charlie shook her head. "You're actually taking Ben's side, aren't you? Unbelievable. Even for you, Pippa."

"All I'm saying is, perhaps he sensed you weren't entirely committed to a future with him. Everyone expresses need in different ways."

Charlie finished her glass of wine in silence. If she erupted now, Pippa would have won.

The timer pinged.

Pippa smiled. "That's the oven heated up. I'll pop our dinner in . . ."

# 7

Monday, September 8

By Kat's feet in the hallway was a suitcase packed with everything Leo would need for the next three weeks, carefully sorted, his clothes folded neatly. As today approached, her heart had grown heavy, knowing that Jake was coming to pick Leo up and it would be weeks before she saw him again.

Leo, oblivious to her anxiety, watched the door, an eager expression on his face.

"Are you sure I can't take Stegosaurus?" Leo said, turning back to her.

"There's not enough room," Kat said. "Your grandma and grandpa will have other toys for you to play with."

Leo sighed, and looked at the door again expectantly.

As they waited, Kat sifted through the post on the mat: a note from the GP's surgery, a takeaway menu and a postcard with a picture of a grand Russian palace on the front. She smiled, knowing who the postcard would be from, and flipped it over.

She showed it to Leo. "Here—this one's for you. Shall we read it together?"

He nodded.

*Dear Leo,*

*Here I am in St. Petersburg in Russia—there's a lot of snow and castles like in your storybooks. I have to rush now to get a train for the next part of my journey.*

*Sending hugs. I miss you!*

*Grandpa*

"I could use my sled in Russia," Leo said cheerfully.

Kat smiled. "Yes, you definitely could."

"When is Grandpa coming back? I miss him."

"Before Christmas," Kat said, silently counting the days. She missed spending time with her dad, but at the same time was glad he had made the trip—it had always been a dream of his. In the weeks leading up to his departure, he had been full of energy and enthusiasm, as if he were a young man again.

"And Grandpa won't mind if I go and stay with my other granddad and grandma?"

"Of course not," Kat said, laughing. "He knows he has to share." She ruffled Leo's hair.

Through the frosted glass, Kat saw a tall figure approach their front door.

"Dad's here," she said, letting Leo open the door. His face brightened instantly when he caught sight of his father.

"Hello there," Jake said. He swept Leo up into his arms and raised him high above his head. Leo let out a loud, gurgling laugh and kicked his legs happily.

Jake's dark brown eyes met Kat's as he lowered his son to the ground, and he smiled at her. For a moment, it was as if everything was the way it used to be. As if Jake was simply home from getting a pint of milk.

"What time's your train?" Kat asked.

"Eleven thirty."

She checked her phone. "You'd better be off, then."

"We're going on holiday," Leo said gleefully.

"Yes, we are," Jake said. "I hope you've got a warm jumper with you. It's cold in Scotland, you know."

"I packed a few," Kat replied. She bent down to Leo's level and gave him a hug and a kiss. "Be good for your dad on the train."

"I will be."

"I'll call you as soon as we get back," Jake said.

Kat wiped a tear away hurriedly, and when Leo looked up at her she put on a smile.

"You OK?" Jake mouthed to Kat, over Leo's head.

"Yes, of course I'm fine," she said. "Go on, or you'll miss your train."

She watched as Leo and Jake walked away from her down the bay. Then, when they were finally out of sight, she closed the door.

# 8

Monday, September 8

Charlie entered the South Cliff Hotel and made her way to the front desk. The grand white building up on the Esplanade had caught her eye as she strolled around town; she'd decided it must offer wonderful sea views if nothing else.

A young, dark-haired receptionist greeted her with a smile. "Good afternoon, how can I help?"

Charlie looked at the receptionist's name tag: *Cally*.

"Hi. Do you have any single rooms available?"

The tension between Charlie and Pippa had worsened, and while she'd tried to be patient, she simply couldn't face the thought of another night under her sister's roof. On the other hand, she didn't feel ready to go home yet—there were tea-rooms here in the north that she wanted to see, and Scarborough was as good a place as any to use as a base.

"Yes, we do," Cally said. "And as we're out of season now, the rates are reasonable—here's our price list."

"Looks fine. Can I book a single for tonight and tomorrow night, please?"

"Of course." Cally took down her details.

"I'll bring my things along later."

"We look forward to seeing you then."

Charlie put her handbag on her shoulder and was about to leave when, on a whim, she turned back.

"It's Cally, right? Could I ask you a question?"

"Of course—fire away." Cally smiled warmly.

"Do you know of any tearooms in the area?"

"Sure. We've got the Hanover round the corner, they do a nice cup of tea . . ."

"Actually," Charlie said, wondering how to phrase her request, "I'm hoping to find somewhere special."

"Ah." Cally seemed to be looking Charlie over, assessing her. "In that case—I know just the spot."

Following the instructions the receptionist had given her, Charlie turned right when she drew level with the rainbow-colored beach huts, and took the path leading up and away from the sea. As she turned, the café came into view: a wooden building with a small clock tower on it, the windows partially obscured by pretty lace curtains.

Inside, she saw a woman behind the counter, taking a cake off a tray and placing it carefully on a stand. She felt as if she should knock before she went in, the scene seemed so intimate. She pushed the door.

"Hi," the owner said, looking up. "Welcome to the Seafront. Table for one?"

"Yes, thanks."

Charlie followed the owner, who introduced herself as Letty, to a corner table with a sea view. The décor in the café was simple, old fashioned, and jazz was playing—it was as if the last few decades had been asked to stop at the front door. Letty passed her a menu and motioned for her to sit down.

Next to her were shelves filled with glass jars of loose-leaf tea. Brown luggage labels with handwritten notes were attached to them: *Jasmine, Polish Rose, Summer Fruits . . .*

A pretty woman with short dark hair was sitting at the table next to hers, studying a newspaper and circling adverts with a pen.

Charlie looked down at her menu, but only briefly—she already knew what she wanted. Letty came over with her notebook. "What can I get you?"

"Your classic afternoon tea, please."

"Of course. What kind of tea would you like with it?"

Charlie's eyes drifted to the jars lining the wall; she was bewildered by the range of options.

"Here, let me show you," Letty said. She brought some jars over to the table and sat down with Charlie. "We've got spiced orange"—she opened the jar and sniffed it herself, before handing it over to Charlie.

Charlie took in a lungful of the sweet, citrusy scent. It made her mouth water.

"Summer fruits is popular too," Letty said, passing her another jar.

After peering at the dried pink and purple petals for a moment, Charlie opened the lid. The scent was light and energizing.

The woman at the table next to her spoke up: "If you prefer something classic, the Lady Grey is hard to beat."

"I'm spoiled for choice," Charlie said, smiling at the dark-haired woman, then looking back at Letty. "I think I'll go for the Lady Grey this time, seeing as it comes recommended."

"Good choice. Kat has impeccable taste," Letty said, nodding toward the other woman. "She's my informal tasting assistant. You'll never meet a woman more passionate about tea."

Kat laughed. "That's Letty's polite way of saying I'm obsessive."

"A tea obsessive," Charlie echoed, an idea forming. "Would you have time to join me? There's something I'd love to talk to you about . . ."

⌒

K at finished her Lady Grey and set the delicate teacup back in its saucer. Charlie scanned her face for signs of interest in her offer, but could find no clues there.

"So, the idea is I'd be finding these tearooms with you, trying them out, and then helping you write reviews?"

"That's right." Charlie nodded. "It's the tea itself I could do with some help on—I've always been more of a coffee drinker, so I'm starting pretty much from scratch for this piece. How did you get interested in it?"

"As a teenager," Kat said. "My dad gave me my first box of tea, and from there I started a collection. When I got a Saturday job during my A-levels I'd save the money and come here on a weekend. I tried all the teas Letty had, then helped her build up the list."

"That's wonderful! So you know all about this area. I need someone like you who knows what they're talking about. Normally I'd do the research myself, but I have my hands full at the moment. I'm afraid I wouldn't be able to pay you much, but it would be enough to cover your expenses with a little extra on top. If food writing is something you're interested in, you'd be learning on the job."

As she waited for Kat's response, Charlie finished the last piece of rose-and-pistachio cake. She had been drawing it out, savoring every bite—rich, indulgent and delicately flavored. It was one of the best cakes she'd ever tasted.

"What kind of places were you thinking of?"

"These." Charlie got out her journal and showed Kat the list of tearooms she'd jotted down. "I could do with your help on the first few." Kat read over the names, nodded and passed the list back. Charlie couldn't shake the feeling that she was the one being interviewed, rather than the other way around. It unsettled her—she was used to being the one in control.

"I'd want to feature this place, of course," Charlie said.

"Here?" Kat's hazel eyes widened.

"Absolutely. It's perfect. This is exactly the kind of place I've been looking for. A real hidden gem. In fact, I'd never have stumbled on it if the receptionist at the South Cliff Hotel hadn't mentioned—"

"Cally told you about this place?" Kat seemed to relax a little then, and for the second time that day Charlie felt as if she'd passed some kind of test.

"Yes. Not right away, though. I got the feeling she was quite reluctant to begin with."

"That's because the Seafront is as close as we have to a secret round here."

"I see," Charlie said, her excitement growing as she considered the potential to change the tearoom's fortunes. "Well, it's one we can share now." She smiled. "With a feature in *Indulge*, we could make this a real destination venue, drawing in customers from all over the country. Send it stratospheric."

"I don't know about that . . ." Kat said, shaking her head warily.

"Why not?" Charlie said, running with the idea now. "An article I wrote in the spring brought huge crowds to the cafés that I recommended. This place may be half-empty now, but it could turn into a gold mine."

Kat glanced over at Letty, who was taking a bill to an elderly couple in the far corner of the room.

"And you think that's what Letty wants?" Kat said, furrowing her brow. "She likes that it's mainly familiar faces in here. That's why Cally didn't direct you here right away."

"But surely everyone wants more business these days?"

"Not everyone. Letty's got a cheap lease on the premises, and she doesn't spend much money on luxuries. If she needs anything else her son, Euan, looks out for her."

"So she keeps the tearoom running because she enjoys it?"

"That's right."

"Oh." Charlie couldn't hide her disappointment.

"Look, Charlie. It's kind of you to ask me to help with your feature, but I don't think—"

Charlie had to act fast. Kat was the ideal person to assist her—she was sure of it now—but if she didn't do something she was going to slip away.

"I'm not asking out of kindness—I need someone like you on board."

"I don't know . . ." Kat was shaking her head.

"Last try," Charlie said, summoning her best negotiation skills. "If I were to leave the Seafront out of the feature—so that this place stays a well-kept secret—would that change your mind?"

The corners of Kat's mouth twitched slightly, and after a moment, a broad smile came to her lips.

"OK," she said. "If the Seafront is out, then I'm in."

Charlie smiled back, relieved and excited. "Brilliant," she said. "Although I have to say it pains me not to include this place—it's perfect."

"Well, now it can stay that way," Kat replied.


Charlie walked back to Pippa's house, full of enthusiasm for the feature she was going to write. She'd arranged to pick Kat up the following day so they could drive to York. With her help, Charlie was confident she could put together an edition of the magazine that would prove she'd make the perfect editor to take the reins from Jess.

Pippa answered the door dressed in a pair of leggings and a lilac top that showed off her slim figure. Her blond hair was neatly blow-dried and she was cradling Gracie in her arms.

"Hi, Charlie," she said nonchalantly. She stood aside and Charlie came into the hallway.

Charlie steeled herself for the conversation she'd been dreading. "Pippa, I don't want to upset you, but I think it might be better for all of us if I stayed in a hotel tonight."

"In a hotel?" Pippa said, looking stung. "Is this because of what happened last night?"

"Partly," Charlie said. "We're too grown up to be squabbling like teenagers."

Pippa bit her lip and looked down. "It sounds as though you've made up your mind."

Charlie walked past her and up the stairs.

"You always have left when things got tough," Pippa called up.

Charlie turned around. "What do you mean by that?"

"I've tried everything I can to make you feel at home here, because I know how much it means to Mum and Dad that the two of us get along." She sounded choked up. "But instead of trying to fix things, you're giving up."

"I have tried. I think we'll get on a lot better if I don't stay."

"Go then," sighed Pippa. "Although I have to say Flo and Jacob are going to be very disappointed."

Charlie ignored her sister, and went up to the spare room, stuffing her clothes and makeup into her suitcase. She was bristling with all the pent-up emotion of what remained unsaid. More than ever, she wanted to be out of Pippa's house and in her own space.

When she came out, she saw Pippa hadn't moved from her spot in the hallway.

"If you carry on pushing people away, Charlie, you may never find anyone to share your life with. You know that, don't you?"

Staying silent, Charlie wheeled her suitcase out of the front door without looking back.


You walked out?" Sarah said.

Charlie pulled her hair back in a ponytail as she spoke with her friend through the laptop screen.

"Yes. I'm in a hotel now. I had to get out of there or I think we would have ended up strangling each other."

"So things haven't got any better?"

"Good God, no. She's still the same old Pippa. In fact, she's worse. I don't know what's happened to her. She's turned into some kind of yummy mumzilla."

"That sounds scary."

"It *is*. I know we're different, but I've always respected her decisions. She shows zero respect for mine. It's all a game of one-upmanship to her. She even started sticking up for Ben at one point."

"You're kidding."

"I drove him away by being too obsessed with work, according to her."

"That's not the way I remember it. Don't want to rub salt in the wound, but wasn't there a lap dancer involved?"

"Urgh. Yes, there was. So classy."

"And Pippa has the cheek to accuse you of driving him

away! That's ridiculous. So, what's the plan now, are you leaving?"

"No, I've already made arrangements to stay on and do some research for the magazine. I've met someone up here who's going to help me out, a woman called Kat—she's an expert on tea. I can't wait to get started."

"That's the spirit," Sarah said. "Good luck."

# 9

Tuesday, September 9

Séraphine kneaded croissant pastry on the worktop, the repetitive motion soothing her. Through Adam's kitchen window, she could see a mist over the park that morning. Only one dog walker was out braving the drizzle: an old man who carried an umbrella as he strode around the lake with his greyhound. Séraphine couldn't help but wonder if the photos of a sunny seaside town she'd looked at online had been of some other place.

Back in France her days started when the twins came and sat on the end of her bed, chattering about cartoons and games they wanted to play. Here in Scarborough, it was the glint of gray morning light through her curtains that greeted her each morning. On her first day, she'd woken bleary-eyed, her fingers touching an unfamiliar quilt. It had taken her a moment to remember where she was.

She'd grown accustomed to her room, but some things had been less easy to get used to.

Séraphine placed the neat pastry crescents she'd made on a baking tray, and put them in the oven. At the sound of Zoe's footsteps on the stairs her heart sank. She told herself to be positive—today was a new day. The day she would make it work with Zoe.

"What are you making?" Zoe asked, calling over from the

kitchen doorway. She was dressed in yellow pajamas, and her long brown hair was mussed from sleep.

"I made croissants," Séraphine said brightly, pointing to the oven. The room was starting to fill with the sweet smell of freshly baked pastries.

"But you know I always have cereal," Zoe said, narrowing her eyes.

Séraphine held in a sigh. "Well, today we're going to try something different. Your dad said you used to love these when you were little."

"Oh? I don't remember," Zoe said, pulling out a chair at the table and slumping down on it.

"You'll enjoy them," Séraphine said, bringing some fresh orange juice over to the table, and a small cafetière of coffee for Adam.

"How do you know?" Zoe retorted, with that expression— tilted head and eyes half-closed with suspicion—that Séraphine had seen so often during her short stay in the house.

"I hope you'll enjoy them, then. Please don't be rude, Zoe."

"I was only asking."

"So, today, after school, maybe we could go for a walk in the park. They said the sun is going to come out later."

Zoe looked at her, silent and unflinching. "Maybe."

"We could read *The Little Prince* when we get back in."

"That book's stupid. I don't even understand it." Zoe pouted. "Can I have my cereal now?"

"OK," Séraphine said, reluctantly getting back to her feet. She stood for a moment and took a breath, composing herself, then got a packet of Cheerios out and poured them into a bowl.

"Morning, Séraphine." She turned to see Adam, dressed in a shirt and trousers, his hair still damp from the shower. "Wow, something smells delicious."

"Thank you. I made croissants," Séraphine said wearily.

"Fantastic."

"That's what I said," Zoe told her father, her eyes brightening. "Fantastic."

That afternoon, Séraphine and Zoe took off their muddy boots in the hallway. "Let's go through to the living room," Séraphine said.

"What for?"

"To study. It's time for your French class."

"No way. I'm going to my room."

"Look, I'm not here to punish you, Zoe. Your dad wants you to learn French, and he's asked me to teach you. Now come with me and let's get started."

Zoe followed her, dragging her heels. In the living room she slouched down in an armchair. "You're not the first, you know."

"Sorry?"

"You're not the first French tutor I've had." Zoe twirled a strand of her long dark hair. "Although I suppose you're the only one Dad has insisted on having actually live with us. None of them have managed to teach me anything."

"You seem proud of that fact."

"I'm not. I just don't care. What am I supposed to do with French, anyway? I'm never going back to France."

"How can you be so sure?"

"I don't know. But I am." Zoe looked down, pulling at the loose stitching on her sock.

"Why is that?"

The girl shrugged. "It's a horrible place."

⌒

"Honestly, Papa. I'm fine," Séraphine said on the phone that evening. She perched on the edge of her bed, towel-drying her hair after the bath. "It's an adjustment. A different culture."

"It doesn't sound like a cultural difference to me, it sounds like bad behavior."

"I'm sure things will improve when we get to know each other better. How are things going with you, anyway?" she asked, anxious to change the subject. She pictured herself with her family—laughing with her mother in the kitchen, reading her little brother and sister bedtime stories—and felt a pang of homesickness.

"We've had a wonderful weekend. Ravi and Anna had a party for their twenty-fifth wedding anniversary on Saturday night, so your *grandmère* looked after the children and your mother and I went along. Hélène made some of her famous tarte tatin. Almost everyone in the village was there. We really enjoyed ourselves."

"I'm glad to hear it." She tried to push aside thoughts of how she'd spent that evening, alone in her room reading.

"They asked if you were enjoying Scarborough. Actually, come to think of it, Anna mentioned something I should tell you . . ." His voice went muffled as he called out into the room. "Hélène, what was it that Anna said?"

Hélène took the phone. "Hello, sweetpea. So, Anna says there is a gorgeous little tearoom overlooking the sea that has the most delicious cakes and pastries. Run by a lovely lady, she said. Lucy or something. The Seafront Tearoom, on South Bay by the beach huts."

Séraphine hadn't walked past the lighthouse and harbor

yet, so that end of the beach was unknown to her, but she'd seen the huts from a distance. "I'll take a look," she promised.

"OK, *ma chérie*," Hélène said. "Dinner is ready, so we'll have to say good-bye. Sending kisses."

This place is boring. I'm going to play my DS," Zoe said, sitting down and immediately getting the game console out of her bag.

After picking Zoe up from school on Wednesday, Séraphine had brought her to the tearoom that her mother had mentioned on the phone, but she was already starting to regret it.

The owner, seated behind the counter, caught Séraphine's eye and gave her a sympathetic look. Séraphine smiled and went up to order. "Could we have some of your scones with jam please?"

"Of course." She reached into the glass cabinet to retrieve a flowered plate piled high with them.

"They look delicious."

"Thank you. My specialty. I'm Letty, by the way." Her voice was kind and welcoming.

"Séraphine."

"You're from France?"

"Yes. And I wouldn't mind being back there now. Is the weather always like this in September?" Séraphine gazed out of the window, where the raindrops dripped heavily from the red awning onto the ground below.

"Oh, we never know quite what we're going to get. Only thing you can rely on is the chill wind."

"Don't tell me," Letty continued, lowering her voice to a whisper. "Even in that rain you'd rather be out there alone than in here, trying to get Zoe to cooperate."

Séraphine laughed in spite of herself. She wondered how

old Letty was. Despite the papery-thin quality of the skin on her cheeks and around her eyes, there was a playfulness about her that defied age.

"Yes. Is it that obvious?"

"You're not the only one to have your patience tested by her," Letty said, cutting the scones in two and placing them on fine china plates, next to a tiny dish of raspberry jam and another of butter.

"How do you know her?"

"Her father, Adam, and my son have been best friends since school. Nearly twenty years now."

"Adam's a fantastic guy."

"Isn't he? Life's dealt him a tough hand, but you'll never hear him complain. It can't be easy for him, bringing Zoe up on his own."

"He's patient. Maybe I need more patience," Séraphine said. "I always thought I was good with children. But this . . ."

"Don't be hard on yourself, sweetheart," Letty said gently, putting a hand on her arm. Séraphine felt the warmth of her touch, and it calmed her a little. "She's a challenging girl, Adam knows that."

"Yes," Séraphine said, biting her lip. Now she'd started talking she was terrified at the way her feelings had come to the surface.

"You miss home, don't you?"

"Very much," Séraphine said, her eyes filling with tears. "It's the little things. I spoke to my family last night and my mum had made tarte tatin—"

"Ooh, delicious."

"It's one of our favorite dishes to make together. I can almost smell and taste it now." She recalled the sweet apple flavor and her mouth watered.

"I've always wanted to be able to make that."

"You have? I can show you."

"Would you? That would be lovely. Why don't you come by on Friday evening?"

Séraphine hesitated. "I think I'm meant to be looking after Zoe then."

"Don't worry. I'll have a word with Adam, he won't mind. And if you enjoy those scones"—she pointed to the plates she had prepared—"I'll share my secret recipe with you."

"You would?" Séraphine said, her spirits lifting. "I'd like that very much."

"It's a date, then. In the meantime," Letty told her, "there are a couple of people I'd like to introduce you to."

Séraphine looked over at Zoe, who was still immersed in her game.

"She'll be OK for five minutes," Letty reassured her. She led Séraphine over to a table in the corner, where two women were huddled over an iPad. A blonde, in jeans and a black blazer, and a woman with cropped brown hair, dressed in a vintage flowered dress and biker boots.

"Kat, Charlie—this is Séraphine. She's an au pair, new to town. I thought I'd bring her over to say hi."

"Hello. Lovely to meet you," Kat said, shaking Séraphine's hand. Séraphine noticed the tattoo on the underside of her wrist: a bold, unbroken circle. Letty smiled and left them.

"Hi," Charlie said. She put the iPad to one side. "Care to join us? That's if you are up for being bombarded with chat about tearooms."

"That sounds fun," Séraphine said, bringing a chair up to their table. "What are you working on?"

"It's for an edition of the food and drink magazine Charlie

works on," Kat explained. "We're going to be reviewing tea-rooms, and we're planning a trip to York tomorrow."

"How interesting. I love reading those kind of articles—you can almost taste all of the cakes and pastries, and yet it's completely calorie-free." Séraphine smiled.

"Exactly," Charlie said. "Although the same can't be said when you're doing the tasting."

"It must be a dream," Séraphine said. "I'm a bit fanatical about cakes. There's bakery similar to this in my village at home—you know that when you go in there you're going to be able to try out something delicious."

"That's exactly the kind of place we're looking for," Kat said.

Séraphine glanced back over at Zoe, to check she was OK. She had put down her DS to eat her scone.

"You're on duty?"

Séraphine nodded. "Yes."

"Where is it you're staying in Scarborough?" Kat asked.

"Over by Peasholm Park."

"Nice. I grew up round there. Is it going well?"

"Polite answer, or honest answer?" Séraphine said quietly.

"Oh dear," Charlie said. "I'm sure it'll get better."

"Do you think so?" Séraphine asked.

"Now that you've found the Seafront, it definitely will." Kat smiled warmly.

"I've got a day off tomorrow, so that will help."

Charlie glanced at Kat, who nodded in silent agreement, and then they both looked back at Séraphine.

"If you don't have plans," Charlie said, "why not come and join us?"

Séraphine smiled. "I'd love to."

# 10

Thursday, September 11

"Ready?" Charlie asked. She and Séraphine were standing in the hallway of Kat's flat.

Kat had a last look in the mirror. Her hair was pinned back on one side with a mother-of-pearl vintage hair comb, and she was wearing an oyster-and-black tea dress with T-bar heels.

"I think I am, yes," she said. "What am I forgetting?"

She checked her handbag quickly. Mobile, lipstick, keys, notebook, pen—it looked so empty without the rice cakes and wet wipes that usually cluttered it up. Her heart contracted a little as she thought of Leo.

"Nothing—as long as you've remembered your appetite," Charlie laughed.

"I've brought mine," Séraphine said.

"No problems there." Kat smiled and closed her door behind her.

They turned onto the side street, and Charlie pressed the button on her keys. The lights flashed on a green MG convertible.

Kat drew in her breath. "That's yours?"

"Yep," Charlie replied proudly. "My pride and joy."

Séraphine got in the back, and Kat climbed into the passenger seat and ran her hand over the cream leather. "Wow, this is nice." She leaned into the plush passenger seat, enjoying the sensation of the leather molding to the shape of her body. "I've never been in a car like this before."

"Wait till we get going."

Charlie turned the key, switched the stereo on and wound down the windows on both sides. A young man walking past on the pavement stopped to admire them, giving a nod of appreciation.

Charlie put her foot down on the accelerator and Kat instinctively held the sides of her seat.

"Road trip, here we come," Charlie said, turning to Kat and Séraphine with a smile.

They listened to music on the journey, and Kat's mind drifted as she gazed out at the fields. It felt strange to be in the company of two women she barely knew, but she was more comfortable than she'd expected. Séraphine, with her warm, down-to-earth nature, was immediately welcoming. Charlie—Kat hadn't quite worked her out yet. She was friendly, of course, and impressively determined in her approach to work. Kat wondered what she made of her, if she thought less of her for not being as ambitious.

An hour later, in the early afternoon, they arrived in York.

"First stop, Betty's," Charlie said. They walked along the cobbled streets until they came to the tearoom. "Not exactly secret, but an essential visit."

"So this is it," Kat said, peering in through the glass of the tearoom in awe. Inside, the tables were made up with crisp tablecloths, waitresses serving in traditional black-and-white outfits. "I've always wanted to come here."

They were greeted by a waitress who showed them to a table in a peaceful corner of the room.

"Thanks," Charlie said. Without looking at the menu, she

put in their order. "We haven't got that long, but could we have full afternoon tea? With—what type of tea shall we get?"

"Don't look at me," Séraphine said with a smile. "You two are the experts."

"Darjeeling," Kat said, without hesitation.

"Right," Charlie said. "That."

A few minutes later, the waitress brought over a white teapot and teacups.

"The champagne among teas," Kat said, lifting the lid of the teapot and drinking in the aroma. "Smell that. There's a trace of blackcurrant in this one."

"Delicious," Séraphine said, leaning in.

A tiered cake stand arrived. Kat took in the finely crafted mix of savory and sweet. Finger sandwiches with delicate layers of cucumber and smoked salmon were placed neatly on the bottom tier, above them a variety of cakes and pastries.

Kat poured the tea out carefully into two fragile white teacups. The light-colored liquid was precisely the shade it should be.

"Let's get started, shall we?" Charlie said.

The three women sipped tea, and each tasted one of the sandwiches, discussing their initial impressions. Charlie ordered a few extra things, and asked the waitress to bring them some water.

"Should we be taking notes?" Kat asked.

"Definitely not," Charlie said. "We don't want them to know we're reviewing, so just relax and enjoy."

"If you insist." Séraphine smiled. "Shall we try these?" She pointed to the macaroons. "They're familiar territory for me."

"Rude not to, really," Charlie said, passing one to Kat and taking one for herself.

Charlie finished hers in two bites. "What do you think?"

"Good—there's an exquisite subtlety to the pistachio flavor," Séraphine said.

"They haven't gone overboard on the filling either. A pretty perfect macaroon all in all," Kat said.

They drank their way through a pot of tea, enthusiastically sharing thoughts on the almond slices and chocolate éclairs. When only crumbs and tea leaves remained, Kat asked Charlie what the next stage of the process was.

"We'll pool our notes, then write up the reviews, and the final stage is to e-mail them over for approval. I'm guest-editing this edition, but Jess, my boss, will still have the final word."

"That sounds good," Kat said. "Well, I've got a lot to say already. I love this place."

"How come you haven't been here before?" Charlie asked her. "You only live an hour away."

Kat toyed with her cup and saucer, stalling. Charlie waited for her to speak, her blue eyes kind, her expression open and relaxed.

"I can't afford this sort of thing," she said. "Since Leo arrived, we can't stretch to much beyond the occasional trip to the Seafront. And even then Letty sometimes helps us out."

"I see," Charlie said. "Letty seems kind."

"Letty's wonderful," Kat said. "She always puts other people first. She helped me out when I needed it most."

"When was that?" Séraphine asked.

Kat paused, looking at Charlie and Séraphine. She barely knew them, but something told her she could talk to them honestly.

"Messy breakup, with Leo's dad."

"What happened?" Charlie asked.

"We weren't ready to have a baby," Kat said. "We'd only been living together a couple of months when I got pregnant with Leo."

"How did he react?" Charlie said.

"Pretty badly. He missed our old life a lot, and I guess he responded by carrying on living it—going out with friends, drinking, coming home late. Having a child brings some people together, but in our case it drove us apart."

"That must have been very hard," Séraphine said.

"It was a lonely time, yes. We didn't talk enough."

"Are things any better now that you're separated?" Séraphine asked.

"They are, yes. We're finding a way, muddling through—he's finally started to embrace being a dad. Leo's staying with him up in Scotland at the moment, the first time that we've done that."

"You seem very forgiving, and strong," Séraphine said.

"Ha ha," Kat said. "I'm not that strong. I just get on with things as best as I can. It does sometimes seem as if everyone else's life is smooth sailing, though."

"I don't know about that," Charlie said, with a wry smile. "Mine certainly isn't. I thought I'd be getting married next spring—that didn't exactly work out as planned."

"I'm sorry to hear that," Kat said. So Charlie's life wasn't perfect after all. It surprised her.

"These things happen." Charlie shrugged. "But I won't pretend it didn't knock the wind out of me. I met him at work, and after a year we moved in together. For the first time in my life, it seemed as though everything was going according to plan." Charlie paused, thinking about Ben. "I've kissed enough frogs, and I was sure that Ben was different. He was a good guy—everyone told me so—and when he asked me to marry him I didn't hesitate. This was it. He was The One. My happily ever after."

She shook her head. "Obviously it didn't work out that way."

"What went wrong?" Kat asked, her voice soft.

"One morning we got up, talked about our honeymoon to Italy over breakfast, and took the bus into the office. I sat down at my desk, ready to start work, same as any other day. Then Jess—my boss—called me and asked me to come into her office. All sorts of thoughts went through my mind—that I'd overlooked some detail or missed a deadline. But no—she'd heard from the sales guys about Ben sleeping with a lap dancer on one of their nights out. Apparently they were all talking about it."

"Ouch," Kat said, shaking her head. "Your boss told you?"

"Yes. As if finding out wasn't humiliating enough in itself. I broke up with him that night, and the next day I stuck every card he'd ever given me into the shredder at work."

"Good for you," Séraphine said.

"There was no way I was going back to him," Charlie said. "Anyway, what's so galling is that I think he was relieved. I guess he'd been looking for a get-out, and that was as good a way as any. I'm glad I'm not with him, I truly am. But I still feel as though it took away part of me. It hasn't been easy, even though I know it was for the best."

"There's a lot to be said for being single," Kat said.

"There certainly is," Charlie agreed, smiling.

Séraphine nodded, but didn't say anything. Kat wondered if it was because she was shy, or if she was holding something back. She seemed comfortable having the conversation, but it was as if she preferred to let Kat and Charlie do most of the talking.

"Spending all evening in the bath with a glass of wine and a good book—you can't beat that," Charlie said.

"Starfishing in bed," Kat said. "That's my favorite thing. Oh, and eating ice cream at midnight."

"Yes. Although for me it's got to be ketchup and chips, in a sandwich," Charlie added.

"Eewww!" Kat screwed up her face.

"Absolutely—try it," Charlie insisted.

"I guess even a foodie's allowed time off. What else?"

"Watching what I want, when I want," Charlie batted back.
"No complaining during *The Great British Bake Off*."

"Time to sew quilts, and cushions."

"I don't seem to get round to any of that," Charlie said,
laughing. "But reading the paper and not having to hand over
the best sections—that's another thing I love."

"Knowing how to fix all the small things in your house.
Because no one else is going to mend them for you," Kat
added.

"Oh yes," Charlie laughed. "I'm even a spider-removal
expert these days."

"There's more time for friends," Séraphine said.

"Yes," Charlie agreed, smiling warmly. "Definitely that."


C harlie paid the bill, and put on her jacket. "OK—our next
stop is over by the river."

"Let's go," Kat said, getting to her feet.

The sun was out as the three women walked through town,
down cobblestone streets and past Tudor buildings that now
housed boutiques and restaurants. A group of tourists stopped
to take photos by the city walls.

"This place is so pretty," Séraphine said.

"Yes, it is. It's quiet though, isn't it?" Charlie said.

"Do you think?" Kat said, surprised. She glanced around
at the shoppers and sightseers, conscious only of the bustle of
activity surrounding them.

"Compared to London, I suppose," Charlie said. "When
I'm away, I always feel as if I'm missing out on something."

"You're not," Kat said assertively. "Maybe now's a good time to talk through the Cardinal Rule of Afternoon Tea."

"Oh?" Charlie said, raising an eyebrow.

"What's that?" Séraphine asked.

"Let's sit down," Kat said, motioning to a bench.

Charlie checked the time on her phone. "Now?"

"Yes," Kat insisted.

"But . . ."

Kat took Charlie's hand, and the three women sat next to one another on the bench. Leaves fell gently onto the grass in front of them, a freshly laid carpet of greens and golds.

"See that cat?" Kat pointed at a tabby that had found a patch of sunlight on a nearby low wall, and was lying in it, content.

"Yes," Charlie said.

"What is it doing?"

Charlie watched the cat, bathing in its patch of warmth.

"Nothing."

"Nothing? Are you sure?"

"Yes. That cat is fundamentally failing to achieve," Charlie said.

Séraphine laughed. "I disagree. It's living slowly. Contemplating. Enjoying."

"Exactly," Kat said triumphantly. "Séraphine's got it."

"That cat's wasting time," Charlie said firmly.

"No, it isn't." Kat shook her head. "And when we take our time over afternoon tea, neither are we. That's the cardinal rule—never rush. Take time to savor it."

Charlie and Séraphine pored over the menu in the Riverside Tearoom and Kat looked around at the mismatched wooden chairs repainted in teal and primrose yellow, admiring the vintage styling. Tiny origami birds were strung from the ceiling, and standard lamps with handmade shades with seventies florals brought a warm light to the room. The window seat, where the three of them were sitting, was strewn with pretty cushions made up of quilted squares.

"You know what, in the name of research—and seeing as we are now officially not in a hurry—I think we go for the champagne option," Charlie said.

"Are you sure?" Séraphine asked.

"Of course," Charlie said, with a smile. "It's research. Besides, when you've worked as many late nights as I have, you don't feel bad about a few expenses."

"Well, if you insist," Kat said, excited at the prospect.

When the drinks arrived, Kat took a tentative sip, the bubbles dancing on her tongue. She smiled. "I could get used to this."

"So, what do you think of this place?" Charlie said, leaning back in her seat.

"It's cool," Séraphine said. "It's trendier, I suppose. I love what they've done with the antique cake stands." She pointed at the display on the counter.

"I like that too."

"I'm not sure about some of the cake flavors, though," Kat said. "Lemon and lavender?"

"It could go either way, I suppose," said Charlie.

The waitress came over to their table with a tray of cakes and dainty sandwiches.

"Here's to afternoon tea," Charlie said, raising her glass.

"And champagne," Séraphine added.

"And to learning how it should be done," Kat added.

After tea, they took a scenic route back to Charlie's car, chatting and laughing together. Kat's mind buzzed with the new tastes and experiences, and in her new friends' company she felt relaxed and free. On the way home, Charlie turned up the stereo and they sang along to the tunes they knew, explaining some of the lyrics to Séraphine. It was early evening, the sky dark, when they pulled up outside Kat's flat by the pier.

"Same time tomorrow?" Charlie said.

"I can't, I'm afraid," Séraphine said. "I'll be working."

"I'm in," Kat said, smiling widely. "This time, the coast."

# 11

Friday, September 12

"Séraphine, I've just nipped out on my lunch break, so I haven't got long. Could I ask a favor?"

"Sure," Séraphine said. Adam was standing in his hallway, the front door still open. There was an anxious expression on his face.

"Could you make a delivery for me?"

"Depends what it is. I've been warned about people like you," she joked.

"It's nothing dodgy, I promise. Come and see."

He led her into the living room, where in the middle of the floor there was a white metal birdcage.

She approached it and bent down to get a closer look. "Lovebirds. How pretty."

"Yes, they're beautiful, aren't they? Very much in love but sadly no longer so loved by their owner."

"You're not keeping them?"

"No. No way. And luckily we have a taker for them already. You're seeing Letty tonight, aren't you? Do you think you could give them to her for me? She said she could do with some company. She's got that flat over the tearoom. I'd take them myself but I've got an after-hours call-out at Flamingo Land. Zoe's going to be at her violin lesson, so I'll collect her on the way home."

"OK. No problem. I'll take them with me this evening."

"Thanks. I'll pay for a taxi."

Séraphine shook her head. "The bus will be fine."

"If you're sure. And there's one other little thing . . ."

"What is it now?" she asked, laughing. "A tarantula? A boa constrictor?"

"Not that bad," Adam said. A bark from the garden gave it away. Séraphine went over to the window.

"A dog." She smiled. "Where did he come from?"

"I just brought him back. He came in this morning. Part beagle. Part something else. And totally mad, from the looks of things. The previous owners couldn't give him the exercise he needed."

"And he's going to . . . ?"

"My friend Euan—obsessed with marathon-training, and totally foolhardy."

"An ideal match."

"I hope so. He's said he'll do a two-month trial period, and I'm hoping it works out, because the alternative isn't that rosy. No delivery needed—Euan will pick him up later. Would you be able to keep an eye on Bagel in the meantime?"

"Bagel?"

"Bagel. The beagle."

"Nice. Yes, sure."

"Maybe you and Zoe could take him out for a walk after school? Euan said he'd pop by at four to collect him."

"OK," Séraphine said, with a little trepidation.

"It'll be fine, honestly."

"You didn't put this in the job description," Séraphine joked.

"Haven't you noticed that I barely put anything in the job description? Because if I had, you never would have come."

Séraphine laughed. "That's probably true. Anyway, don't worry, your animal hotel is in safe hands with me. Have a good day."

"You too. And sorry about all this."

"No problem. But try not to bring anyone else home tonight."

S o here are the different shops in the town," Séraphine said, pointing to a picture of her village in the hope she could engage Zoe's attention. *"Patisserie, boul—"* The doorbell interrupted her.

"Saved by the bell," Zoe said, springing to her feet. "I bet that's Euan." She looked out of the window. "Yes it is. You get the door, I'll get Bagel."

Séraphine went to answer the door. The man on the doorstep was around Adam's age, with dark-blond hair.

"Hi," she said. "You must be Euan. I'm Séraphine."

"Pleasure to meet you," he said. "Adam's told me all about you."

"Good, I hope."

"Yes. All of it good."

"You're here for the dog, aren't you? Zoe's just getting him."

"Euan," Zoe bellowed through from the garden, "he won't move!"

"Oh dear," Euan said. "That doesn't sound a very promising start."

The beagle was pressing himself up against the garden wall and whining. Zoe had hold of his collar, and was tugging at it, but the more she did so, the more determined Bagel seemed to stay put. He was letting out a high-pitched whine.

"Look, Euan, he won't move," Zoe said. She threw the lead to the floor, exasperated. "You try."

Euan stepped forward and crouched down next to the dog. He spoke to Bagel in soft tones. "Hey there," he said. "We're not going to hurt you."

He turned around and looked at Séraphine. "Have you got anything we could lure him with? Any food?"

"Cheerios?" Zoe said.

"Not ideal," Euan said. "Doesn't Adam have any Pedigree Chum? Or dog biscuits?"

"I don't think so," Zoe said. "We used up the biscuits last time."

"Last time?" Séraphine said.

"There've been a few," Zoe said. "Staffordshire bull terriers mainly. But we had a husky, and a Chihuahua."

"This is the first one that Adam's succeeded in getting me to say yes to, Séraphine," Euan said, with a smile. "He knows I've got a weakness for beagles. I've always admired the way they can learn to get into fridges on their own."

"What about a madeleine?" Séraphine said. "No one can resist a madeleine."

Bagel was letting Euan stroke him, but wasn't moving an inch.

"OK, a madeleine it is. Whatever that might be," Euan said.

"You try one first," Séraphine said. She ducked into the kitchen and came back with the biscuit tin, handing a madeleine to Euan. He took a bite and nodded appreciatively. "Not bad."

Bagel started to sniff at the food and bark loudly. Euan got to his feet. "OK, I'm going to lay a trail of crumbs. Zoe, you stay here, so that he can't get any farther away, and Séraphine, could you stand by the front door to stop him dashing out?"

The three of them worked together for the next quarter of an hour, tempting Bagel with crumbs until he was safely in Euan's hatchback.

"Thank you," Euan said.

"That's OK." Zoe shrugged.

Séraphine was starting to see a different side of her in Euan's company. Softer, quick-witted and kind.

"I wish you two a very happy life together," Séraphine said to Euan. "And if either of you ever want any more cakes, you know where to find me."

Séraphine got off the bus and walked toward the Seafront. The town looked different at night, the reflections of lights twinkling on the water. She glanced down at the cage she was carrying and smiled. The lovebirds had attracted quite a lot of attention on the journey. It felt good to be out on her own in town, talking to local people, and now, with friends, and somewhere to go. Kat had texted her earlier to say that she and Charlie would be at the tearoom that evening too.

Letty opened the tearoom door to her, and Séraphine greeted her, waving over to Kat and Charlie, who joined them at the door.

"Hi, everyone. Letty, I brought you something—from Adam," Séraphine said, setting the birdcage down gently.

"Wow," Charlie exclaimed, smiling. "I really wasn't expecting that."

"Oh, aren't they gorgeous?" Letty said, crouching to admire the birds.

"So pretty." Kat peered into the cage. "Are these yours now, Letty?"

"Yes. I expect they'll be no end of trouble, flying around upstairs, but I can't bear to think of them in this cage all the time." She lifted the cage. "Thanks for bringing them over. I'll take them upstairs and get them settled. See you in a moment," Letty said, walking off with the birdcage toward the staircase at the rear of the tearoom.

"How's it all been going?" Séraphine asked Kat and Charlie. "Did you have a good trip today?"

"It's been great," Kat said. "We wanted to give Letty an update. I think she's slightly envious that she hasn't been able to join us. Today we went to see some tearooms along the coast and found a beautiful place cut into the rock of a cliff—it took us about an hour to get to it, but the tea and cake were totally worth the long walk."

"Sounds wonderful," Séraphine said. "Have you finished, or are there more places to visit?"

"We've got a few more to see," Charlie said.

"Then I'll be back to looking for a permanent job." Kat wrinkled her nose.

"Put off reality as long as you can," Séraphine said, smiling.

Letty reappeared, without the birdcage this time.

"So, you two. Guess what Séraphine's going to teach me to make?" she said.

Kat turned to Séraphine. "Let me think . . . Not croissants—Letty can already make those. Something with fruit? A tart?"

"That's right," Séraphine confirmed. "This is Tarte Tatin 101. And Letty's giving me a scone workshop. Why don't you join us?"

"I'd love to," Kat said. "A cup of tea wouldn't hurt."

"I should get back, I'm afraid," said Charlie. "I've got a ton of e-mails that need my attention. Another time perhaps." She smiled and said good-bye.

"Come through to the kitchen," Letty said. The women filed past the till and out to the back room.

"I've been looking forward to this," Séraphine said. Even the lesson with Zoe had been manageable that day, due to the knowledge that she'd soon be enjoying a break, doing what she loved most in the world—baking. There was something about Letty's calm, melodic voice that put Séraphine at ease.

She lifted a canvas shopping bag. "I picked up the ingredients on the way over."

"You're a star," Letty said. "Now, empty that bag up here on the counter and let's get started."

Letty and Séraphine worked together in the kitchen, aprons on and sleeves rolled up, while Kat chatted to them from her seat.

"You know how this dessert came to be?" Séraphine said.

"I don't think so," Kat said. "What happened?"

"The story goes that one of the Tatin sisters was making an apple tart, but she accidentally left it too long in the oven. In trying to salvage it, she turned it upside down. Her guests loved it."

"How wonderful. Some of the best things come out of mistakes, don't they?" Letty said.

"Yes. My brother and sister, for example," Séraphine replied, with a mischievous smile.

"Is that so?" Kat said.

"I'm sure of it." Séraphine nodded emphatically. "There's almost fifteen years between us—I don't think anyone plans a gap like that! My parents would never admit it, but me and my brother Guillaume have always been pretty certain that Mathilde and Benjamin were a happy accident."

"I bet they wouldn't change a thing now," Letty said.

"Definitely not. They're spoiled awfully by all of us," Séraphine said.

Kat took a sip of tea and watched as Séraphine worked on the fruit for the tart.

"So, you peel the apples, then halve them this way—" She held one up to show Letty. "Then scoop out the middle, the seeds and the core."

Letty got to work, preparing the apples on a wooden board.

"Heat up the pan, and this is where you'll be making the caramel. I add a vanilla pod and the seeds, scraped out. When you add the apple, you get that lovely . . . how do you say . . . toffee thing as it softens."

Making the tart, Séraphine realized she felt something she hadn't since arriving in England—at home.

"I always thought it was terribly complicated, this one. But you make it look easy." Letty smiled.

"I grew up with it. It feels strange, talking you through it, because for so many years it's been something my mum and I have done without a recipe—without even needing to talk about what we're doing."

"How lovely. I must say, I adore French baking. As much as I'm proud of our English cakes—and I still think you can't beat a good Victoria sponge—I'm glad that afternoon tea is such an international affair these days. Millefeuille, éclairs— we've had some good imports from over the Channel."

Séraphine laughed. "I've only recently learned how to make those things myself. In the village next to mine, we have a fantastic pastry school. It's world-renowned. For my last birth- day, my father gave me the best present I could have wished for—a week staying there and studying."

She smiled at the memory. Those had been some of the hap- piest days of her life. Covered in flour, and fretting over oven temperatures, yes—but in good company. She'd been paired with Carla, who had come over from Barcelona to take the course.

"Was this something you always wanted to do?" Séraphine asked, as she loaded the tart into the oven. "Run your own tearoom?"

"Oh no," Letty said. "Much as I love it, it was the family business. To be honest, it never crossed my mind to do anything else." She smiled. "Nowadays that must seem strange, I suppose."

"Not at all. I think it's nice to have something that you share with your family. That continuity," Séraphine said. "Will you pass the place on to Euan?"

"Oh no." Kat smiled. "I mean, he wouldn't be interested, would he, Letty?"

She shook her head. "He helps out from time to time, but he'd never run the Seafront, no. He put far too much effort into his architectural training for me to want to see him running the tearoom." A wistful look came into her eyes. "I would have liked to pass the place on though, if things had been different . . ." She paused for a moment, then picked up a bag of flour. "But things are as they are. Now, these scones won't make themselves, will they? Are you ready to learn my secret recipe?"

An hour later, Kat had left, and Letty and Séraphine were sitting at a table in the tearoom, tasting the scones and tart that they'd made.

"The tarte tatin is delicious with crème fraiche. But I couldn't find any so we'll have to make do with some vanilla ice cream," Séraphine said. "It's not a bad option, actually."

"And for the scones—strawberries and clotted cream," Letty said.

She watched as Séraphine helped herself to fruit and cream.

"No. More than that," Letty insisted, stopping Séraphine

as she raised a scone to her mouth. "You haven't got nearly enough on there."

Séraphine laughed. "More? I've already piled it high, Letty."

"Definitely more. And come on, there's barely anything of you. You could do with some calories."

"I knew there was a reason I wanted to come to England." Séraphine smiled, adding an extra layer of cream and topping it with jam. The past days with Letty, Charlie and Kat had helped her to relax and brought back some of her natural optimism. Instinctively, she felt she could be herself with them, without any fear of judgment. Her feeling that she'd made the wrong decision in coming to England was gradually being replaced by a certainty that she'd been right to be brave and step out on her own.

"I'm rather proud of that tart," said Letty.

"You should be," Séraphine said. "You did well turning it out. That's quite tricky when the caramel is so hot."

"I think I'm going to add it to our menu," Letty said, holding up a slice and admiring it.

"Are you serious? What an honor. My mother will be delighted."

"Good," Letty said, putting her fork down for a moment. "Now, tell me. How are things at Adam's? Is Zoe still making your life a misery?"

"It's not much better," Séraphine said. "She simply does not want to learn."

"I wonder what the problem is. Zoe does know some French—I remember she used to speak it all the time with her mother."

"She did?"

"Yes. I'm sure Adam will have told you that they lived in France when his wife, Marianne, was alive. They'd still come here for holidays though, to visit Adam's parents and to see Euan. During those trips, Marianne would always bring Zoe in here. They'd take that table in the corner and chatter away over slices of strawberry shortcake."

"I see."

"Then Marianne died, which was incredibly sad. She was so very young. Adam and Zoe moved back to Scarborough so that he could have the support of his parents. He still brings Zoe in from time to time, like you did the other day, but she's a different girl now. Not surprising, given what she's had to cope with."

"How did she die, Zoe's mother?"

"It was a horse-riding accident. In the countryside near their house. Her favorite horse startled, and she was thrown."

"That's awful."

Séraphine thought of Zoe—her hostility and coldness. Given what she'd heard, it wasn't hard to understand why the girl would be resistant to having a stranger in her house, and why she might resent Séraphine's attempts at friendship. Perhaps by trying to ignore, rather than acknowledge, the palpable absence in the house, Séraphine had been going about building a relationship with Zoe in the wrong way.

"It was. Adam was very much in love with Marianne. I remember Euan said he thought he'd never get over it."

"And now?

"Well, he still isn't over it—I'm not sure you do get over something like that. But Euan seems to think he's found a way to move on. Focusing on Zoe must help."

"So him wanting Zoe to speak French—it's about more than education."

"Oh yes, far more. It's about fulfilling a commitment to his wife: the one thing he can still do for her."

⌒

On Saturday, Séraphine and Zoe walked back from the supermarket together. Séraphine asked questions, and Zoe gave monosyllabic answers, dragging her heels. But after her conversation with Letty, Séraphine realized she'd found the patience she'd been missing.

That evening they ate together, and when Zoe went off to read in her room, Séraphine stayed to clear up.

"You don't need to do that," Adam said.

"It's no problem," she said, putting the plates in the dishwasher. "I prefer to be busy."

When it was full, she filled the sink to wash the pans she'd cooked dinner in. "I'll wash, and you dry?"

"Deal," Adam said, picking up a tea towel.

They joked with each other for a while, until Séraphine got up the courage to raise the issue that had been on her mind.

"I get the impression Zoe understands quite a lot of French. More than I expected."

Adam looked up, surprised. "She's started talking to you?"

"No." Zoe shook her head. "Unfortunately not. But I can tell she understands."

"Yes. She knows some. But it's been a few years now since she spoke it, which is why I thought you might be better off starting from scratch."

Séraphine rinsed a pan clean and stood it on the drying rack. "If she does understand, and she could speak it once, why do you suppose she doesn't want to speak it with me?"

Adam rubbed a pan with his tea towel as if drying it were the most important task in the world. Séraphine let the silence sit between them, resisting the urge to fill it.

"It was her mother she used to talk to," Adam said finally.

"I sometimes wonder if it's difficult for Zoe to go back to that time. I don't find it easy myself. Maybe hearing the language her mother spoke brings everything too close."

"That's possible," Séraphine said. "Do you talk to her about it?"

"I used to, when she was younger. We'd remember together the times we shared with Marianne, the holidays we went on. Zoe used to enjoy doing that. But in the last couple of years she's started to shut down." There was emotion in his voice, and Séraphine instinctively put her hand over his.

"Thanks," he said, clearing his throat. "It's always there, I guess, just below the surface."

"Of course."

"Maybe it's my fault that she's being so difficult with you now."

Séraphine shook her head. "It isn't. And it's not too late to change things. Do you have any more photos of Marianne? Because I think perhaps I need to get to know her a little better myself."

"Let's go into the living room," Adam said.

He went over to the bookshelves and took down some photo albums. "We haven't looked at these much recently," he said, brushing the dust off them. "I don't know why. When we first moved back here, when Zoe was seven, we used to look at them all the time. But now—there just never seems to be the right moment. Here—" He sat down next to Séraphine. "This is Marianne when she was pregnant with Zoe."

He pointed to a picture of a pretty woman in a yellow sundress with a large baby bump, her hand resting tenderly on top of it. Her long dark hair was loose, and her gaze was direct. Séraphine could imagine Adam taking the photo. There was an easy, relaxed smile on her face.

"And here's Zoe, when she was a newborn."

"She was beautiful."

Séraphine turned the pages of the album, studying photos of Zoe cradled on her sleeping father's chest, Zoe lying on a picnic rug in a yellow bonnet . . .

"She used to love it when Marianne played guitar for her— even when she was tiny. And the two of them used to paint together."

Séraphine leaned in to look at the photo of mother and daughter painting together on a low wooden table, brightly colored splashes adorning Zoe's arms and face.

"They seem to be having fun."

"They were a real team. Oh, and look, here they are with the horses. Marianne used to lift Zoe up to stroke them. Zoe loved being around them."

Adam turned the pages, and Zoe grew before Séraphine's eyes, stumbling with a baby walker, riding a small red trike, her own bicycle.

"A lovely family."

"We were happy," Adam said. "It went by so quickly. We didn't have long enough."


On Sunday, Zoe and Séraphine were in the living room. Séraphine had put her usual teaching materials to one side.

"I thought we could do something different today," Séraphine said. She braced herself. This could either go well, or very, very badly.

She took out the photo album Adam had shown her, the one with pictures of Zoe as a toddler. "This is yours, isn't it?"

"Yes. Those are photos of my family."

She passed the album to Zoe. "Why don't you tell me who is who?"

Zoe opened the album and stared at it for a while. Séraphine wondered if she was doing the right thing.

After a minute, Zoe pointed at a photo of her mother playing the guitar.

"That's my mum."

She looked up at Séraphine. Her eyes were sad, but there was a proud smile on her lips.

"*Très belle*," Séraphine said.

"*Oui.*"

"And she looks very kind," Séraphine continued, in French.

"*Oui.* She was. She was the best."

"What was she like? Tell me more about her."

"She would tell me silly jokes. Sometimes we'd talk behind Dad's back, say things in French that he couldn't understand. And *elle adorait chanter*, she loved to sing. Terribly, but all the time. In the shower, to the horses, to me."

"She sounds fun. I wish I could have met her."

"*Maman* made us laugh a lot." Zoe's voice caught.

"Do you miss her?"

"*Elle me manque tellement.* I miss her so much," Zoe said, brushing away the tears that were spilling onto her flushed cheeks. "I hate not having a mum. Being different from my friends. I hate that Dad is lonely sometimes."

A lump formed in Séraphine's throat as she listened. The hard expression on the young girl's face had disappeared completely, replaced with a gentleness, a vulnerability.

"But more than that," Zoe continued, her voice thick with emotion. "I miss her because of who she was. Her hugs. The songs she sang to me to get me to sleep. It's been years, I know, but I miss her every single day."

# 12

Sunday, September 14

"Hi, Mummy," Leo said, his voice clear and bright over the phone. Kat's heart lifted.

"Hello, darling. How was your day?" She perched on the edge of the sofa, holding the phone close to her ear.

"Excellent," he pronounced.

"Yes? What made it so excellent?"

"I went with Grandma and Grandpa to feed the ducks."

"You did? And what were they up to?"

"Quacking. Flapping their wings. They were hungry. I think it was feeding time."

Kat heard a voice in the background: Diane, Leo's grandmother, was talking to him. "Nearly your feeding time," she said.

"Are you having your tea?"

"Yes, but I'm not eating bread like the ducks. I'm having fish fingers. That's what penguins eat."

"Lovely. You eat those all up. Is Daddy there?"

"Yes. I'll get him."

"OK. Bye. I love you," said Kat, biting her lip and trying not to cry. "Sending a triceratops-sized hug."

"I'm sending a brontosaurus one. Love you too. Byeeee . . ." His voice trailed off as he passed the phone to Jake.

"Hi, Kat."

"Hey. Sounds as if he's been having a wonderful time. Everything going OK?"

"It's fine. He's having fun." He sounded distant.

"How has work been?"

"OK. Not bad. Listen, Kat. We're about to have dinner. Can we chat tomorrow?"

"Of course," Kat said. "Bye for now."

Kat made a cup of Earl Grey, and brought the teacup and saucer over to the kitchen table. It had been good to hear Leo's voice. He seemed so happy with his dad and grandparents.

And of course for her, it meant more time and space to think. She got out a pen and notebook, opened it on a blank page and began writing out her thoughts for the tearooms reviews. She sipped her tea as she went, conjuring into her mind the tearooms they'd visited—the décor, how the waiting staff had treated them, and—her favorite task of all—the delicious flavors they had tasted.

Kat hadn't wanted to admit to Charlie that e-mailing wasn't that easy when you didn't have a computer to do it from. She'd had to sell her laptop in the summer—it was old anyway, and she'd promised herself she'd get a better one when she had the money. But she'd manage; she could write by hand then send half on her phone that evening and then go down to the library the next day and write up the rest. There was something she enjoyed about writing freehand anyway.

As the words flowed from her pen, Kat forgot about grocery shopping and paying bills, and even—for a short while—about being a mum. She was totally caught up in the moment. She remembered the last time she'd felt that way—staying up through the night to meet a deadline for her university dissertation, with only her dreams and a steady supply of biscuits to keep her going.

Perhaps work didn't have to be just a matter of figures on a payslip. She'd once thought she could do something that tied in with her passions in life. Was it too late to hope that might still be true?

J ess, hi," Charlie said, moving over to the hotel window where the reception was better. "It's Sunday again, sorry, I expect you're at home—but you said to call and update you."

"Yep, fire away. And don't worry, I'm in the office anyway, having an absolute nightmare with the October edition—somehow the printers got hold of the wrong file and we've had to pulp the first batch. Our MD's not a happy man."

"Oh no—is Louis there with you?"

"No, he's left me to sort it out. Thank God you're back tomorrow. So, how's the tea stuff been going?"

"It's coming along nicely. I've found a wonderful new writer who's been helping me out with some of the research, and we've discovered some real gems along the Yorkshire coast. We should be on track. I'll be back in the office early afternoon."

"Not a moment too soon—I could use your help with getting this sorted. I left Nicky in charge while you were away, and the whole thing's been a complete disaster."

"Oh dear. Well, don't worry—we can fix it. I'll see you tomorrow."

Charlie hung up the phone and laid her shoes on top of the rest of her clothes in her suitcase. Whatever the chaos in the office, it couldn't be worse than dealing with her sister.

⌒

Séraphine popped downstairs to make some hot chocolate. She could hear Adam and Zoe in the living room together, laughing and joking.

"Hey, Séraphine," Adam called out.

She put her head around the living room door. "Hello, you two."

"Hi," Zoe said. "You got a package. Our neighbor just dropped it by. I left it for you on the hallway table."

"It's a big one too—looks interesting," Adam added.

"Oh? How exciting. I wasn't expecting anything."

She found the parcel in the hallway and examined it. The stamps, and the handwriting, were distinctively continental, but the return address wasn't legible. She took it upstairs to her room and closed the door.

Sitting down on her bed, she unwrapped it. Inside was a packet of homemade madeleines and a CD from her favorite jazz singer.

The card was a black-and-white photo of a riverbank.

She read the message:

*i hope you enjoy the madeleines, i made them myself—perfect with a cup of English tea. And— i'm sure you remember—ha—this CD was playing when we first kissed. i miss you.*

Inside was a photo of the two of them: Séraphine and Carla, looking up at the camera as Carla held her phone out. Both smiling, Carla's dark hair merging with Séraphine's blond.

Séraphine remembered the moment it was taken. The completeness that she'd felt that day.

"I miss you too," she whispered.

# PART TWO

. . . even a tea party means
apprehension, breakage.

—VIRGINIA WOOLF,
*The Diary of Virginia Woolf*

# 13

Monday, September 15

Pippa was in her hallway in a white dressing gown, Gracie wailing in her arms. "Don't just stand there on the doorstep, Charlie. Come in."

Charlie stepped inside, wondering if she'd made a mistake in coming to say good-bye. She stuck her head round the living room door and Flo and Jacob waved and yelled from the floor. It looked as though they'd been painting pictures, but the green and orange paint wasn't only on their paper, it was all over the plush cream carpet.

Charlie turned back to her sister. "Have you seen what they're doing to the—"

Pippa nodded. "I don't care." Charlie noticed then that her cheeks were red and blotchy, and there were dark circles under her eyes.

Charlie closed the living room door behind her and turned to face her sister. Pippa had lifted Gracie up onto her shoulder and was patting her back gently. The wailing quietened to a gentle grizzle. "What's going on?"

Her sister mumbled, "Nothing."

"Doesn't look that way to me. Come on, sit down and let's talk." They went into the kitchen, and Pippa placed Gracie in a bouncy chair.

"OK, tell me what's happened," Charlie said, thrown by her sister's disheveled appearance. "You look—"

"Don't," Pippa said, shaking her head. "I look like crap, I know. And I feel even worse."

"Why, what is it?"

"I haven't slept in two days. I mean at all. Not a moment."

"That doesn't sound good. Is Gracie OK? I realize babies aren't known for being big sleepers, but that does seem extreme."

Pippa looked up, her eyes red-rimmed and shiny with tears. "It's not Gracie."

Charlie paused, confused. "What then?"

"It's Luke. He's moved out."

"What?" Charlie sat back in her seat, trying to process what her sister was saying. Luke—loyal, kind Luke? It didn't seem possible that he would walk out on his family. "Why?"

"Because he's married to me, and I'm an idiot," Pippa said, her voice cracking. She put her hands up to her face and covered her eyes. "And I know you won't disagree with that."

"Come on, Pippa," Charlie said. "Don't say that. Tell me what happened."

"I messed up."

Flo burst into the room, a paintbrush in hand.

"Auntie Charlie—you're back! Are you coming to stay again?"

Charlie looked at Pippa, who had turned away, shielding her face with her hand and swiping the tears from her cheeks so that Flo wouldn't see her crying.

"Maybe," Charlie said. She wanted to hear the full story from Pippa, but it was impossible to ask her with the children present. "I'm here for today, at any rate. Your mum needs some rest, so I'll be looking after you two. That means you'd better be on your best behavior."

"Yay!" Flo jumped up and clapped her hands together. Jacob rushed in to find out what all the fuss was about.

Charlie made a mental note to call Jess at the earliest opportunity; better to face up to postponing her return sooner rather than later.

She turned to Pippa. "You—upstairs. I'll bring you a hot-water bottle and some camomile tea in a minute. Before we do anything else, you need to sleep."

"OK," Pippa said, too weak to protest. Pulling her dressing gown more tightly around her, she got to her feet.

"There's some expressed breast milk for Gracie . . ." she murmured vaguely, her eyes glazed. "We're nearly out of nappies. In fact, I think we are completely out . . . God. I'm normally so on top of this stuff."

"Don't worry," Charlie said calmly. "I'm sure we'll be fine."

Pippa walked out of the room, whispering a barely audible "Thank you."

Flo turned to her aunt, concern in her eyes. "Is my mum OK?"

"Yes. She's feeling sleepy, that's all," Charlie told her. "Babies are exhausting, you see. We're going to see she gets some rest today."

On cue, Gracie let out a wail. Charlie bent to pick her up. The little body seemed awkward in Charlie's arms, impossibly fragile. She tried to mimic the way that Pippa held Gracie, but felt as if the slightest wrong move could break her. Her crying escalated and Flo blocked her ears.

A couple of feet away, Jacob pressed a green crayon into the pale fabric of the dining chairs. "Coloring in," he announced proudly.

Flo took a sniff of air near Gracie's bottom. "Phew-wy," she said, waving her little hand back and forth. "She's done a poo."

⌒

"Kat, it's Charlie." Sitting on the bathroom floor, Charlie leaned back against the bath and pressed the phone to her ear, relieved to hear Kat's voice.

Her niece Gracie was on the changing mat, clean but nappyless, wrapped up in a makeshift fashion in a towel, gurgling contentedly.

"Everything OK?" Kat said. "I thought you were driving back to London today?"

"I was. But now I'm not. Listen, could you help me with something?" Charlie had searched through every cupboard in the bathroom and nursery, and there wasn't a single nappy to be found. The towel was working out for now—more or less—but it wouldn't do the job for much longer and she couldn't bear to wake Pippa any more than she could face the thought of taking all three children to the shops to buy nappies. "I wouldn't ask if it wasn't—"

"AUNTIE CHARLIE!" Jacob bellowed from the bedroom. "I'M HIDING, COME AND FIND ME."

Flo put her head around the bathroom door, a worried expression on her face. "Jacob's got the cat, Auntie Charlie. Mummy said he's not allowed to hold her, not after last time."

"Last time?" Charlie said, moving the phone away from her ear.

"He HURTS her."

"OK, Flo. Go and tell him I'll be right out—and he'll be in big trouble if he touches Venus. Sorry, Kat," Charlie said, returning the phone to her ear.

"Everything OK?"

"Yes. I mean, no. Sort of." Charlie rubbed a hand over her brow. Out of the corner of her eye she saw that Gracie had managed to squirm out of the towel construction. "Could you do me a huge favor and stop by my sister's house on Victoria Road?"

"Of course. Is there anything you need?"

"Yes. Some newborn nappies. And a dose of sanity."

Charlie opened the door to Kat fifteen minutes later, a wave of relief washing over her.

"Nappies, m'lady," Kat said, holding out a shopping bag.

"You're a lifesaver," Charlie said, taking them gratefully, paying Kat and then scanning the outside of the packet. "They have instructions on them, right?"

"Why don't I get her changed for you?" Kat said kindly. "It looks as though you might have your hands full with those two."

Charlie followed Kat's line of vision to where Jacob and Flo were tugging the living room curtains while jumping up and down like a pair of demented bell-ringers.

"Stop that," she called out to the kids, while handing Gracie over to Kat and pointing at a changing bag in the corner of the living room. "Thanks, Kat."

Kat expertly changed and dressed the baby, and a few seconds later was holding her and swaying gently, making her smile.

"Any solutions for them?" Charlie asked, pointing at Jacob and Flo.

"Yes. Emergency measures." Kat located the TV remote and put on some cartoons. The children reluctantly let go of the curtains and settled on the sofa.

"So how come you're in charge?" Kat asked.

"You seriously think I am?"

⌣

While Jacob and Flo were engrossed in an episode of *Peppa Pig*, Charlie grabbed the opportunity to prepare some milk for Gracie.

"I'll get the kettle on," Kat said. "You look as though you could do with a pick-me-up."

"She said something about expressed breast milk," Charlie said, rummaging in the fridge and finding only vegetables, yogurts and chickpea salad.

"It might be in the freezer," Kat said, scanning the shelves and retrieving some bags full of creamy-white milk. "Bingo."

"Frozen? That's weird."

"Means you always have some. Did your sister not tell you where it was?"

"There wasn't time. She hasn't slept for a couple of days and looked as if she was about to pass out. I sent her upstairs to get some sleep."

"Must be tough with three of them."

"Yes, but it's more than that. Her husband's left."

"For good?"

"No—I mean, I don't know. I'm not sure what happened, I've barely had a chance to talk to Pippa about it."

"I hope she's OK," Kat said. "You've decided to stay then?"

"I think so." Charlie thought of the missed calls on her phone from Jess. She'd only had time to send a hasty e-mail explaining she wouldn't be returning as planned.

"Let's concentrate on getting through today. Between us we can see to it that the kids have so much fun they won't realize anything's amiss."

# 14

Monday, September 15

Séraphine walked along the South Sands, the autumn sunshine glinting on the water and couples in thick coats strolling arm in arm. In her bag was the photo she'd received from Carla. She thought of the last time they'd seen each other, just before she'd made the decision to come to England, cutting short their relationship.

They'd been by the river, Séraphine sitting back on the picnic blanket and Carla smoking a cigarette, slowly blowing the smoke out of her mouth.

"You shouldn't smoke, you know," Séraphine said, turning onto her side.

Carla raised an eyebrow and smiled. "And you never do anything you shouldn't, Miss Perfect?"

"Not often, I suppose."

"Not often enough, more like," Carla teased her.

Séraphine laughed. They were the same age, twenty-three, but somehow Carla seemed older. Wiser. More comfortable in her skin. It was the first thing Séraphine had noticed about her when they were paired up on the patisserie course. While she had been consumed by worry that she would mess up the recipe, Carla was naturally confident, not seeming to notice or care what others thought. They'd worked well together, and the teacher had called the entire class over to taste their blueberry brioches.

"Have you ever done anything your parents wouldn't approve of?" Carla said, playfully curious. "I mean, before you got together with me?"

"No," Séraphine said, feeling a little embarrassed that she'd never stepped out of line. "Is that very boring? We've always got along well, so I've never wanted to upset them. I guess Guillaume did the rebelling for both of us."

"But this time it's you going against their wishes?"

"Yes. It's not easy for me to keep such a big secret from them."

"Does it have to be a secret? Couldn't you tell them about us?"

Séraphine shook her head. "No. How could I?"

"I don't know," Carla said, shrugging. "Open your mouth, say the words—"

"It's not that simple," Séraphine said. "They've always assumed I'd marry a nice boy from the village, stay here, have lots of children."

"You can still have children," Carla said matter-of-factly.

"I know. But it's not only that. They wouldn't be able to take it in. They wouldn't understand—and I don't think the rest of the family would either."

"They might surprise you," Carla said. "My parents took the news better than I expected."

"Your parents sound pretty laid-back, though. It wouldn't be the same with my family."

"It still wasn't easy telling them," Carla said. "It was a big adjustment. It's OK now, but it took them a long time to get used to it."

"How old were you?"

"Sixteen," Carla said.

"You were sure then?"

Carla nodded. "I've always known."

"I envy you," Séraphine said. "I put a lot of energy into trying to change myself. If a boy at school asked me out, I'd go, hoping that my feelings would turn from fondness or admiration into something else, that maybe I'd start to understand what all my friends were getting so excited about."

"And did that ever happen?"

"Never," Séraphine replied, smiling. "So, here I am. With you. All those years, I had no idea what my friends were talking about. Now, finally, I get it."

"Before me, you never went out, tried to meet other women?"

"Have you seen our village?" Séraphine laughed.

"OK, yes." Carla smiled and put her hands up. "I see what you mean."

"Barcelona must be quite different from here."

"It's the polar opposite," Carla said. "More open-minded. Sometimes I wonder what I was thinking, coming here. This beautiful, crazy place. But then I did get to meet beautiful, crazy you."

Then they'd kissed.

Séraphine smiled at the memory. She looked down at the imprints that the soles of her shoes made in the soft, wet sand on the beach. However far you went, there were some things you couldn't outpace.

# 15

Monday, September 15

When Jacob and Flo were finally tucked up in bed, Charlie saw Kat to the door. Kat had shown her how to strap on the sling and she'd grown to enjoy the comfort of Gracie's small body against her chest, close enough that she could feel the gentle rhythm of her breathing.

"Thanks for everything," Charlie said.

"Any time," Kat replied. "I enjoyed it. I've been missing Leo, and Jacob reminds me of him when he was that age."

"Well, it was good of you to come."

Kat waved it away. "It was nothing. Anyway, I hope things get better for your sister soon."

"Me too. Maybe I'll be seeing more of you now."

They said good-bye and Charlie closed the front door. She went upstairs to her sister's bedroom and knocked gently.

"Come in . . ." Pippa's voice, groggy with sleep, came from behind the door.

Pippa was sitting up in bed. Her eyes were dark with smudged mascara, but color had returned to her cheeks.

"God, how long was I out for?" she asked, rubbing her eyes. Without another word she held out her arms for Gracie, and Charlie passed the baby over.

"Most of the day. You must have really needed it."

"I guess I did." She looked down at Gracie lovingly. "She looks happy."

Charlie smiled. "I did my best." She perched on the end of Pippa's double bed. "Thankfully, I had some help."

Pippa was stroking her daughter's hair gently, and Charlie noticed a single teardrop fall onto Gracie's face.

"Are you going to tell me what happened?"

Pippa looked up, shaking her head. "I feel such a fool."

"A fool? Well, tell me about it—I have quite a lot of experience in that area." She brought her legs up onto the bed, moving closer to her sister.

Pippa smiled weakly. Slowly, she began to speak: "I'm lucky to be married to a man like Luke, I know that . . ."

She paused, her brow creased with anxiety.

"I can't tell you why I don't feel happy, Charlie. But each day when I wake up—if you can call it that; it feels as though, since Gracie was born, I've barely shut my eyes—anyway, the kids are clambering on me, demanding my attention. Luke goes off to work, and then I'm on my own. Getting everyone ready. Cleaning. Tidying. Trying to make everything seem as if it's perfect. A lot of hard work goes into this illusion."

Charlie thought of the times she'd envied Pippa—the expensively decorated, tidy house, her happy marriage. It seemed such a thin façade now, Charlie couldn't believe she hadn't seen through it.

"I love them, Charlie," Pippa said, her voice laden with guilt. "Don't get me wrong. But I never thought it would be this hard."

"Have you told Luke how you feel?"

"No. Even now. I'm a good actress, I suppose." She said the words numbly, as if she were stepping outside herself. "But Luke knows something's wrong. He knows what he read."

"What he read?"

"E-mails I should never have sent." Her cheeks flushed with shame.

"Oh God. Who to?"

"Will."

"Will Mortimer?" Charlie said, wrinkling her nose, surprised. She hadn't heard her sister mention him since they were teenagers.

"I know." The tears were running down her face now. "It's ridiculous. The whole thing. I haven't seen him since we were nineteen and I was still studying."

"What were you e-mailing him about?"

"He e-mailed me, out of the blue, said he'd been thinking about me. I sent a reply, just chatting, you know. I thought, any day now, I'll get a friend request on Facebook. That way I wouldn't have to spell it out—he'd see the photos of me and Luke, our wedding day, he'd see the photos of Gracie, Flo and Jacob."

"So he knows now?"

"No. The thing is, the friend request never came. Turns out he doesn't even have a profile. So then I realized I didn't have to tell him everything."

"What did you say?"

"I started writing to him in the middle of the night, when Luke was asleep and I was feeding Gracie. That three-in-the-morning stillness where you think there's no one else in the world who's awake. It turned out that Will was, though—and so we e-mailed back and forth. I told him about my job as a solicitor . . ."

Charlie raised an eyebrow.

"You wouldn't believe how glamorous it is, Charlie. Media law. Very high-flying. A lot of posh lunches on expenses, and drinks in town after work." She gave a wry smile. "Not here, of course. I'm in Manchester."

"OK," Charlie said, taking it all in. "So you got a little creative with the truth, and said you had a job that you don't. That's not the most awful thing in the world, is it?"

"That was the start." Pippa rearranged Gracie on her chest. The baby's breathing had deepened and she was snoring softly now. "I sent him photos of me—I guess they were about five or six years old."

"You didn't mention Luke?"

"No. Or the kids. I edited them right out of my life."

"You didn't say *anything*?"

"Nope. You see what I mean? I'm a pretty awful person. And you know what makes it worse? I felt better, Charlie. I felt better being that woman, the one I invented."

Charlie took a deep breath. "Did the two of you meet up?"

"No, never. He wanted to—but I kept putting him off. I didn't want to meet him. I just wanted to have that taste of freedom once in a while. But last night when Gracie wouldn't stop crying, Luke went off to sleep in the spare room. He does that occasionally, when he has a big meeting the following morning and needs a good night's sleep. The thing is, I didn't realize I'd left my phone in there, still logged into my e-mail. I suppose he must have suspected something was going on, because he checked my account."

Pippa stroked the back of her daughter's head.

"He waited until this morning to confront me. Over breakfast with the kids, he asked me who Will Mortimer was. I felt sick. I didn't know what to say, so I didn't say anything. He went upstairs, so calm, packed his bags. He said he needed some space to think, told the kids he had to go on a business trip and walked out."

"Oh God. That's awful."

Charlie thought back over the past week. How had she missed things being so wrong in the house? Sisters were meant to have some kind of special intuition, weren't they? But she'd been too caught up in her own annoyance with Pippa to see through her behavior to the underlying cause. Her marriage was in serious trouble, and what she needed wasn't someone to pass judgment but a good friend and listener.

"How do you feel now?" Charlie asked.

"Bloody awful. Like everything's been turned upside down." Pippa started to sob again.

"Do you still love him?"

"Yes," Pippa said, wiping her nose hurriedly with her hand. "I think so. Yes."

"Then we have to find a way to fix this," Charlie said, trying to focus her mind on a solution. "What about one of those counseling hotlines? Relate, maybe?" She picked up her phone to find the website.

"Don't," Pippa said, putting a hand on her sister's arm to stop her.

Charlie paused and put down the phone.

"You know what I actually need at the moment, most of all?" Pippa said. "Time. To think. Get my energy back. Someone to help with the constant cycle of school runs and laundry and washing up. There's so much to do, I never stop to give any thought to what's wrong in my marriage, in my life. I need to work this out, but I can't do it alone."

Charlie looked at her sister. Pippa's forehead was creased with worry, and there were fine lines around her eyes. She wasn't perfect. She wasn't even trying to be anymore.

"I know I've been a cow," Pippa continued. "And I don't

deserve for you to do this. But would you stay with me? I could really do with your company."

Charlie saw the desperation in her sister's eyes, then glanced down at Gracie, nestled in her mother's arms. She wondered what would happen to them both if she left.

"Don't worry," Charlie said. "I'm not going anywhere."

# 16

Tuesday, September 16

"Charlie, you can't just not turn up!" Jess said, furious. "I told you we needed you here. Where the heck are you?"

"I'm still in Scarborough. Something's come up."

"Something that means you want to throw your career away? Because it looks as though that's what you're set on doing."

"I'm sorry, Jess, but it's unavoidable. I've got weeks of holiday stacked up and I'm going to have to take some of it. I'd be happy to do whatever I can by e-mail—"

"I need you in the office, Charlie. That's why you're employed to work *in the office*."

"I can't leave right now. I'm sorry, but I have to stay another week at least."

Overnight, it seemed as if Pippa had gotten worse instead of better. She'd sat up sobbing for hours, barely saying a word. Luke had called a few times but she'd refused to speak to him; she was convinced that he was only calling to tell her it was all over, that she'd ruined things between them.

"How am I supposed to trust you with the next edition? We're due to go to print in a few weeks and we have no articles or reviews yet—you do realize that, don't you?" Jess said sternly.

"Yes, I do," Charlie said, lowering her voice so that Pippa

and the children wouldn't hear her. "And I'm working on it. But I'll have to do it from here. I'm sorry, Jess, but this is a family emergency."

Jess sighed. "I took a leap of faith allowing you to guest-edit this issue, and now I'm having to make excuses for you. I thought you were serious about this."

"I am," Charlie said, trying to keep her voice calm despite the mounting sense of desperation. "I'll do most of the reviews while I'm here and have them edited and ready for when I get back."

"You're going to do all that on your own, while dealing with your 'family emergency'?"

"Yes. I am."

"Fine . . ." Jess paused. "OK, I hope I don't end up regretting this, but let's talk next Wednesday. You need to have most of the content ready for subbing by then, and the absolute outside date I can give you for the rest is Monday the twenty-ninth. And that's it, Charlie. If you let me down, there is no way I will be able to recommend you to take over as my replacement."

"Don't worry, I'll have everything done. Thank you." Charlie felt a wave of relief wash over her. "I won't let you down, Jess. I promise. This is going to be the best edition of the magazine yet."

"I certainly hope so."

# 17

Wednesday, September 17

Charlie had had it all planned out—she'd pick Jacob up from nursery, then Flo up from school and they'd all go to the playground together. That would keep them occupied for at least an hour, giving Pippa some relative peace at home with Gracie.

"It's raining!" Flo protested, covering her head with her hands theatrically. "We can't play. The swings are all wet."

"It's *raining*," Jacob said, echoing his sister's whine. "We can't play."

For once, Charlie had to admit that her niece and nephew had a point. Storm clouds were thick in the sky, and the current drizzle looked like it was only going to get worse. She looked around for other options, and with delight and relief, caught sight of the Seafront.

Inside, at Letty's stool by the till, there was a man about Charlie's age. Broad-shouldered with dark-blond hair—the kind of guy Charlie might look twice at if she didn't have other things to think about right now.

Flo rammed her scooter into the glass cabinet, shaking the cake stands. A couple of customers looked over and Charlie cringed.

"Flo, Jacob—see that table by the window? Let's see who can get there fastest, shall we?"

Her niece and nephew skidded across the floorboards, and then clambered onto chairs.

"Sorry about them," she said to the man. "I promised we'd go and play but then the heavens opened."

"Don't worry," he said. "It's fine."

"Is Letty not here today?"

"She's had to go out, but she'll be back later this afternoon."

"And you are . . ."

"Euan," he said, holding out his hand for her to shake.

"Letty's son?"

"Yes," he said. "Has my reputation preceded me?"

"No." She laughed. "It's just . . . You look like her. Your eyes." They were a striking light blue.

He smiled. "Yep, people sometimes say that."

"She mentioned you to me. Said you were the real self-starter in the family."

"I keep myself busy, I suppose," he said. "Although I kind of enjoy it when Mum asks me to help out here. Time seems to go slowly. And the Seafront is my second home—I practically grew up in these four walls, after all."

"You're lucky."

"So, what can I get you?"

"Could I have a cup of . . ." She looked at the jars on the wall, recalled the distinct aroma of each one when the lid was opened. "I think I'll go for the jasmine tea today, please."

"And for the kids?"

"Two of your finest gingerbread men, please." She pointed at them in the glass cabinet.

"Three, did you say?" Euan said, a glint in his eye as he brought the plate out.

"Three would be even better. Rainy-day rules, right?"

"Absolutely. These are freshly made too. Busy day?"

"You could say that. Up at six, and yet I still didn't have time to eat anything."

Euan arranged the gingerbread men on a tray.

"And could you do a couple of babyccinos?"

"Baby whats?" Euan wrinkled his nose and laughed.

"You know. Mini cappuccinos, for kids. Frothy milk, chocolate sprinkles?"

"Sure," he said, getting some cups down. "Babyccinos, eh? And I thought I'd heard it all."

When Charlie went up to pay, Euan was serving a middle-aged couple. He chatted easily with them. Laughter-lines formed at the corner of his eyes as he smiled. His shirt sleeves were rolled up to the elbow, revealing strong, tanned forearms and hands, as if he worked outside. He glanced over at Charlie fleetingly and caught her eye.

As she waited, she noticed a scrapbook lying on the counter. On the front were the words: *The Seafront: 1913 to the present day*.

She opened it—inside were newspaper cuttings dating back to the early days of the tearoom. The first photo showed men and women constructing the building.

"Sorry to keep you," he said. "Is it the bill you're after?"

She nodded. "This is fascinating stuff," she said, pointing to the scrapbook.

"Oh yeah. The whole history's in there," Euan said. "This place has stood through two world wars."

"Is that so?"

"Yes. The year after my grandparents opened the tearoom, the town was bombarded by German warships. Nineteen people died, the lighthouse was destroyed—but the tearoom survived."

"Impressive," Charlie said, continuing to browse through the pictures.

She turned the page, and saw a photo of Letty when she was young, in a pair of flares and a flowery blouse, a man with a mustache by her side.

"He's handsome," Charlie said, pointing at the man.

"That's my dad, John."

"Is he still around?"

"Very much so." Euan smiled cheekily. "Why, are you interested?"

Charlie laughed. "I'm surprised I haven't seen him in here, that's all."

"He and Mum are separated. He doesn't come here. Hasn't for years."

"Oh, I see. Sorry, I didn't mean to pry," she said, sensing that she'd touched on a sensitive subject. She closed the scrapbook and rummaged in her handbag for her purse.

"It's OK," Euan reassured her. "I've never believed in having secrets—but Mum, well, she's different in that way. You won't find the personal side of the story in that scrapbook."

Charlie heard a hammering on the window and looked around to see Flo's face, mouthing demands for her to come out.

"I'd better be going."

"What was your name?" Euan asked. "So I can tell my mum you dropped by."

"Charlotte—Charlie." She smiled. As she turned to leave, she found herself wondering if he might still be watching her.

To: Kat
From: Charlie

Hi Kat,

Please tell me you have some free time? The reviews
you sent over are fantastic—you're a natural. I knew
you would be.

The deadline is approaching so quickly and I need to
have all the content ready soon, but things are still crazy
over here.  School runs. Glitter. Mud. I'm struggling to
get anywhere farther than the Seafront at the moment.

Any chance you could get out and see some of the
other tearooms on our list? Maybe Séraphine could
join you? We still have some room in the budget, so I'll
make it worth your while, I promise!

Charlie x

_____

To: Charlie
From: Kat

Hey Charlie,

Of course! It would be a pleasure. Call me when you
get a minute and we can talk it through. I'll have a word
with Séraphine in the meantime.

Kx

# 18

Wednesday, September 17

"My mum painted these for me," Zoe said, pointing to two square canvases. One painting was of an elephant, the other of a little house, in yellow, pink and purple. "She used to paint all kinds of things. Mostly from her imagination."

"*Ils sont très beaux*," Séraphine said. She picked up the elephant canvas and took a closer look. "She's chosen some lovely colors, hasn't she?"

"*Oui—violet, rose et jaune* . . ." Zoe switched effortlessly between English and French as she spoke, describing the painting, not even seeming to notice when Séraphine spoke to her in her native language.

"Where did your mother do her painting?"

"She had a room, it was next to the stables—she said the light there was good. That's what she'd say, but me and Dad both knew it was because she could see the horses from there. She was happiest when she was near them . . ."

Zoe paused, and then continued.

"*Maman* would paint when Dad was looking after me. Sometimes she'd go to that room after I'd gone to sleep. I could see from my bedroom that the light was still on in her window."

"Where did you find these paintings?"

"In a box under my bed. I didn't want to put them up when we got here. But maybe now . . ." She glanced down and Séraphine thought for a moment that she might cry. Instead, she looked back up and nodded her head determinedly. "I think I'm ready."

"Right. Well, why don't we do it then?"

"OK," Zoe said, getting up. "Will you help me? Dad keeps the hammer under the sink."

"Let's go."

An hour later, the two pictures were up on Zoe's wall, the little house hanging over her dressing table and the elephant by her bed. After their first conversation about Marianne, it had taken Séraphine aback how quickly Zoe's attitude had changed her. It was as if there was a reservoir of emotion that had been waiting for the right person to tap into it. The frostiness had disappeared and made way for warmth. Something had happened that she'd never imagined could—Zoe was opening up to her.

"It's quite babyish, isn't it?" Zoe said, touching the painted elephant's trunk. "But I don't care."

"I think it looks lovely," Séraphine said, straightening it slightly.

"I was smaller when she painted it."

Zoe sat back on her bed, and pulled one of the purple satin cushions onto her lap.

"Do you enjoy painting?" Séraphine asked.

"Yes." Zoe shrugged. "I'm not very good though."

"I bet you are. Did you see that there's one space left?" She pointed to a blank area of wall by the door.

"Do you think I should paint something?"

"Yes. You've got some paints, haven't you?"

Zoe nodded.

"Paint anything you'd like."

"I want to do a picture of my mum. How I remember her."

# 19

Thursday, September 18

At eight in the morning, the sky lightening to a gray-blue, the South Bay was quiet. The shutters on the shops and restaurants were down, and the only sound was the gulls overhead.

Charlie needed a run to clear her head. How Pippa did it, she had no idea; the last few days had left her completely exhausted. Back in London she would put her iPod in and jog by the canal before work, dance music prepping her for the day ahead. She hadn't wanted to run with music today, though. Up here, away from the city, it was quieter. She didn't want to block out the world and create a bubble, as she usually did.

*Thud, thud, thud.* It felt good to hear her feet on the tarmac, the sound of her efforts. After a few hundred meters, her skin grew warm.

*Thud, thud, thud.*

Sweat began to trickle down her back, but with each step she took, calm returned.

*Thud, thud—*

BAM.

Charlie's body buckled.

Something had knocked the backs of her knees sharply, pushing her legs out from under her and knocking her hard onto her Lycra-clad side. She grazed her elbows as she hit the floor.

"HEY," she called out, shocked, her elbows and hip stinging and sore.

She looked around, dazed, and was met by a furry muzzle and a pink tongue licking her shoulder.

"Wha—" she began, pushing the animal away.

"Bagel! Bagel! Get off her!" Euan grabbed the dog by its collar. "Charlie, I'm so sorry, are you OK?" He helped her to her feet.

Her shorts had a rip at the side, and there was grit in the scratches on her elbow and thigh. "Just about."

"Thank God," he said. "I'm so sorry." Then, turning to the dog: "Sit, Bagel. SIT." Reluctantly, the dog sat down, tongue still lolling.

"What happened?" She leaned against the sea wall, trying to get her breath back.

"He ran into you. I've only had him a week and I haven't quite worked out this extendable lead yet. Well, I've worked out how to extend it, but not how to . . . Again, I'm so sorry."

Charlie looked at the dog suspiciously.

"He's on probation," Euan explained. "He's a rescue. My friend Adam is a vet and took him in. I'm up for a challenge, but I have to say I'm wondering whether I've bitten off more than I can chew this time. So to speak."

The dog whined and tilted its head.

Charlie crouched to the dog's level. "Can we start over?" she asked. Bagel raised a muddy paw and she shook it.

"OK," she continued. "He's forgiven. But you? You might have to work a bit harder. How do you intend to make it up to me?"

Charlie and Euan were sitting outside Rosa's, a coffee shop by the pier, with croissants and two cappuccinos. Bagel was barking at seagulls nearby, his lead held tightly by Euan.

The seafront was slowly starting to wake, with one or two people emerging from their houses, and in the distance Charlie could see the lights go on in Letty's tearoom.

"It's good you get time to run—are your children at home this morning?" Euan asked.

"No. I mean, yes, they're at home—but no, they're not mine." She smiled. "They're my sister's kids."

"Oh, right, I see." His face relaxed and he smiled. "I just assumed."

"I'm the super-auntie." She laughed. "Or something like that. They've been keeping me pretty busy. There's Flo—she's the eldest, then Jacob, and finally the new baby, Gracie."

"A new baby, that's lovely. Is that what brought you up here?"

"Yes—or at least it was . . . It's a long story."

He opened his mouth to speak and she shook her head.

"I won't ask," he said.

"It's a lot to explain, but suffice to say my sister needs a hand at the moment."

"So did you get time off work to come here?" Euan asked, breaking off a bit of croissant.

"I'm actually still working—kind of." She smiled. "I persuaded my boss I could do my research here. I write food and drink reviews, and I'm editing the next magazine, which has a section dedicated to tearoom."

"Cool job," said Euan. "Now I understand why you were so interested in Mum's tearoom."

"Exactly. Although Kat's persuaded me to leave them out of the feature. She thinks some things are best kept a secret, and I'm starting to understand what she means."

"Yes. I'm not sure how Mum would cope with a flood of gastronomic enthusiasts quizzing her about her scones. She's happiest when she has time to chat to the regulars. I tried to talk her into building a website last year, but she just laughed and said why try to fix something that's not broken."

"It's true. What she does, she does well."

"I know. I leave her to it these days," Euan said.

Euan smiled at Charlie, and she felt her shoulders, hunched from the stress of the past few days, start to soften. There was something about him that put her at ease. They were silent for a moment.

"Do you enjoy the reviewing?" Euan asked gently. "It sounds a dream job."

"Oh yes. I love it. I've always been obsessed with food, so getting paid to try out other people's cooking works for me."

"You must get a lot of perks."

Charlie nodded. "I get invites to new restaurant openings in London, pop-ups on rooftop terraces, boat parties, that kind of thing, and I'm working my way up to . . ." Charlie paused, suddenly aware that she was reeling off a spiel that sounded hollow.

"What is it?" he said.

She laughed wryly. "I'm not going to lie, it's the same as any job. It has its great points, but a lot of the time I'm commuting, answering e-mails at midnight and stuck in pointless meetings when I want to be writing."

"I know exactly what you mean," Euan said.

"What is it you do?"

"I'm an architect. See the cinema?" He pointed to the building on the corner nearest to them. "We're turning part of it into a restaurant."

"It's a fabulous building. Art Deco, right? You're not going to knock it down, are you?"

"No, definitely not. It's a conversion—we'll be retaining

the period features, but enabling the space to work in a very different way."

"I like the sound of that. I'll have to come back and see it when it's done."

"Should be finished by the summer, hopefully, although the buyers want it yesterday. I enjoy the planning stage, but negotiating with them is the part of my job that reminds me it's work."

"How do you find time to help out at the tearoom?"

"I make time, when I can. I'd rather work late once in a while, if that's what it takes. Although, to be fair, often I'm just enjoying the scones along with the rest of you, so it's not all hard graft."

"It must be nice for Letty, having you nearby," Charlie said. She thought briefly of her own parents and how rarely she saw them these days. It was easier that way, of course—not to have to deal with her mother's questions and her dad's unpredictable outbursts, but she was also dimly aware that one day they wouldn't be there, and that then she might feel differently about it all.

"I think it is, especially since she and my dad separated," Euan said. "She's always given me space to do my own thing, but as it turned out I chose to stick around in Scarborough."

"I can understand that."

"Do your parents live in London?" Euan asked.

"No. They live in Bristol, where Pippa and I grew up. We're scattered all over the country these days."

"What are your family like?"

Charlie bit the inside of her lip, wondering where to start. "My mum is lovely. She's kind of an old-fashioned mum, runs around after all of us, cooking and organizing. Dad and Pippa are pretty high-maintenance. We're very different people." She paused, then smiled. "That, or we're exactly the same and I'm in denial about it."

Euan was listening to her calmly, an empty coffee cup in front of him. In a gray hoodie and T-shirt, his hair ruffled, he looked completely relaxed. She was aware of her torn Lycra running gear, and the fact that her hair, coming loose from a ponytail, was a mess. This wasn't something she did—sitting with a man she barely knew, still sweaty from a run, talking about her family. Saying things she'd never said to anyone other than Sarah.

Unsettled, she switched the focus back to him.

"I bet you had a great childhood, growing up here."

"It was good, lots of time outdoors. Mum's a magpie and she used to drive Dad mad collecting things. When I was young she brought home a broken old rowing boat, complete with oars, and set it up in the garden for me. I loved it—Adam was always round, playing in it with me. We'd pretend we were sailing out to a secret island, like in *Swallows and Amazons*."

"That must've been fun."

"It was. I had friends round a lot. I think Mum and Dad were worried about me turning out weird, being an only child. But I reckon I turned out all right." He wrinkled his nose. "At least, I hope I did."

"You seem relatively normal." Charlie smiled. "To be honest, I'm not sure having a sibling makes you any saner. Probably the opposite." She glanced at her watch. "Speaking of siblings, mine will be wondering where I've got to," she said. "I told Pippa I wouldn't be long." Charlie tipped her croissant crumbs onto the floor next to Bagel, and he snuffled them up quickly.

"Sure, of course," Euan said.

As he asked for the bill, Charlie wondered if she'd said too much. When she'd been with Ben, they hadn't ever talked about family—it was something they had both chosen to overlook, preferring to focus on going out, enjoying every high-octane, indulgent moment in the city's bars and clubs when work was done. Yet here she was, opening up to someone she had only just met.

"Thanks for being so understanding about this terror." He pointed at Bagel.

"It's fine. As long as he's learned his lesson." Charlie stroked the dog's ears. "Behave yourself," she said to Bagel. "He can still give you back, you know."

She got to her feet. "Thanks for the coffee," she said.

"It was good talking to you," Euan said. "See you again, I hope."

"Yes," said Charlie, secretly hoping the same. "That would be nice."

# 20

Thursday, September 18

Kat spread an ordnance survey map out on the tearoom counter.

"Over here in Whitby there's a lovely place run by an old friend of mine," Letty said, tapping her finger on the map. "The Alexandra Tearoom. You should give that a visit. And then up here"—Letty's finger moved up a centimeter to the port—"you'll find the loveliest little tea shop. The Hideaway, I think it's called. Doesn't look much from the outside—and I haven't been there for years—but I seem to remember they do the most delectable strawberry tarts."

"Sounds perfect," Kat said, marking the spot with a Post-it.

"I'm rather envious. You and Séraphine are going to have a wonderful trip."

"I'm looking forward to it."

"It seems to suit you, this work," Letty said. "I haven't seen you this excited in a long time."

"I have been enjoying using my brain again, as well as my taste buds." Kat smiled.

"You were always cut out for great things, Kat."

"Thanks. I feel a little out of my depth, to be honest—but Charlie seemed happy with the reviews I've written up till now, so hopefully I'm on the right track."

"I'm sure you are," Letty said. "You've always had a knack for writing."

"When I sat down, the words simply flowed," Kat said. "I didn't think it would come so easily to me. You know how it is when you've got a young child—the last few years I've struggled to find time to read a grown-up book, let alone do any writing. But once I got started, it was as if something clicked in my mind and the cogs starting whirring again. Perhaps those years at uni weren't wasted after all."

"Of course they weren't," Letty said. "You'll find the right job for you. And as long as it involves tea, I'm sure you'll be happy."

"You know me too well."

"Talking of tea—I've christened the lovebirds Lady and Earl Grey. What do you think?"

"Perfect!"

"They're settling in rather nicely. Not quite as sophisticated as the names make them sound. They're more than happy to watch telly." She smiled. "They're nice to have a chat to though, when I'm making my dinner. They fly around and then rest up on the rafters—always together."

"How sweet."

"Yes. They're very romantic, a real team, won't be separated."

A thought came to Kat. The tearoom was quiet, and now seemed a good time to ask Letty something she'd been wondering about. "I don't suppose anything's changed—with John. The two of you still aren't talking?"

"No, love," Letty said, shaking her head. "We've gone too far for that. I hear the occasional thing from Euan about what he's up to: fishing trips they've taken together, or a new car he's taken on to repair. I don't mind hearing about him. It was a long time we were together, a lot of them happy years. I'll always care about him. But it's easier this way. Better two happy parents than an unhappy home—you know all about that, of course."

"Yes," Kat said.

"It's must've been harder for you, though, with Leo so young."

"I don't know if there is such a thing as a good age where that's concerned. But children are resilient, I think—I hope. I felt bad about it at first. But when Jake left . . . well, I felt lighter, somehow. I suddenly remembered how to have fun again."

"You certainly seem happier," Letty said.

"I am. And this time alone, while Leo's with Jake, has reminded me of all the things I used to enjoy doing. I realize now that I don't have to give up being me in order to be there for Leo. If anything, I'll be a better mother to him if I know what I want."

# 21

Friday, September 19

"I was so happy when I got your call," Séraphine said to Kat the following morning, as they boarded the bus for the journey to Whitby.

"I'm glad you had time to come."

"Adam's pretty easygoing as a boss. He knows I've been working hard with Zoe, and he says he wants me to be able to see some of the country while I'm over here. Especially now the weather's good."

That day, Kat had woken to sunshine pouring in through the slatted blind in her bedroom window, warming her face. After a week of gray days, she'd almost forgotten how it felt. She'd put on a denim jacket and an orange scarf that morning, and walked to the bus station where she met Séraphine.

"Where exactly are we going again?"

"The fish-and-chip capital of the northeast," Kat said, unfolding the map to show Séraphine the places she'd marked with luminous Post-its. "And hopefully the home of some fine tearooms too."

"OK. Interesting . . . The Hideaway—I like the sound of that one."

"Me too. We can start there."

"It's a plan." Séraphine took out her guidebook and opened it at a page with a smaller local map. "I have a friend back home who would be so envious. She's obsessed with English tea, cakes, all that kind of thing."

"You'll have to try everything out for her," Kat said.

"I suppose it's my duty," Séraphine said, with a mischievous smile.

"How are things at the house?"

"They're getting better, actually."

"What's changed?" Kat asked.

"I've got to know Zoe better, and I think she's starting to trust me. We've been talking about her mum, who was French, and she's begun to open up. We've also been painting together, and she seems to enjoy that—we'll chat together but without the pressure of a class."

"Sounds as if you're doing a good job. How old is she again?"

"Ten. Going on sixteen."

"It's a tricky age, ten, isn't it? You're stuck in the middle. I remember when I was ten, I'd be looking at my cousins, who were teenagers, and wanting desperately to go out with them, but to them I was just a kid. Books were the thing that saved me. I'd go up to my room and read—whether it was Jane Austen or Sweet Valley High, it gave me an escape."

"I know what you mean. With a good book, you can enter into whichever world you want. When I find the twins still reading under the covers late at night, sometimes I can't bring myself to tell them off."

"It's a magical time, discovering that."

"That's part of what makes me want to be a teacher."

"Is that what you're going to do?"

"Yes. Teaching English. I'm qualified already, so I'll look for a job when I get home. I came here because I wanted to polish up my English conversation and pronunciation. I feel it's become quite rusty."

"Your English sounds great to me. I'm sure you'll have no trouble finding a teaching position."

"I can't wait to start."

"Children or teenagers?"

"Teenagers, I hope. Seems more of a challenge. Although I doubt anyone could be a bigger challenge than Zoe." She laughed. "Have you got any photos of your son, Kat? I'd love to see one."

"Sure. Yes. Here's Leo." Kat took out her phone and showed Séraphine her screen saver, a picture of Leo on a swing, his hair golden in the sun. "He's three. No reading under the covers yet."

"He's gorgeous."

"Thank you. He's pretty good. The terrible twos certainly lived up to their name, but, fingers crossed, I think we're coming out the other side." She bit her lip, recalling it. "This past year it's been tantrums in the supermarket, refusing to get in his buggy, climbing into my bed every night. It nearly drove me crazy. But now he's sweet as anything."

"I remember that time with the twins. Being so much older, I'm more like a mum to them than a sister. I Skype them when I can. They're far better with gadgets than I am."

"Leo's the same."

"You must miss him a lot," Séraphine said.

"I do. Even though him being away gives me the freedom to do things like this—I still can't wait for him to come back. Isn't it silly? When he's here I'm usually desperate for a minute to myself. I dream about being able to pop out to the shops, or go out with a friend without having to beg a favor off someone.

Even to read a magazine in peace. But the moment he's gone, I wonder what I ever did without him."

This can't be it, can it?" Kat said, peering in through the windows of a shabby-looking tearoom by the water. She and Séraphine had arrived in Whitby shortly before midday, and walked down to the port in search of the café Letty had mentioned. There was only one place that it could be.

"It does say The Hideaway," Séraphine said. "Look."

Kat looked up at the sign, where raised lettering reading THE HIDEAWAY had been crudely whitewashed, with the new name painted over it. Another sign hung in the doorway announcing that it was under new management.

"Not quite what I pictured," Kat said. "But appearances can be deceptive, can't they? Let's give it a go."

They went inside, and found a table out toward the back. A man in his fifties, with gray hair and a mustache, came over to them.

"What can I get you, ladies?" he asked kindly.

"Hi," Kat said. "Could we have a pot of tea and two of your strawberry tarts, please?"

"Coming right up."

"Can I ask a question?" Kat said, as he turned to go. He smiled and nodded. "Have you just taken this place over?"

"Yes. A couple of months ago. Me and my wife fancied a project. It's uncharted territory for us, this tea business, but we've always enjoyed a cuppa. We're getting on OK so far."

"I see," Kat said.

"That's the missus"—he gave a nod in the direction of a stressed-looking woman juggling pots in the kitchen—"trying out a new recipe."

He left to get their order.

"The décor could do with some sprucing up," Kat whispered when the owner was out of earshot. She pointed to the faded wallpaper, with a repeat pattern of ships just visible on it.

"It feels quite damp in here too," Séraphine added.

"It doesn't matter. Letty said not to expect much from the surroundings."

"Yes. Of course."

The teapot arrived a few minutes later, with the tarts on plain white plates next to it.

Kat only needed a quick look. "Shop bought," she said, disappointed.

"Oh dear." Séraphine took a bite and nodded to confirm Kat's suspicions. "You're right. The jam's not good at all."

The door swung open and a man with a gray ponytail lurched into the café. "How's it going, Steve?" he called out.

"And who's this?" He made his way over to their table and Kat noticed the strong smell of whisky. "Haven't seen you two around here before."

"We're visiting," Séraphine answered politely. "It's our first time here."

"A Frenchie, eh? Oooh la la." He pulled up a chair, turned it around and sat with Kat and Séraphine. "You seem friendly enough, though. Don't mind if I join you, do you?"

"Actually we were—" Kat started.

"Charming conversation with a local lad, you can't beat that, can you? Now let me tell you how I came to be here . . ."

Kat rolled her eyes at Séraphine discreetly and Séraphine's mouth twitched as she tried to hold in her laughter.

"I used to work in the merchant navy," he drawled. He then burst into song, forgot the words and suddenly remembered he'd started a story. "I've been all around—Singapore, Malaysia, Germany. You name it." He pulled up the sleeve of his shirt and showed them his arm, patterned with dark-blue tattoos. "A few memories these bring back."

"Nice," Kat said.

"You've just got the one"—he pointed at the tattoo on Kat's wrist—"and I bet you it wasn't as painful as these ones. An old pen—do you know the way?"

Kat looked over at the owner, hoping for rescue, but he was talking to his wife in the kitchen.

"Grew up in Ireland, I did," the man continued. "One of ten. I was one of the lucky ones. Two died from TB, we were crammed into a room, all of us and . . ."

His drunken drawl slowed as once again he lost track of what he was talking about.

Kat wolfed the last of her tart and raised her eyebrows at Séraphine. "I'm afraid we have somewhere we need to be."

"Do we?" Séraphine asked innocently. Kat widened her eyes. "Oh yes—of course we do," Séraphine said, pulling on her jacket. "So sorry," she said to the man. "But we must be going."

Kat left money to pay the bill on the table and they headed for the door. As soon as they were outside on the pavement, they both collapsed in giggles. "God—I didn't think we'd ever get away from him," Kat said.

"He'd have enough stories to keep going all day, that's for sure."

"Oh dear. Not the most promising start. But the only way is up. Where next?"

They looked at the map, getting their bearings. "How about the Alexandra Tearoom?" Kat suggested. "That looks a safe enough bet. Don't hold me to that, though."

⌐

The Alexandra Tearoom was a short walk away and had a terrace overlooking the sea. The tables were filled with a mix of elderly couples and younger day-trippers in groups.

"I think we're safe," Séraphine whispered, making Kat laugh.

They ordered the full afternoon tea and Séraphine put on her sunglasses, looking out at the water. "It's beautiful here."

"Yes, stunning. What a view—completely unobscured. I thought Letty had the best view going, but this—"

"I'll tell her you said that," Séraphine teased.

"Don't you dare!"

The teapot and cake stand arrived, and Kat poured out tea into their two cups.

"It's a lovely tradition, this," Séraphine said.

"Do you know how it all started?" Kat asked, taking a finger sandwich.

"No, how?"

"In the mid-nineteenth century a woman called Anna—a duchess, I believe she was—wanted a little something to pep her up in the late afternoon. You know that post-lunch lull when you can't find the energy to do anything?"

"Yes. I normally just want to sleep. I think the Spanish have the right idea."

"Well, Duchess Anna requested a cup of tea and something to eat, and before long her friends were doing the same. The idea caught on and spread."

"Then here's to our friend Anna," Séraphine said, raising her teacup. "She was a very smart woman."

"Would you ever be tempted to come and live here?" Kat asked. "More permanently, I mean?" Séraphine seemed so at ease in England, relaxed and confident.

"I don't think so," Séraphine said. "There are things I'd miss." Her eyes took on a distant look.

"People?" Kat asked gently.

Séraphine nodded.

Something in her expression told Kat not to pursue the line of inquiry any further.

"Well, we'll just have to see to it that you enjoy your time here as much as possible," Kat said.

In the afternoon, after two more tearoom stops, Séraphine and Kat browsed the antique shops in the town, picking up small trinkets and souvenirs.

"Are you hungry?" Kat asked. "I mean, a macaroon is only so filling. Do you fancy some fish and chips?"

"That would be great. I've never had any before. Not proper English ones, anyway."

"Then it's settled. Let's go."

They bought portions of cod and chips wrapped in paper and took them down to the sea. On a bench, they ate the warm chips with wooden chip forks.

"These are good," Séraphine said.

"Incredibly healthy too," Kat said, with a smile.

"Oh yes, all that salt and ketchup in particular."

"We used to have these when I was growing up. Every Friday, Dad and I would go down to the harbor and pick them up. He'd get fish and I'd get a battered sausage."

"Do your parents still live in Scarborough?" Séraphine asked.

"My dad does. At least, that's where his house is. He's away traveling at the moment—and having the time of his life, if his postcards are anything to go by. He deserves it. He's worked hard ever since he left school."

"What about your mother?"

"She passed away when I was young."

"I'm sorry to hear that."

"Thanks. I wish I could remember her better. To be honest, I barely have any memories of her." Kat shrugged. "I was four when she died. Dad and Letty—who was a friend of hers— have told me a few things. They both say that she wanted desperately to be a mother, and that having me completed her in a way. Apparently she was kind and generous, and funny."

"Are you similar to her? Do they ever mention that?"

"No." Kat shook her head. "Apart from the kind and funny bit," she joked. "But seriously? No, not at all."

"How can you be sure?"

"Mum was curvy, as much as I'm not. Red hair, freckles . . ."

"Really?" Séraphine raised her eyebrows.

"Yes," Kat said, with a smile. "It's not as surprising as it seems, though. I'm adopted."

"Oh, I see."

"I should have said that at the start. Sometimes I forget, Dad is so much my dad. He could have been lost on his own when Mum died, but he wasn't. He was OK. It wasn't regular, our little setup, but it's worked for us. What about your family?"

"They're pretty conventional." Séraphine smiled. "Perhaps a little too conventional."

"Too conventional?"

"Yes. Although perfectly normal for where we live. Church on Sundays, don't say or do anything to upset the others in the village—that kind of thing."

"Does it bother you?" Kat asked.

"It didn't always. But lately, yes. I sometimes wonder how they'd react if they knew the real me."

Kat wanted to ask—she could see that Séraphine was holding something back, but at the same time she was wary of pushing too much. "Do you think it holds you back?" she asked.

Séraphine considered the question, then nodded. "I suppose it's easier to carry on pretending to be what they want me to be."

"You only get one lifetime to be the real you," Kat said. "You can't afford to miss that chance, you know."

That evening, Séraphine sat on her bed and put her canvas bag down beside her. The fresh air had left her relaxed and pleasantly tired—but what had affected her most was the conversation with Kat.

Her parents were already halfway through their lives, and had been lucky enough to spend a lot of those years in love. Was it fair that she should deny herself that same happiness in a bid to please them? When she met Carla, she felt as if she were coming alive—every interest, each silly joke or childhood memory was received with delight and matched by one of Carla's. Their synergy was effortless and natural. Séraphine had clumsily pushed Carla away by escaping to England, and yet she could see now that Carla was strong enough in herself not to turn her back on the woman she loved. Séraphine sensed that the door might still be open. Perhaps it wasn't a case of saying either yes—in its whole, messy entirety—or saying no. Maybe it was also possible to say yes in a slower way. *Yes, but I need time.*

She laid out the objects she'd collected.

A smooth white-and-peach-colored shell.

Two jars of tea leaves—Darjeeling and Lady Grey—that Kat had recommended she buy.

A tin of pinwheel cookies that she had made with Zoe.

A vintage scarf, with a diamond-ring print on it.

A postcard of Scarborough.

She wrapped them all up in bronze paper and tied the packages with string before placing them in a padded envelope. On the back of a photo she'd printed, a self-portrait taken on the South Sands, she wrote a message to go with the gifts:

Salut, ma belle,
Où que je sois, tu es avec moi.
Je t'embrasse,
Séraphine x

Wherever I am, you're with me.

# 22

Saturday, September 20

"You look OK like that, you know," Charlie said. "Reminds me of when we were teenagers. Before you started nicking my eye shadow."

Pippa was dressed in tracksuit bottoms with tea stains on the knee, and her hair was pulled up into a rough ponytail, her face clear of makeup. As the week wore on, she was sleeping a little better and some of the color had returned to her cheeks.

Pippa smiled. "I couldn't be bothered," she said. "I'll dig out my mascara when I'm ready to go out of the house again."

"I hate to mention it, but you do remember that Mum and Dad are coming today? They're due at midday."

"Oh God, I forgot," Pippa said, putting her hand to her mouth and looking around the living room. "This place is in chaos."

"They won't care."

"Can't we quickly uninvite them?"

"They'll be almost here by now. Anyway, they're our parents. And they've been worried about you. They're not expecting to be entertained, they've only come to see you and the kids."

"Well, I should probably put some proper clothes on, at least," Pippa said, looking down at her scruffy tracksuit bottoms. "Dad won't think much of this outfit."

"You go upstairs and get ready, and I'll have a quick tidy in here."

"OK," Pippa said. She turned her head as she walked out. "Tell me it's not going to be awful?"

"It'll be absolutely fine," Charlie reassured her.

Pippa, darling!" their father said, giving her a hearty bear hug. He pulled away and looked at her, dressed now in lilac jeans and a white blouse. "You look OK to me. Charlie said you were in a right state."

"I never said that," Charlie whispered to her sister.

"Only teasing," Henry said, ruffling Pippa's hair. "Got to have some fun at times like these, haven't you? Can't have everyone falling apart."

"I'll get the tea on, shall I?" their mother volunteered.

"A glass of brandy for me, would you, Paula dear? You've got some back there, I expect?" Henry asked Pippa. She nodded.

"It's only midday, Henry." Paula frowned.

"Details, details."

Paula shepherded her grandchildren out of the front room. "Now, Flo and Jacob, do you think you could help me find a biscuit or two to go with our tea?"

Pippa sat in the armchair by the window, near where Gracie was sleeping in her bouncy chair, leaving the sofa for her father and Charlie.

"So where is he?" Henry said. "That husband of yours? Still cowering somewhere?"

"He's staying with a friend," Pippa told him.

"The other woman, you mean."

"Dad, that's not the way it is." Pippa shook her head.

"Well, however it is, I've half a mind to wring his neck. Who does he think he is, walking out on his family? Turning his back on his responsibilities? Not a man at all."

"You don't know the full story," Pippa said, crossing her legs. "It's complicated."

"Doesn't sound it to me," Henry said. "Your husband leaves you and you're here making excuses for him?"

"I'm not making excuses, Dad . . ." Charlie saw that tears had sprung to her sister's eyes.

"Dad," Charlie said, laying a hand on her father's arm and encouraging him to settle back on the sofa. "Pippa doesn't need this right now."

"If you ask me, what she needs is the good sense to get the locks changed."

Pippa put a hand through her hair anxiously.

"She needs some space—time to think," Charlie said.

"Fine," he said, sitting back and seeming to calm down a little. "I suppose the alternative isn't too tempting. Not with three children. Bad enough having one grown-up daughter with no one to look after her."

Charlie felt a dull thud in her stomach. She'd heard it before, but that didn't mean it didn't hurt. Pippa's eyes widened. "Dad! You can't say that."

Pippa's words took Charlie by surprise.

"No point dancing round the subject, is there? You think in your retirement you'll be able to relax, but with one daughter still on the shelf, and the other—"

"On the shelf?" Pippa repeated.

"It wouldn't have happened in my day, all this farting about with a career rather than settling down. Pippa, things might have gone arse over tit for you now, but at least you had the good sense to—"

Pippa straightened in her seat. "Say what you want about my life, but don't speak about Charlie that way. You're in my house today, and I won't have her being bullied."

Charlie felt a swell of delight as her sister jumped to her defense. Only a few days ago Pippa had been saying almost the same things about her. The change in her sister filled Charlie with pride. It seemed Pippa was gathering strength, transforming before her.

Their father puffed out his cheeks and then let out a stream of breath.

"Charlie's happy. And I for one admire her for working hard, doing something she loves."

Henry paled. He opened his mouth to reply but no sound emerged.

Paula came back into the room with a tray of drinks. "Here's your brandy, darling." She put a glass down in front of her husband. "Now, who's for a nice cup of tea?"

There was silence in the room. Charlie suppressed the urge to giggle.

"Did I miss something?" Paula said. "Henry, you look as if you've just seen a ghost."

God, I'm glad that's over," Pippa said with a wry laugh. She and Charlie were in their pajamas that evening, with glasses of wine and the Saturday-night TV on low in the background.

"Me too," Charlie said. "Maybe I shouldn't have asked them. I sort of forgot how bad it was. Has Dad always been like that?"

"I think he's worse than ever. I put it down to being retired and having more time on his hands."

"Is it awful that we can't stand our own father?" Charlie said, taking a sip of her drink.

"No. We still love him, don't we?"

Charlie nodded and smiled. "Just about."

"But honestly, I can't believe the things he came out with today." Pippa laughed. "No way I'm putting up with that anymore."

"I nearly fell off my chair when you talked back to him."

"He took it though, didn't he? Kept quiet after that." Pippa smiled cheekily.

"I appreciate you sticking up for me."

"Least I can do. Listen, Charlie, I'm sorry about the way I acted when you got here. Jealousy's a funny old business."

"You? Jealous?"

"Of course. You seem to breeze through life, while I'm busy saying the wrong thing and winding people up without meaning to."

"Oh, believe me, I do a fair share of that too," Charlie said, smiling. "I guess some of Dad's, er, 'charm' filtered down to both of us."

"Ha. Perhaps." Pippa laughed.

"Poor Mum. She has to deal with it all the time, doesn't she?"

"Oh, she can fight her corner. In fact, I'm pretty sure that behind closed doors she's the one calling the shots."

"Still, being married to a man as demanding as he is—it's got to be hard work."

"Yes. It must be." Pippa nodded, a pensive look on her face.

"Are you thinking about Luke?"

"Yes."

"What about him?"

"That I miss him. That I love him. That I could have done a whole lot worse."

Pippa picked her phone up off the table and passed Charlie the remote control. "You know what, I'm going to leave you in the capable hands of BBC 1. I've got a phone call I need to make."

# 23

Saturday, September 20

"Over to you," Séraphine said, passing the laptop to Kat in the kitchen at Adam's house. "I've set up the document, but you're the writer, so now it's down to you to make all that"—she pointed at the notebook of scribbled ideas that lay between them on the table—"into something intelligible."

Kat took the laptop from her and started to type. "Here goes. Now, the Alexandra Tearoom—four stars?"

"I think that's fair, yes. It lacked a little something that would bring it up to five."

"I agree. The service was polite but quite slow. The meringues are worth a mention though." Kat typed up their thoughts, then moved the screen so that Séraphine could see what she'd written. "Does that sum it up?"

"Perfectly, yes."

"God, what on earth do we say about The Hideaway?"

Séraphine grimaced, then laughed.

The front door opened noisily and the hallway filled with the sound of excited chatter. Kat glanced up from the screen.

"Hi, Séraphine," Zoe said, coming into the room. She was wearing jeans and a purple-striped hoodie, her hair up in a topknot.

She looked at Kat curiously. "This is my friend Kat," Séraphine explained.

"Hello," Kat replied. "You must be Zoe."

Zoe put down the bag she was carrying and shook Kat's hand politely. Adam followed her through the door.

Kat recognized him immediately, and felt the warm glow of familiarity. It had been years—back at school, and waiting for the same bus in the morning—but that ruffled brown hair and the expression, somewhere between confident and shy—he hadn't changed at all.

"Kat," Adam said, a smile breaking out on his face.

"You two already know each other?" Séraphine asked, confused.

"Yes," Kat said. She tried to recall the last time they'd seen each other. "And no. It's been years. But we used to live on the same street."

She remembered him and Euan chatting to each other on the bus, skating up and down the street. In those days she'd longed for Adam to talk to her, wished she was the kind of girl who was brave enough to engineer an excuse to speak to him. She never had, but on the days that he smiled at her, or even nodded in her direction, she'd be carried along on a cushion of happiness all day.

"You lived with your dad," he said.

"Yes. And you and Euan Hill were always in trouble, I remember that."

Adam smiled. "I'm sure your memory's deceiving you," he said, glancing at Zoe.

Zoe looked up at her dad, wide-eyed. "Is that true? Were you and Euan very naughty?"

"I had my moments. Nowhere near as wild as you, though," he said, playfully ruffling her hair.

"Adam's a vet," Séraphine said.

"And I run an unofficial sort of animal refuge," he added.

"You know the lovebirds that Letty has?" Séraphine turned to Kat.

"They were from you?" Kat looked up at Adam, smiling. "Ah, now things are making more sense."

"Is she getting on OK with them?" Adam asked.

"Yes. She's grown quite attached to them already. She says she loves having their company. She's determined that they have some freedom, but one nearly flew out the window the other day—luckily she managed to catch it again."

"It's good that she's letting them fly around."

"We've had dogs in here too. And a tarantula. He's gone now," Zoe said.

"Right," Kat said, raising her eyebrows.

"That was a one-off," Adam assured her.

As they talked, Kat warmed to Adam, just as she had all those years before.

"Dad—can I watch *Despicable Me*?" Zoe asked.

"Again?"

She pouted. "Please?"

"Oh, go on, then." He shook his head.

"Thanks!" Zoe left and went through to the front room.

"Not that a ten-year-old calls the shots in this house or anything," Adam said.

Kat laughed.

Adam studied her face intently. "You haven't changed."

"No?" Kat said.

"I mean, the last time I saw you you had purple hair . . ." He smiled. "But apart from that."

"That was years ago," Kat said, laughing. "I must have been fifteen then."

"You and your dad were in the corner terrace—and in the summer he'd give me a fiver to wash his car. Does he still live round here?"

"Yes. He's traveling at the moment, but his home's here."

Kat thought how small Scarborough seemed sometimes. It was strange that their paths hadn't crossed until now.

"I see Euan quite often, but you . . . ?"

"I was living in France for a while," he said. "And my hours at work tend to be rather antisocial."

"Speaking of work," Séraphine said, coughing and pointing at the computer. "I hate to break up this reunion, but Kat and I have a lot to do. The reviews I told you about, Adam."

"We have to get these finished for Charlie." Kat smiled apologetically. "Another time."

"Don't let me keep you," Adam said. He held Kat's gaze for a moment. "It was good to see you again."

K at walked home that evening, wondering if it was possible for chemistry to be a one-sided thing. While she'd only seen Adam briefly, the feelings she'd had a decade ago had come back almost immediately, an attraction that meant she had wanted to stay close by. She'd felt good talking to him. She was too old to have crushes, she told herself, shaking it off.

She let herself into her flat, set up some food for her dinner and called Jake.

"Is Leo around?" she asked.

"You're a moment too late, I'm afraid. He's in the bath."

"On his own?"

"No, what do you take me for?" Jake laughed. "My mum's with him."

"Ah, that's a shame," Kat said. "I was looking forward to talking to him."

She felt a pang of regret. She should have gotten home a little earlier, or called on her way. She was desperate to hear her son's voice, and for him to know she was thinking of him.

"Do you think you could call me back when he's out?" she asked.

"We should put him to bed, I think—he's tired out today."

Kat resisted the urge to ask again. Leo was with Jake, and therefore he was in charge—even if his decisions didn't suit her.

"So what have you guys been up to?" she asked brightly.

"Dad and I took him to a funfair in town; he went on the dodgems with me and won a massive teddy bear in hook-the-duck. I helped out with that."

"Lucky Leo." She smiled at the image.

"He enjoyed it a lot."

Kat tried to rein in the emotion, the longing to hold her son in her arms again, kiss the top of his head, smell his famil-iar smell—Johnson's baby shampoo and clean skin. Even though at moments like this it was hard to be apart from Leo, she felt reassured that she had made the right decision. He and his dad were bonding, and he was spending quality time with his grandparents. What kind of a mother would she be if she begrudged him that?

"Sounds as if he's enjoying his holiday with you," she said.

"We're having fun. He hasn't forgotten you yet, though, don't worry."

She smiled. "That's good. I thought he might not have forgiven me for telling him his stegosaurus was too big for his suitcase."

"He's moved on already," Jake said. "My dad bought him a pterodactyl to make up for it."

"Fickle, fickle child." She laughed.

"It's nice talking with you, like this," Jake said.

It was true, Kat thought. Things had got easier between the two of them, with time. His tone hinted at something more than that though.

"What do you mean?" she asked.

"I mean relaxed, having a laugh, the way we used to," Jake said.

He was right. Sometimes of an evening when she was on her own in the flat, it was impossible not to recall the time they'd spent together, drinking wine and talking. Among the difficult days, there had been a lot of good ones.

"I miss that," Jake said. "I really do."

# 24

Sunday, September 21

Charlie parked up the pram by the window in the Seafront Tearoom. Tucked in with a pale yellow blanket and her bunny comforter, Gracie was fast asleep, breathing gently.

"Are you meeting Kat and Séraphine today?" Letty asked her.

"Yes—they're coming at two to fill me in on their trip to Whitby. I'm early. This little one needed some fresh air."

"Do you know how it went?"

"Good, from what I can tell. They've written up the reviews already. Interesting stuff. Talking of interesting—I was looking through the scrapbook on your counter the other day. There are some wonderful things in there."

"This place has seen a lot, that's true. I'm glad you had a look. Most of the people around here don't give the history a second thought. They just assume we've always been here and always will be."

"I think it's fascinating."

"I've got a couple more things, if you'd like to see them? While you wait for the others to arrive, and the baby's sleeping?"

"I'd love to take a look."

Charlie took a seat at one of the tables, and Letty brought over the tea she'd ordered and a large cigar box. "It's a bit of a muddle, but who knows, you might find something that you and Kat can use for inspiration."

"Thanks."

Gracie stirred, and Charlie rocked the pram to get her back to sleep. With her free hand, she opened the box and looked through the papers and photos.

The first thing she came to was a menu. She couldn't see a date on it, but it was pressed between letters dated from the late 1960s.

The sweets—now this was what she was really interested in:

Chocolate éclairs, cream sandwiches, almond tarts, butter-cream, Battenberg squares . . . Viennese cakes. In all the years the tearoom had been running, some things hadn't changed.

"What did you do to celebrate the centenary, Letty?" Charlie asked out of the blue.

"Nothing," Letty said. "That's rather sad, isn't it? It sort of passed me by. It was an awful year for the Seafront, to be honest. We started the year with a break-in, and then in February part of the roof came away. Euan and I were too focused on getting that sorted to think about a party. All in all, it didn't seem the right time for a celebration."

"What a shame. It's such a milestone."

"I suppose it would have been nice to mark it," Letty said, tilting her head as she considered it. "Too late now, though."

Charlie immersed herself in the postcards and photos from the early days of the Seafront. She stayed like that for a while, ideas drifting through her head. She was nudged out of her daze by a man's voice.

"Hello there."

Her eyes flicked up from the page and met Euan's. A smile came to her lips as she saw him standing by her table. "Hey," she said.

"How's it going?" His gaze drifted to the baby, who was now smiling and wide awake, her blue eyes button-round and bright. "I'm guessing this is the famous Gracie."

"The very same," Charlie said, putting the papers down and peering into the pram. "This is her. My youngest niece."

"She's lovely."

"She is beautiful, isn't she?" Charlie said, carefully lifting Gracie out of the pram and holding her close. "I'm allowed to say that because she's not mine." She smiled.

"Ha, yes."

"How's the work on the cinema going?" Charlie asked.

"Good, thanks. There's a slight issue with one of the plans, but I reckon we've worked out a way to fix it."

"The buyers have got a real catch. That place is going to make an incredible restaurant."

"I think so," Euan said. "The venue is on everyone's radar already, so there'll be a lot of interest around it when it opens. I wish it were going to nicer people though—it's one unreasonable demand after another with these buyers."

"Intense?"

"Yes. Hence the scone break." Euan smiled. "What are you up to?" He looked at the papers on her desk. "Research?"

"Yes. And meeting some friends."

"Euan, have you got a minute?" Letty called over from the kitchen. "Only the tap's broken again."

"Yep, sure." He rolled his eyes playfully in Letty's direction. "Duty calls."

"See you later," Charlie said. As he walked back into the kitchen, she found it difficult to look away.

We're not late, are we?" Kat said, pulling out a wooden chair and sitting down opposite Charlie. Séraphine sat down with them.

"No, don't worry, we said two," Charlie said. "I left the

house early for a walk with Gracie. Luke's come round today to talk to Pippa and I wanted to give them some space."

"So they're talking?" Kat asked. "That sounds positive."

"I think it's a very good sign. Pippa called him yesterday and he agreed to come to talk things through. She apologized—which is quite a big deal. Pippa doesn't back down easily. Fingers crossed, they'll be able to work it all out today. The kids miss him terribly."

Letty brought Kat and Séraphine their cups of tea. "Here you go, you two. Our blend of the day."

"Thanks, Letty," Séraphine said.

"And I suppose you need to get back to your job soon," Kat said to Charlie.

"Too right. My boss isn't exactly thrilled with the situation. But I'll try and fit in with whatever Pippa and Luke decide."

Euan came out of the kitchen to get something from the counter, and waved over to Kat, who said hello back.

"You know Euan?" Charlie asked.

"Yes." Kat shrugged. "Everyone knows Euan."

"In a good way, or a bad way?" Charlie tilted her head, feigning disinterest.

"Ha." Kat smiled. "In a good way. Why do you ask?"

"No reason," Charlie said quickly.

"Yeah, right," Kat laughed.

"Anyway. Your trip," Charlie said, changing the subject. "I want to hear all about it."

"Were the reviews OK?" Séraphine asked.

"Yes, they were terrific," Charlie said. "I've made a few small changes, but nothing major. I'm happy with everything—thank you."

She'd been pleasantly surprised when she read the reviews—they were far more concise and honest than the ones she usually had to deal with, even from experienced food writers. There was something about Kat's voice that was instantly engaging and her vivid descriptions brought the tearooms she'd visited to life. The only problem was, due to her own lack of input, there still weren't enough of them.

"So, are you on track now?" Séraphine asked Charlie.

"Almost. Nearly," Charlie said, biting her lip. Then she realized there was no point lying about it. "By which I mean, not at all."

"Do you want us to help with some more?" Kat offered.

"Would you? It would really help me out. I'd need them by the end of the week."

"Sure," Kat said. "That's fine. All right with you, Séraphine?" Séraphine nodded.

"Phew, that's such a relief," Charlie said. "I'm only getting snatches of time at the moment, and to be honest I feel horribly unfocused. A couple more reviews from you guys would make all the difference."

"Sure. We can do another trip," Séraphine said. "We still have a few places on our list."

"Excellent. Then it's all coming together," Charlie said. "I've just been doing a little research. Look at these mementoes of Letty's—they're wonderful. Check out this old menu."

Kat took it from her and read it. "How funny. Tongue? They served that?"

"I know," Charlie laughed. "Gross, right? Letty's certainly improved the menu."

"These photos are nice," Séraphine said. "Look at this picture of Letty and . . . Who's that? I suppose it must be her husband."

"John," Kat said. "Euan's dad. They're not together anymore."

"They look as if they were happy back then," Séraphine said. "I wonder what happened."

"I don't know," Kat said. "She's never talked about it as far as I know."

Charlie pulled out a newspaper article that dated back to the middle of the Second World War. "There are so many stories about what the tearoom went through. So much history here, and Letty's family have been here since day one. Over a hundred years of serving tea."

"A hundred years?" Séraphine said, her eyes widening.

"Yes, it was a shame that we didn't get a chance to celebrate," Kat said. "Letty had a run of bad luck that year and it put a damper on things."

"Are you sure it's too late?" Séraphine asked.

Charlie smiled. "What's a year or two between friends?"

"Maybe the three of us could do something for her?" Séraphine said. "Throw a party?"

"That's a lovely idea," Kat said. "But you know Letty, she never wants a fuss."

"Maybe she doesn't get a say in it," Charlie said mischievously.

"I like the way you're thinking," Kat said. "A surprise party, here at the tearoom. How are you two fixed the Saturday after next?"

"It looks as if I've got a party to go to," Séraphine said, smiling.

Shhh," Pippa said with a smile, putting a finger to her lips. "Gracie just went down, and I swear her hearing is super-sensitive."

"I thought you were still up with the kids."

"No, they're all in bed."

"How did it go today, with Luke?" Charlie asked.

"Not bad," Pippa said, tilting her head. "Better than I expected."

"Did Flo and Jacob realize you were meeting up?"

"No. I didn't mention it. It'd only confuse them, so as far as they're concerned he's still away on that business trip."

"Did you get to explain everything?"

"Yes. And thank God he seems to believe that nothing ever happened between me and Will. He says he wished I could have said something to him earlier rather than reacting in the way that I did—and he's right, of course."

"Where's he staying?"

"He's still at a friend's. He says he wants to spend another couple of nights away."

"And how are you feeling?"

"Oh, I don't know," Pippa said. "I miss him. More than I thought I would. I mean, honestly, what was I thinking?"

"You're allowed to find things hard every now and again."

"Perhaps. But I hurt him, Charlie. He still sees it as me trying to write him and the kids out of my life. He thinks that's what I really want. But it isn't. The thing is Gracie was a shock. For both of us. I thought if I could escape from it for a few minutes, I might be better able to handle real life. Adjust."

"Does he understand that?"

"He's beginning to. We didn't fix anything, but it feels as if we've made a start. I've messed things up too much to fix in a day."

"Nothing is ever one person's fault completely."

"Perhaps. But it was me who wrote the e-mails, wasn't it?"

"Is there anything Luke could've done—could do now—to help you? So that you're not on your own with the kids so much?"

"I don't know." She furrowed her brow. "Not work week-ends, I suppose." She shrugged. "But that won't happen."

"How can you be so sure? Why don't you try asking him?"

Pippa seemed to mull it over. "I suppose it's worth a shot."

That evening, Charlie looked through one of Pippa's recipe books, deciding what she was going to bake for the cen-tenary party and reflecting on her day. The time with Kat and Séraphine had been a tonic. Since Sarah had moved to New York, she rarely got to socialize with her real friends, and while she and Sarah still talked on Skype, the time difference meant one of them was usually about to go out. Charlie didn't open up easily—she never had. What was there to enjoy about being vulnerable? And yet she could feel it starting to happen with Kat and Séraphine. She felt relaxed in their company, safe.

As she flicked through the pages of cakes and muffins, she thought of the other encounter she'd had that day—with Euan. The buzz she'd felt at seeing him again. There'd been something between them. Or had she imagined it?

Kat's name flashed up on her phone and she picked up.

"Hey, Kat, how's it going?"

"Good, thanks," Kat answered brightly. "So, I'm calling about the party."

"Perfect timing," Charlie said. "Help me decide something. I'm torn between healthy date-and-raisin muffins and indul-gent white chocolate and cranberry."

"Come on, that's a no-brainer," Kat said.

"That's true." She flagged the white chocolate muffin page with a Post-it note. "Now, what was it you wanted to ask?"

"I called Euan to tell him what we had planned."

The mere mention of his name sent a tingle down Charlie's

spine. She berated herself—she was a grown woman, not a teenager, and she ought to act like one.

"He's going to sort the music," Kat continued, "and he also says he can get his hands on some discounted wine for us."

"That's terrific."

"There's just one thing . . ."

"Oh?"

"He's asked me for your number. Said he wants to talk it all through with you," Kat said.

Charlie's heart thudded in her chest. She hadn't invented it. The connection she'd felt had been real.

"What do you think?" Kat asked, a smile in her voice. "Shall I pass it on?"

# 25

Tuesday, September 23

Dinner at mine tomorrow night? Kat had texted Séraphine and Charlie. Bring a dish, your party-planning skills and a readiness to drink wine x

It had been a while since Kat had had visitors, and it showed. Leo's toys were scattered around the living room, and in her bedroom clothes were strewn on every available surface. She put on music and began tidying things into their proper places, throwing away what she could as she went. There was an hour to go until the women arrived, and as they'd all agreed to bring a dish, it wouldn't take her long to get her part of dinner ready. As she tidied, dusted and cleaned, she looked forward to the evening ahead. Being with Séraphine and Charlie was easy and relaxed; it was as if she'd known them far longer than a fortnight. It was good to have friends round again; that had been one of the first habits she'd let go when Leo arrived.

She answered her ringing phone with one hand, still tidying with the other.

"Hi, Jake," she said.

"Hey. Is now a good time?"

She glanced at the clock. "It's not ideal. Is it about Leo?"

"Yes, sort of," he said.

"OK, sure." She laid down the pile of clothes she was carrying. "What's going on?"

"It's about Leo . . ." He hesitated. "But actually more about us. About you and me."

Kat furrowed her brow. "Us?"

"Yes," Jake said. "Us."

"Right," she said, waiting for him to elucidate.

"I meant what I said the other day, you know. I miss how we were together. I miss you."

Kat's heart sank. They'd been through all of this.

"Who's to say we couldn't be a proper family again?" he said.

"Jake, we've tried," she said calmly. "You know that. We've tried and we've tried."

"Have we though, really?"

"Yes, we have," Kat said. She remembered every moment of it—the date nights with their long, awkward silences, the family days out where they made the effort to be cheerful for Leo's sake. By the end it had all fell stilted, forced.

"I mean, I know *you* tried—but I don't think I ever put my heart into it. It was as if I was numb."

"Right." She took a deep breath.

"Things change, don't they?" he said, his intonation rising in hope. "Look, I'll admit it—I wasn't ready for the responsibility that came with having a baby, not then. But I am now."

"The time for that's passed," Kat said firmly.

"I feel completely differently now," Jake insisted. "Isn't that worth talking about?"

Kat glanced up at Leo's painting on the fridge, remembered painting it with him, how proud she'd been, how they'd both ended up covered in glue and glitter. She might not get it right all the time, but they had a lot of fun together. Her home was a safe haven for the two of them. There had been something missing for a while, but now there wasn't. As the two of them had grown closer, and other friends and relatives had come into their lives, that gap had disappeared. She and Leo were coping. More than that—these days, they were getting on just fine.

"Sorry, Jake, I don't want to go back."

"Is that how you see it? Don't you think it could be going forward?" The hope in his voice was tinged with desperation.

"We can both be there for Leo. But I'm sorry, Jake, there's no us anymore."

Kat was relieved when Charlie and Séraphine arrived, bringing distraction and fresh energy. Talking with Jake had revived memories of the two of them at their worst, and even though she'd tried to end the conversation on a positive note, she could tell that the rejection had felt like a fresh blow to him.

"Hey," Charlie said, coming inside and glancing around Kat's living room. "Nice place."

"It's a lovely flat," Séraphine added. "Cozy."

"Thanks," Kat said, glad that the rush job she'd done on tidying had made a difference. "We're fond of it. It never normally looks this tidy actually, but with Leo away I thought I'd have a go at stemming the tide of chaos."

"It's got tons of character," Charlie said. "I love this table," she added, running her hand over the wood.

"Thanks," Kat replied. "I got lucky with this one; a pub was closing and getting rid of all the furniture. I painted it with chalk paint, then rubbed away at it. Those chairs in the corner are from the same place."

Kat remembered the day, a month after Jake had finally moved out, when she'd resolved to make the flat her own, and decorate it exactly how she wanted.

"Quite the upcycler," Charlie said, impressed.

"Keeps me out of trouble." Kat grinned. "But enough small talk," she said, leaning in toward Charlie. "Spill. Did Euan call you?" she asked eagerly.

"Euan?" Séraphine echoed.

"Yes," Kat explained to Séraphine. "He's totally into Charlie. Made up the flimsiest of excuses to ask me for her number. It was very cute."

She turned back to Charlie. "So did he?"

"He might have," Charlie said, blushing.

"And how was it? What did he say?" Séraphine asked.

"It was nice talking with him," Charlie said. "We barely talked about the party at all, though. He got straight to the point."

"And . . . ?" Kat said.

"We're going on a date," Charlie said, unable to contain her excitement. "Tomorrow."

"Great!" Kat and Séraphine said at once.

"You think it's a good idea?" Charlie said, furrowing her brow. "It all seems a bit crazy, as if I'm planning a holiday romance or something. I'm meant to be here helping Pippa."

"You are helping Pippa. But why shouldn't you have some fun at the same time?" Kat said. "You're only here for a while."

"That's true, I suppose," said Charlie.

"Live a little," Kat said. "I'll give the disclaimer, though— Euan's lovely, but from what I know, he's not particularly serious about relationships."

"Fine," Charlie said. "That suits me perfectly."

⌐

This is the way to eat dinner," Charlie said as they settled down at Kat's table, "everyone doing a little bit. It's so much easier, isn't it?" She heaped her plate with the butternut squash salad Kat had made, and the pasta bake that Séraphine had brought.

"I do this with friends back home," Séraphine said. "I love finding out what people's special dishes are."

Kat turned a page in her spiral-bound notebook as they ate. She tried to focus on the list she'd made for the party at the Seafront, even though thoughts of her conversation with Jake were still nagging at her.

"So, the centenary party. Now, as you know, it's all a secret from Letty. I've spoken to a few people and got them on board. Euan has volunteered to sort the music and booze."

"I'll do the invites," Séraphine said.

"Great—I'll give you the names and addresses," Kat said, writing a reminder. The steady process of listing and ticking was helping to restore a sense of order where just a couple of hours ago it had felt as if there was none. "Some of Letty's friends have already volunteered to bring cakes and savories."

"More cake and muffins over here," Charlie said, putting her hand up. "Plus anything that needs arranging on the night."

"So . . . what else?" Kat looked down the list. "Decorations—I'll do that." She made a note.

"That leaves Project Get Letty Out," Charlie said.

"What's that?" Séraphine said.

"We need to be able to set up without her realizing what's going on," Charlie explained, "which means someone needs to whisk her away."

"I'll speak to her friend Sue," Kat said. "She's excited about the party, and I think she'd be more than willing to lie if it was for a good cause."

"We're getting there, aren't we?" Charlie said.

"She's going to love it," Séraphine said.

At midnight, the three women moved into the living room, Charlie carrying their second bottle of wine, now half-empty.

"Are you OK, Kat?" Séraphine asked, as they sat down. "You seem a little distracted."

"I'm fine," she said. "I just had a weird phone call before you arrived."

"Jake?" Charlie guessed.

"It's always Jake. Even now, when we're supposed to be living separate lives. Out of the blue, he asked me if I wanted to get back together."

"And do you?" Séraphine asked.

"No. Not at all. I've gone through it all in my head, more than once. There are no more what-ifs. I told him it wasn't going to happen."

"How did he take it?" Charlie asked.

"OK. It's hard to tell on the phone. I suppose with Leo up there he's been doing a lot of thinking. I always got the impression when we broke up that he wasn't fully taking everything in—maybe he's having a delayed reaction."

"They never know what they've got till it's gone," Charlie said.

"Exactly," Kat said. "I guess it's a necessary stage you have to go through. He's just taken longer to get there than I did."

"But it can't be easy having all that stirred up again," Charlie said.

"That's it." Kat took a sip of wine. "I feel that Leo and I are the team now, and I want to concentrate on getting on with that. Life with Jake was always so complicated."

"It's good that you know what you want," Séraphine said.

"That certainly helps," Kat said.

"What about you, Séraphine?" Charlie said gently. "I don't think we've asked—are you seeing anyone?"

Séraphine's cheeks flushed instantly.

"Ha!" Charlie said, smiling. "You're a dark horse. Tell us everything."

Séraphine shifted in her seat uncomfortably.

"You don't have to," Kat said. "Just because Charlie's being nosy." She threw a playful look in Charlie's direction.

"I prefer to call it curious, not nosy," Charlie said huffily. "And I'll have you know it's a professional requirement. So I'm guessing from your reaction that there is someone?"

"Kind of," Séraphine said.

"Ah, it's complicated," said Kat.

"Very complicated."

"We've all been there," Charlie said.

"Not here, you haven't," Séraphine told her. "Or I very much doubt it anyway."

"Try us," Charlie said.

"No." Séraphine shook her head.

"We won't bite," Kat chimed in.

Séraphine looked at them for a moment, as if she was trying to work out if she could trust them. She breathed out, seeming to relax, and spoke again.

"You have to promise not to judge me."

"Of course we won't," Charlie said. "Go on, then. You've got us on the edge of our seats."

"Right . . ." Séraphine bit her lip. "Oh God, I can't. It's . . .

I don't know. I hardly know you two. I probably shouldn't say. I don't want you to think differently of me."

"Would it help if we confessed something to you first?" Charlie offered.

"Maybe," Séraphine said, her embarrassment coming out in a laugh.

"OK, go on then . . ." Charlie said, nudging Kat. "You first, Kat."

"Me first? How's that?" She mock-glared at Charlie. "Oh fine, right . . . So, is your confession worse than spending a night in jail?"

"You didn't," Séraphine said, her jaw dropping.

"I did so."

"What for?" Charlie asked.

"Drunk and disorderly. It was fresher's week and I was a Jägerbomb casualty. They had an ice fountain at the fresher's ball and someone persuaded me to open my mouth at the bottom of it. Seemed a good idea at the time."

"Oh God," Charlie said.

"Apparently I was singing the theme tune from *The Bill* all the way to the station in the back of the police car," Kat said, laughing. "I covered myself in glory that night."

"And you look as if butter wouldn't melt." Charlie laughed.

"So, what about you?" Kat dared her. "I bet you can do better."

Charlie looked up, searching the recesses of her mind, weighing one story against another.

"I snogged a teacher once."

"No," Séraphine said, her jaw dropping. "How old were you?"

"I was a sixth former." A cheeky smile crept onto Charlie's face. "Mr. Fletcher. He was only in his mid-twenties. Not one of those ancient teachers. Not that it makes it that much better, in retrospect. But he was cute. Poor guy, he was terrified."

"Of being found out?"

"No, of me in general, I think. I sort of pounced on him."

Séraphine laughed. "I can picture it."

"I was quite fearless about relationships in those days. Don't know what happened. Well, I do. Ben, my ex, happened. I used to be more carefree, trusting. I can't imagine being that way again."

"I bet that side of you is still there, just under the surface," Kat said. "The right person will bring it out again."

"I don't know," Charlie said. "I've built some pretty hefty barriers. I find it quite hard to let them down these days."

She paused, her gaze turning to Séraphine. "But I'm distracting attention from the matter at hand. Last call. Who else for the confession box?"

"All right," Séraphine said, raising her hand. "Seeing as you two have shown willing. But you can't tell anyone. Seriously."

"Scout's honor," Charlie said, putting her hand on her chest. "I mean, Brownie's honor."

Séraphine raised an eyebrow, confused.

"She means we promise," Kat chipped in.

"I am seeing someone. More than that, I think I'm in love. But no one back home knows anything about it."

"You haven't told anyone?" Charlie said.

Séraphine shook her head.

"Why not?" Kat asked.

"It's a . . . She's a woman," Séraphine said, the words rushing out.

"A woman?" Kat said.

"I knew I shouldn't have said anything," Séraphine said,

her cheeks flushing anew. She looked down at the floor. "It was stupid."

"No," Kat said kindly, touching Séraphine's arm. "So that's it? That's your confession?"

"Yes," Séraphine said, looking back at them again. "I'm in love with a woman."

"What's her name?" Kat asked softly.

"Carla."

"And what's she like?" Charlie asked.

Séraphine hesitated, gaging their reactions before continuing.

"Beautiful. Inside and out. Funny too. When she walks into the room it's as if the party's started."

"She sounds lovely," Charlie said. "Lucky you."

"Yes," Kat added, giving Séraphine a nudge. "Now get on with being happy, for goodness' sake. Don't waste any more time feeling bad about it."

"You don't think differently of me, now that you know?" Séraphine asked.

Charlie and Kat shook their heads. "Of course not," Kat said.

Slowly, Séraphine started to smile.

# 26

Charlie heard the knock at the door and dashed to answer it before Pippa could get there. As far as her sister knew, she was going out to see Kat—she couldn't deal with any questions. It was challenging enough shutting off the voices in her own head. As she'd got ready that evening, putting on a red top with black skinny jeans, she'd felt a buzz of excitement about seeing Euan again. Her mind ran with possibilities.

And then the doubts would come—she hadn't dated anyone since Ben. Was she even ready?

"Hello," Euan said. He was standing on the doorstep in a shirt and a leather jacket, a smile on his face. "That was quick."

"I don't mess about," she said, her pulse quickening at the sight of him. He looked even more gorgeous than she'd remembered. "Shall we head out?"

"Sure. I'm just over the road. Although I'm wondering now how I can compete with that. Is that your sister's car?" He pointed at her MG.

"Nope, it's mine," she said.

"Nice," he said, nodding. "I'm a little embarrassed about introducing you to my ancient Fiat right now."

"Not that I care about riding in a Fiat, but do you fancy driving mine?"

"Are you serious?" His eyes lit up.

"Sure, why not?

"That would be amazing."

"Here you go," Charlie said, passing him the keys. "She could do with a run around."

Euan got in and turned the key in the ignition. "I could ruin our date right now, couldn't I?"

"You won't. I trust you," Charlie said.

He drove them through South Cliff and down to the seafront, deftly steering around the curves. Charlie put some music on.

"It's nice to be able to get up some speed," Charlie said. "In London I'm usually creeping between red lights. I still love driving around though. It's such an escape."

"I feel the same way about getting out on the water. Not that I've got my own boat—that'd be the day—but I love to go surfing, windsurfing, sailing with friends. I've never felt the same thrill about driving, but perhaps I could get used to it."

"Don't go getting too attached," Charlie said cheekily. "So where are you taking us tonight?"

"It's a seafood restaurant, pan-Asian. Nice conservatory with sea views. Sound OK?"

"Sure. Sounds perfect."

Charlie and Euan were sitting in a quiet corner of the restaurant, and had ordered their starters. With low lighting and a laid-back atmosphere, friendly staff and an original menu, Charlie noted that it was exactly the kind of restaurant she would have chosen.

"How are things going at your sister's?" Euan asked.

"Magic at times, with the kids, but far more tiring than my normal job."

Charlie thought of how she'd now be at Pippa's longer than

she'd planned. Her talk today with Jess hadn't been the easiest, but she'd finally managed to negotiate a few extra days away, given that she'd already submitted some of the content. She was happy she'd now be able to make the centenary party.

Euan smiled. "I've always fancied being an uncle—you get all of the good bits then, don't you?"

"You get a lot of cuddles," Charlie said, "but also glitter on your face, and plastic spiders in your bedsheets."

"I have to confess when we first met, and you were with Jacob and Flo, I thought—damn, she's already taken."

Charlie smiled.

"I'm probably saying too much," Euan said. "I don't know why I find it so easy to do that with you."

"Ha. That's the journalist in me. I don't have to say a word and people think I can tell what they're thinking. I'll tell you a secret . . ." She put her hand to her mouth and whispered: "I can't."

"I'll play my cards closer to my chest from now on, then. So what do you fancy eating?"

"Anything—I'm starving." She looked down the menu. "So long as it's not potato waffles or fish fingers. I've been eating far too much of Flo and Jacob's leftovers lately."

"Can't have those standards dropping."

"I know, can you imagine?" She put on her poshest voice. "'Yes, this chic eaterie in Broadway Market has steak freshly imported from Argentina, but there was NO alphabetti spaghetti on the menu.'"

Euan laughed. "Do you cook a lot at home?"

"No. Ironic, isn't it? I've always enjoyed cooking—don't get me wrong—but with the hours I do I'm usually too tired when I get home. I love cooking for friends when I do have the chance though. What about you?"

"The same. I like to make simple dishes, fresh ingredients, nothing fancy, but food that's good for the soul, I suppose. And of course I enjoy eating out. Have you ever thought about going in the other direction—running a restaurant rather than reviewing them?"

She paused before answering. The truth was it had been on her mind for the last year or so. When she visited restaurants she often had ideas ticking away in her head—what she would do if she had a place of her own, how a menu she put together might look. But she'd never said it out loud before.

"Yes. I've thought about it a lot."

"What's stopping you?"

"Oh, it's not that easy." She shook her head and smiled. "I couldn't do it. It's a pipe dream."

There was the money she'd need to set the whole thing up, the dog-eat-dog world of urban restaurants—and then, of course, the fact that she had no experience whatsoever of running a business.

"Where would we be without those?" Euan said with a smile. "I didn't take you for someone who'd be put off because something wasn't easy."

"What do you mean by that?" she said.

"That you seem determined, ambitious—I admire that." He looked at her and held her gaze for a moment. A shiver of anticipation traced its way up her spine.

"Thank you," she said. "I think."

Shortly after ten, Charlie and Euan walked out of the restaurant into the cool autumn night. She felt pleasantly full from the meal, and content. Considering this was the first date she'd had since breaking up with Ben, it had all gone surprisingly smoothly.

"I guess we'll be getting taxis home, then," Charlie said. "That wine was far too nice."

"It goes down pretty well, doesn't it?" He smiled mischievously.

"You're a bad influence." She shook her head.

"I don't seem to remember you needing that much persuading." Euan laughed. "So, shall I call you a cab?"

"There's no hurry. Let's go for a walk." The wine had left her feeling slightly fuzzy-headed; some fresh air would do her good. Plus she'd enjoyed talking to Euan. No reason to cut things short.

"It's pretty cold—are you sure you wouldn't rather go on somewhere, a bar or something?"

Charlie looked up the bay and saw the old cinema on the corner. A smile crept onto her face. "You haven't got the keys to that place, have you?"

"Erm . . ." he said, narrowing his eyes. "What exactly did you have in mind?"

"Show me around?" Charlie said playfully. "So I can see what it looks like inside?"

"I can't." Euan shook his head. "It's a building site—I can't take you in at this time of night."

"Oh, go on," she said, nudging him. "Please?"

He seemed to be on the verge of refusing for a second time.

"Pleeease?" she said. Now that she'd got the idea in her head, she wasn't about to let it go. She was in the mood for an adventure.

"You get what you want a lot, don't you?"

She laughed. "At times."

"OK, OK," he conceded reluctantly.

They walked the block together, and his hand found Charlie's naturally. There was a thrill at his touch, yet at the same time the warmth of his skin against hers relaxed her. It felt easy, being with him. They reached the building, and he turned to whisper an instruction to her.

"Now follow me and be careful."

"All right, all right, Mr. Health and Safety," she teased.

He unlocked the building and let them both in. Inside, he put a yellow hard hat on her, and took one for himself.

"I feel like Bob the Builder in this," she said, tapping the top of it.

"No taking it off," he said sternly.

"Yes, sir. So, what's the plan, what are you going to do in here?" She gazed at the interior of the building.

"We're going to knock this wall down, and we're building a glass-roofed area over here."

"Cool." Charlie looked up. "Can we go upstairs?"

Euan frowned. "We shouldn't."

She raised an eyebrow.

He sighed. "But then we shouldn't be in here at all. Come on, then."

He led her up a staircase to a domed roof with tiny windows.

"It's beautiful up here," she said, looking out on the white lights of the town and the bay beside it. From their vantage point, it looked as if the streets were lined with little dolls' houses.

"It's a lovely view, isn't it?" Euan said, looking out with her. "This dome was one of the things that made me want to take on the project. We're going to retain it and make it more of a feature."

"Nice setting for cocktails," she said, looking around.

"Trust you to think of that," he joked.

"I'm only trying to assist you with the plan," she said.

She turned toward Euan, and her arm brushed against his. As their skin touched, she felt the rush of attraction.

Euan cupped her face with one hand and ran his thumb gently over her lips, and instinctively she covered his hand with her own. She looked into his blue eyes, feeling closeness. Excitement. But as he leaned in to kiss her, the excitement blended swiftly with something less comfortable—panic.

*What was she doing? How had she thought she was ready for this?*

She froze, and he sensed it right away, before their lips touched.

"I must have read that all wrong," he said softly, moving back. "I'm sorry."

"You didn't." She shook her head. "I wanted you to. But . . ."

She searched for the words to explain what she was feeling. That she wanted him—so much it ached. And yet something was standing in her way.

"You don't need to explain. Look, let's forget it even happened." He smiled at her kindly. "Why don't I finish showing you around?"

"Yes, let's do that," she said, her voice catching in her throat.

She'd messed it up. She'd missed the moment. And she only had herself—and the stupid walls she'd built—to blame.

# 27

Thursday, September 25

"The Copper Kettle was gorgeous, wasn't it?" Kat said, tucking her legs up under her on Séraphine's bed.

"Yes, I loved the little touches: the crisp white tablecloths, that beautiful silver cutlery—and the pink-and-yellow cake. What's that called again?"

"Battenberg." Kat smiled. "You can't beat a good Battenberg."

Séraphine and Kat had spent the day on the coast, stopping at tearooms from the list they'd put together with Charlie. In the early evening, tired but still buzzing from the new discoveries, they were in Séraphine's room, typing up their notes.

"The Cove was my favorite, by a long way," Séraphine said.

"Yes—and the long walk you had to take to get there made it even more special. Worked up our appetite for the scones, didn't it?"

"I could have eaten four of them! That freshly made strawberry jam was out of this world."

"It was incredible."

"The styling was imaginative too—that reupholstered chaise longue and the antique armchairs."

Kat started typing again. She might remember the scones and the styling for a few weeks—maybe months—but she knew already that what she'd recall most of all were the conversations she and Séraphine had had. They'd talked easily while they were walking along the coast, the wind blowing through their hair, and savoring the hot tea at the end of their journey. They'd laughed together, and they'd shared things that mattered. Kat felt privileged that Séraphine had opened up to her about Carla, and told her that in the past couple of days they had spoken on the phone and begun to rebuild the relationship that they'd had in France. The change showed in Séraphine—it was as if a cloud had lifted, leaving her eyes bright and her face relaxed, with her natural beauty showing through.

When they'd finished the reviews, Séraphine got to her feet and walked over to her wardrobe. "Kat, I was thinking—you know that dress you were looking at the other day? In Whitby?"

"The crazily expensive one?" Kat said. "I love that with window-shopping there's no budget."

"Yes. I have something similar that I think would suit you. We're pretty much the same size."

She rifled through the hangers in her closet and pulled out a vintage tailored dress, black with Hawaiian flowers on it. "What do you think?"

"It's beautiful," Kat said, getting to her feet and touching the fabric.

"Go on, try it on," Séraphine urged.

"No, honestly, it's fine." Kat shook her head.

"Seriously," Séraphine said. "Just try it on, see how it looks on you."

"But it's yours," Kat said, embarrassed. Perhaps she shouldn't have mentioned to Séraphine how rarely she got to buy new things.

"I never wear it. Ever."

"OK," she said. "If you're absolutely sure."

Kat pulled off her T-shirt and put the dress on over her leggings. Séraphine zipped her up and they looked together in the mirror.

"Wow!" Séraphine said. "You look stunning."

"It fits well, doesn't it?" She smiled, twisting to the side to see how the dress looked at the back.

"It fits perfectly. It's meant to be yours. Have it."

"Are you serious?"

"Absolutely. It's never suited me. I'm not even sure why I brought it over."

"That's very kind. Thank you."

Someone knocked on the bedroom door, and Kat startled.

"Just a second," Séraphine called, doing the zip on the dress up all the way. "OK?" she asked Kat. She nodded.

"Come in," Séraphine said.

Adam opened the door, wearing jeans and a gray cashmere sweater. He paused for a moment, looking at Kat, their eyes meeting. Kat felt conscious of the way she looked, and wished she was back in her T-shirt.

"Nice dress," Adam said.

"Thanks," Kat said. "It's Séraphine's."

"It's yours now, I told you," Séraphine said, nudging her.

"Well, whoever's it is, it suits you," Adam said, with a smile. "Dinner's nearly ready. Will you join us, Kat?"

Kat checked her watch—it was still early. There was no harm in staying for dinner. It would be nice to spend some more time with Séraphine, and with Adam. She could always call Leo on the way home. "Yes, I'd love to."


"Help yourself to more," Adam said, pointing to the remaining slices of pizza.

"I'm full," Kat said, glad that she'd changed back into her

own clothes, which were stretchier and more accommodating than the dress. "But thank you, it was delicious. I'm impressed you made this, Zoe."

"Thanks. Dad barely did anything," Zoe said. Her dad gave her a sideways glance. "OK, he did a little bit of chopping. But the toppings and smiley faces on the pizza were my idea."

"You're a natural," Kat said.

"A hidden talent," Séraphine agreed. "I'm going off duty more often."

Zoe smiled proudly.

"There's dessert too," Zoe said. "Dad helped with that."

"Apple crumble," Adam told them. "The apples are from the garden."

"A couple had worms in—we left those out," Zoe said, smiling mischieviously.

"What? So we're missing out on all that protein?" Kat said.

Adam laughed, and their eyes met for a moment.

"My son, Leo, loves worms," Kat said. "He'd probably want those ones most of all."

"Boys are sooo disgusting," Zoe said, wrinkling her nose.

"She's right," Adam said. "We're horrible. It doesn't get better with age. Is Leo into nature?"

"Oh yes. Madly. He loves animals—fish, penguins, whales . . . oh, and dinosaurs, though they're less easy to come by these days."

"It's been a while since I've had any of those to treat." Adam smiled. "You should drop by the vet's surgery with him one day. We get all sorts of animals in there."

"He'd love that."

They chatted happily over dessert, Kat and Adam sharing memories of the school they'd gone to and finding out friends that they had in common. Kat felt as if she already knew him, even though all they'd exchanged at the time was an occasional lingering look. Not even a word had passed between them when they were teenagers, and yet chatting now they were older was so easy. When they'd all finished the crumble, Kat helped Adam clear the plates while Séraphine and Zoe tidied up the kitchen.

"Do you want to stay for a coffee?" Adam asked.

"I'd love to, but I should get back. All the adventures Séraphine and I had today kind of tired me out."

"Understandable. It sounds as if you covered a lot of ground."

"We found some really nice places. We're both pleased with how it went."

Kat gathered up her things and looked in to say good-bye to Séraphine and Zoe.

"I'll see you out," Adam said, holding the kitchen door open for her and following her through it into the hallway.

"I meant what I said—pop into the surgery with Leo any time. We're over on South Street."

"Thanks. I will do. He's in Scotland with his dad at the moment, but he'll be home soon." Kat slipped into the jacket Adam was holding out for her and turned to give him a good-bye kiss on the cheek.

"Listen, thanks for having me this evening, I enjoyed it."

Adam nodded. He hesitated, then said, "It was a pleasure."

They stood there, looking at each other, not saying anything, until Adam broke the silence.

"It would be good to see you again."

Kat nodded, then inspiration struck: "The party," she said. "Has Euan mentioned it? Saturday after next, at the Seafront. You should come."

"He did mention it, yes," Adam said, a smile coming to his lips. "OK, I'll see you there."

⌢

Kat got home and plugged her phone in to charge. She'd tried to call Leo on the way home, only to discover that her battery was dead. If she let it charge now for a minute or two she might still catch him in time.

As her phone returned to life, a message buzzed through from Jake.

You didn't call. Where are you?

No friendly sign-off, nothing but the bald statement and question. She rang through to his phone, feeling a little unsettled.

"Didn't you get my message?" Jake said coldly.

"I just read it. Sorry, I tried to call but my battery ran out."

"And you clearly had more important things to do than call and speak with Leo."

"I was at a friend's for dinner, that's all."

"Anyone I know?"

There was a sharpness in his tone that made her anxious, as if whatever she said next wouldn't be the right answer. The contentment she'd felt over dinner at Adam and Zoe's house had all but gone.

"No one you know. Why?"

"Just seems strange that you'd forget to call."

"I didn't forget. My battery was out—I told you."

Jake said nothing. Even over the phone, she could sense the hostility from him.

"Jake, what are you trying to say?"

"Nothing . . . Look, I don't get what's going on here. Were you out with a guy?"

"No," she said bluntly.

"OK," he said.

"Would it be any of your business if I was?"

"It is my business, because it could affect Leo."

"Well, I wasn't—so this is irrelevant."

"You wouldn't usually miss a call to Leo. You're different these days."

"Jake, don't guilt-trip me. So I'm not perfect, who is? I don't want to play this game, but if I have to . . . You went weeks without seeing Leo—"

"We're back to that, are we?"

His voice was harsh. She recalled how he had been in the days after Leo's birth—an edge to him that left her feeling she was walking on eggshells. She'd done her best to please him, but had never seemed to be able to. She was in no hurry to let history repeat itself.

"Jake, you're snapping at me."

"So I can't ask you anything anymore?"

"Look, is everything all right?"

"Fine, Kat. Never been better."

"OK," she said. But a feeling of unease had settled in the pit of her stomach. Something wasn't right here. "Is there something you want to talk to me about?"

"There is, yes," Jake said.

"What's that?"

"It's Leo. I've been talking to him, and my parents have too. He doesn't seem happy."

"What's wrong?"

"I mean, he's fine here—that's not the problem. He says he wants to spend more time with me."

"I see." Kat drew in her breath. She couldn't take it personally. Perhaps there were things they could do to make the situation easier for Leo.

"Well, we can arrange that. You having him regularly at weekends—we always said that was the plan in the long term."

"Yeah . . . but I think he needs more stability, Kat. That kind of arrangement would only unsettle him."

"So what are you suggesting?"

"That he lives with me, full-time."

"Sorry?" Kat choked. Her mind raced. She must have heard him wrong. "Are you saying you want custody?"

"Yes."

Her jaw fell open. "Where on earth has this come from? You can't just do that."

"I can. And I will. I'll do whatever is best for Leo."

Jake hung up, and Kat, stunned, let the phone fall from her hand. This couldn't be happening. Leo was everything to her. A life without him—it didn't bear thinking about.

# 28

Friday, September 26

Charlie scraped the last bit of Weetabix off the tiled kitchen floor, and felt a hand in her hair. Gracie's fingers, sticky with her brother's cereal, were wedged into her freshly washed hair. She fought to keep her patience. It wasn't even seven o'clock yet and she already felt worn thin.

"Oh dear, I'm sorry," Pippa said, when she saw what had happened. "That's a first." She lifted Gracie out of harm's way.

Charlie got to her feet and picked the bits of cereal out of her fringe. That morning, Flo had woken her at 4 A.M. after having a nightmare, and insisted she needed to talk it through in minute detail.

"You look as if you need a break," Pippa said.

"It's fine, honestly."

"Go on, I'm serious. Go out for a bit. God knows you've helped me enough. I don't want you going home exhausted. We'll be OK."

"You're sure?"

"Absolutely. Go on—get out while you can." Pippa grinned.

"All right. Thanks."

As Charlie walked upstairs, she thought about the night before last. She and Euan had had such a good time, right up until the moment she pushed him away. The more she'd talked to him, the more she found herself attracted to him—if she could only get past feeling so damn scared about the whole thing, maybe she could make things right.

She thought of her conversation with Kat. Spending time with Euan was supposed to be a bit of fun, nothing to get stressed out about. She wasn't going to be here long enough to get hurt again. Steeling herself, Charlie got out her phone and sent him a text.

Morning. Fancy a run?

Then, as an afterthought:

Provided Bagel has a new lead.

Her phone buzzed with a message.

Sure. Give me half an hour. Meet you by the scene of B's crime.

Charlie jogged up to the stretch of pavement where Euan was standing with his dog.

"Morning," she called out brightly.

"Hello, Charlie." He smiled.

She jogged on the spot alongside him for a moment. "Race you to the lighthouse," she said, then set off before Euan could reply.

"Hey—you didn't give me a chance," he protested, running to keep up. Bagel let out a bark of excitement and raced along beside them.

She could hear Euan's footsteps, rapidly gaining pace. She glanced back and saw he was only a meter or so behind her.

Charlie gathered her reserves and ran harder, keeping the lighthouse in her line of vision as her trainers pressed down on the wooden boards. She continued to build up speed as she ran along the pier.

"I thought you meant a friendly jog," he said, overtaking her. He turned around and jogged backward, brushing his hair out of his eyes.

As he slowed, she saw her opportunity and grabbed it, running faster and getting to the lighthouse a moment ahead of him, touching the white building and then bending to catch her breath.

He caught up seconds later, Bagel panting by his side.

"A friendly jog?" Charlie said, with a smile. "That just goes to show that you don't know me very well at all."

Charlie sat back on the sofa in Euan's lounge, sipping from a glass of fresh orange juice.

"Do you fancy Eggs Florentine?" Euan asked. "I think we've earned it."

"Sounds delicious."

He got the ingredients out, and Charlie turned slightly in her seat so that she could still talk to him in the open-plan room.

"Nice place you've got here."

"Thank you. I only moved in a couple of months ago, but it's been great finally having my own space."

"After . . . ?"

Euan smiled. "I've been flat-sharing with friends for the last few years. What's with the question?"

"No reason." She shrugged.

He worked away in the kitchen, and Charlie watched him. Being in his house felt surprisingly comfortable.

"Here you go." Euan brought over Charlie's plate a few minutes later, and laid it on the table in front of her.

She took a big bite of the muffin and egg. "Good hollandaise."

"Thanks. I try."

Bagel sat down next to Charlie, resting his head in her lap. "He's after my breakfast." She tapped him gently on the nose. "Not a chance, mate." He whined and lay down.

"He's not that discerning when it comes to food."

"This would definitely be wasted on him, then. How's his probation period going?"

"I think we're stuck with each other." Euan grinned. "I'm getting used to having him around."

Charlie nodded, and stroked the dog. "Good. I'm pleased to hear that."

"It feels as though we came into each other's life for a reason," Euan said.

Charlie looked up, startled by what he'd said. Had he really meant that? As their eyes met there was a spark of chemistry between them, diffused by his smile.

"Me and Bagel," Euan said, putting her straight.

"Of course," Charlie said, with a smile. "I knew that."

# 29

Saturday, September 27

Hi Charlie, Séraphine—have you got time for a tea?
Something's happened. I need to talk.

Kat x

Kat walked toward the Seafront Tearoom, hoping that this early in the morning the place would still be quiet. The rush of waves on sand seemed louder today, abrasive even, and the wind whipped at her face. After Jake's phone call on Thursday night, she'd barely slept, restlessly playing their conversation over and over again in her mind as she lay in bed. The previous day she'd tried to distract herself, focusing on research and trying not to think the worst, but now all she could think about was going up to Scotland and getting Leo back.

Letty opened the door to her, tidying her loose gray hair with a Kirby clip. "Kat—what's wrong? Are you OK?"

"I've been better." She allowed Letty to usher her inside, but the usual calming effect when she walked through the door of the Seafront was absent today. The adrenaline was still coursing through her and leaving her unsettled.

"Come and sit down," Letty said, putting a reassuring hand on Kat's arm. "Charlie and Séraphine are already here— they came as soon as they got your message."

She looked across to their usual table and saw the expressions of kindness on her friends' faces.

Letty poured Kat a cup of tea and handed it to her, but she shook her head and sat down.

"What's happened?" Charlie asked.

"It's Jake," Kat said, her eyes welling up. "He wants Leo."

"What do you mean he wants him?" Charlie said.

"He called me on Thursday, after I got back from dinner with you, Séraphine. He said he wants full custody. That Leo would be better off with him." Kat's voice cracked as she spoke. Saying it out loud made the threat seem so much more real.

"That's terrible," Séraphine said, putting a hand on Kat's arm. "I'm so sorry."

Letty was shaking her head. "That's not right. Not right at all."

Charlie's voice cut in, matter-of-fact. "It's ridiculous, obviously. He'll never get custody."

"How can you be so sure?" Kat asked her.

"The courts would favor you as the mother," Charlie said. "And on top of that Leo's been happy here with you since he was born."

"Anyone who knows you would vouch for that," Letty said, nodding vigorously.

"Think about it, Kat: what case, if any, does Jake have for saying he'd be a better parent?" Charlie said.

"You've got a point," Kat said. "It's not as if he's seen Leo that often—his visits have always been fairly erratic."

"Plus didn't you say he hasn't even been supporting you lately?" Letty said.

Kat nodded.

"So there you are," Charlie said, reassuringly. "That's not going to help his case."

"But there are . . . things he could say," Kat said. She felt raw even thinking of it—the things he might bring up. But she knew she couldn't afford to ignore the possibility.

"Like what?" Charlie asked.

"After Leo was born, I was very down for a while. Letty, you remember," Kat said, glancing over at her.

"You struggled at first, as so many mothers struggle," Letty said softly. "It's not easy, especially at the beginning, and it seemed to me Jake wasn't there for you as much as he could have been."

"I wasn't clear in my mind," Kat said. "I don't know if I was depressed or what it was, but everything seemed so difficult."

It pained her to remember it. All she could think about now was how desperately she wanted to hold Leo again, to have him back with her. But there had been times in those early weeks and months when she'd felt as if part of her had disappeared. Days spent in the maternity ward, anonymous in her blue gown, a baby next to her who she'd thought would fill her heart with joy, and yet seemed at that point to be little more than a small, wrinkled, dependent stranger. Jake had been pacing the hospital corridor, texting on his phone. It seemed to Kat as if he was avoiding them.

"At home, when Leo cried, I sometimes had to stop myself from walking out of the flat to escape it," Kat said, recalling the sound and the way it had echoed off the walls and tugged at her very being. When Jake went out in the evenings, when the grizzling and crying was at its worst, she'd started to wonder if she'd made a terrible mistake. "I kept going, but some days it was all I could do to get out of bed. I tried to tell Jake how I was feeling, but that only seemed to make him withdraw even further. I had to talk to someone about it, so I came here to talk to Letty"—she glanced over at Letty, who nodded for her to continue—"and we went together to the GP. He prescribed me antidepressants. I don't know if they helped or not. But in time me and Leo bonded, and things got easier. For Jake though, the pills were confirmation that something was wrong with me. I think that's stayed in his mind."

"It sounds as though you had it very hard," Charlie said. "It's a tribute to you that you've come out the other side so strong." She reached out to clasp Kat's hand in her own. "Feeling down or being depressed—those aren't failings. And you worked through it. In terms of Jake's case, I can't see that what happened back then would be of any relevance whatsoever."

"I'm not so sure. He's brought it up in the past, when we've argued. He might find a way to use it."

Charlie shook her head. "I know I've never met the guy, but I have to say I'm not warming to this Jake. He should have been there for you—and instead he's judged you for finding it hard?"

Kat shrugged. "I didn't question it at the time. I was too busy trying to focus on bringing Leo up as well as I could. Perhaps I should have got out sooner than I did."

"He shouldn't be doing this to you," Letty said, sitting down opposite Kat, a frown on her face. "I'm not sticking up for him, but I did think he was more sensible than this."

"Me too," Kat said. "What gets me is that he says his parents are with him on it. He says his only concern is what's best for Leo, and all three of them have noticed that Leo's not happy, and that he's said as much. If his parents feel the same way, perhaps there is something in it."

"If Leo's upset, they should be talking to you constructively, not behaving like this," Séraphine said. "It sounds as if they know you're a good mother."

"You know what the worst part is?" Kat said, her voice cracking. "I've even started to doubt that myself."

"Don't," Séraphine said, putting her arm around Kat's shoulder. "You mustn't."

"I don't understand," Kat said. "Why is he doing this to us?"

Later that day, Kat was on the station platform, her coat wrapped tightly around her. In her bag was Leo's stegosaurus. She thought back to the day he'd left, how he'd wanted to take it to Scotland, but Kat had said no. She wished now that she could have that moment again.

After leaving the tearoom, she'd gone home to collect a few things, then gone straight to Scarborough station. Charlie had advanced her some of the payment for the review work so that she was able to buy a return ticket.

Kat pictured the town house by the meadows where Leo would be staying with his grandparents. All she wanted was to be there and to hold her son in her arms again.

The tone in Jake's voice had sent a chill through her. Her mind had been racing ever since, picturing the various scenarios—a drawn-out court case, lawyers picking over her private life, legal bills to add to all the others that were piling up in her hallway. What did she know about the law? She'd have to learn quickly.

And all the while a quiet fury burned beneath. To think that the man she'd once loved could do this to her.

On the train, she put her book to one side and stared out of the window, watching the scenery go by in an effort to take her mind off the what-ifs. The carriage was quiet and empty and for once she wished it were fuller—anything to distract her.

It had been good to talk to her friends, to get some perspective on the situation. To a point it had reassured her that Jake's case for sole custody was weak. But still Kat felt vulnerable, and she knew she wouldn't rest until she had Leo back at home.

When she and Jake had broken up she'd made a promise to herself that she would build a safe haven for Leo. Now she was more determined than ever to keep to it.

The meadows were scattered with fallen leaves, and as Kat walked through them, she remembered the walks she and Jake used to go on when they visited his parents. Back when she was at uni, it had seemed as if nothing could overcome or stand in the way of the love that they had for each other. But their tiny newborn had exposed the cracks in their relationship, and with each broken night those cracks had grown. It had been a slow, insidious thing. Jake hadn't wanted to change his lifestyle, and had convinced her that they didn't need to make compromises. She had been overwhelmed by her love for her son, torn by the need to keep Jake happy as well, and had ended up feeling she was spread too thinly.

Nothing could bring back the days when they had been happy together, but she had truly believed they'd found a new balance, a way to be parents even though they were no longer lovers. Perhaps she'd been naïve to believe it was possible—that they could be friends after everything they'd been through.

Diane, Jake's mother, opened the door. "Kat," she said. There were lines on her forehead and her usual smile was absent.

"I'm sorry to turn up unannounced."

"No, I'm glad you're here. Please, come in."

"Is Leo here?" she asked. She listened out but couldn't hear anyone in the house. Panic rose in her. "He is here, isn't he?" she said quickly.

"Yes," Diane said. "Don't worry, he's in the other room. Leo!"

They went through into the living room, where Leo was sitting on a playmat in the middle of the floor, a network of train tracks surrounding him, and Kat put her hand to her heart and smiled, full of relief at seeing him again.

"Mummy!" he said, jumping to his feet and running over to her.

She opened her arms and embraced him, bringing his small body into the warmth and protection of her own. She breathed in the smell of his hair and pressed her face against the blond strands. The skin of his shoulder and neck, where his T-shirt had stretched in the hug, was impossibly soft. Hot tears spilled down her cheeks and trembled on the sill of her upper lip. She squeezed him, then realized how tight she was holding him and loosened her grip. She didn't want him to know how worried she'd been. She owed it to him to make life as normal as possible.

She let him go, and as he stood back, she looked at him standing in front of her. "You've grown. Again!" She laughed. "How on earth am I expected to keep up?"

"I missed you, Mummy," Leo said.

She ran a hand over his cheek. Words couldn't describe how it felt now they were back together. She pressed him tightly to her.

"I'm going to show you something Grandma got me," Leo said, pulling away.

Diane leaned forward and whispered to Kat. "We need to talk. It's about Jake. He's gone."

⌐

Diane and Kat were sitting on the sofa in the living room. Sun streamed in through the bay window and dappled the red Persian rug. Leo was upstairs with his grandfather Andy. He'd bounded upstairs, saying they needed to introduce his stegosaurus to his new dinosaurs. Kat was relieved that she'd have a moment to talk to Diane openly.

"I'm so sorry about what's happened," Diane said. Her hands were in her lap, and she was twisting her wedding ring nervously. "We don't know what's come over him."

"So it's not true, what he told me about you supporting him?"

"No, no . . . not remotely. He started talking about wanting custody the other day, out of the blue, and we've both been doing all we can to talk him out of it. We wouldn't want Leo to be put through that ordeal any more than you would. Besides, we know you're doing a wonderful job bringing him up—you only need to look at him to see that."

The relief Kat felt at hearing Diane's words was overwhelming. "That means a lot to me. I was really worried that you were on his side with all this."

"No, love," Diane said, shaking her head. "We wouldn't do that to you."

Kat's relief was short-lived, as the gravity of the situation came back to her. Jake, her son's father, was still missing. "So you say he left last night?"

"I went into his room this morning and his bed hadn't been slept in. He disappeared without leaving a note, or anything," Diane said, shaking her head. "Given his state of mind, we're quite worried."

"He did seem upset when we talked on the phone. He spoke about us getting back together, but after everything—"

Seeing the hurt in Diane's eyes, Kat stopped herself. "I mean, we made our decision."

"Of course. And there's no point confusing Leo by trying to repair things only to break up again."

"Do you have any idea where he might be? Have you asked his friends?"

Diane nodded. "No one's seen him."

"And the police?"

"It's too early for that."

Leo's voice, chattering away to his granddad, could be heard on the stairs, and Kat turned instinctively in the direction of it.

"Could we stay here tonight, the two of us?" Kat asked.

"Of course, Kat," Diane said.

"I don't want to go until we've found Jake. I can't leave with things like this."

# 30

Sunday, September 28

"I found a note on the mat for you, Auntie Charlie," Flo said cheerfully. "I know it's for you. It has your name on it." She passed the white envelope over to Charlie in the kitchen.

Charlie looked up from the pile of laundry she was sorting and took it from her, studying the handwriting on the front, no address, just her name. It must have been hand-delivered. "How strange. Thanks." She'd been thinking about Kat—she'd called that morning to say that Leo was fine, but that his dad had now been missing for two nights. She'd sounded stressed, and Charlie wished that there was something more she could do to help, but Kat insisted that having her there on the end of a phone was what she needed.

Charlie opened the envelope, pulled the paper out and unfolded it.

"Mummy, Charlie's got a letter!" Flo called out behind her.

"What does it say?" Flo said, peering past her aunt's shoulder.

Charlie's gaze dropped to the signature at the bottom.

Pippa peered around the door, carrying Gracie in one arm and holding Jacob's hand in the other. "A letter?" She smiled. "What is this, the nineteenth century? Who's it from?"

"It's nothing," Charlie replied quickly.

"You're blushing!" Pippa teased.

"God, you lot are terrible," Charlie said, pouting. "I'll be upstairs if anyone needs me."

She went up to the bathroom and shut the door behind her, relishing the moment of silence. She sat down on the edge of the bath and unfolded the note.

HI CHARLIE

IT WAS GOOD TO SEE YOU ON FRIDAY. ARE YOU FREE THIS AFTERNOON? MEET ME BY THE BOATS IN PEASHOLM PARK AT 3 P.M.

EUAN

She smiled in spite of herself. He wanted to see her again.

Hey," Euan said, as Charlie arrived to meet him that afternoon. The lake and park were calm and quiet, with only a couple of boats out on the water.

"Hi," Charlie said. "I got your note."

"I guessed that," he said, smiling. "I'm glad you could make it."

"I had a bit of spare time," Charlie said, trying to sound nonchalant.

There was no need to mention the whirlwind she'd created getting everything sorted at Pippa's so she could leave in time to meet him. As she'd gotten ready to go out she'd felt a steady build of excitement at the prospect of seeing him again. After the jog, and breakfast at his on Friday, she'd found she couldn't get him out of her head.

She was starting to wonder if maybe something could happen between them—that perhaps she could start to let go.

"I thought we could work as a team this time," Euan said, passing a ticket to the man handling the boats and pedalos. "Which is of course my way of saying that I don't want to lose to you again after what happened at the lighthouse."

He got into a rowing boat and held his hand out for her to join him. She took it and climbed in beside him. As their skin touched, Charlie felt a rush. She wanted to be closer to him.

"Water isn't exactly my natural environment," she said lightly. "You would have stood a good chance of winning."

They rowed together, sunlight flickering on the water on the crisp autumn day. "It's lovely out here."

"Isn't it?" Euan said. "It's meant to be relaxing, by the way. You don't need to put yourself out with the rowing, we'll end up going round in circles," he laughed.

"Oh," Charlie said, easing her grip on the oar. "Sorry, I didn't realize."

As they drifted past the island, Charlie looked up at the large Japanese pagoda.

"Let's go over there," Euan said, pointing toward a part of the island that was thicker with trees, and where the shrubs extended over the water.

The wooden boat butted against the side of the island. "Why do I get the feeling you're taking me somewhere we shouldn't be going?" Charlie said.

He tied the boat to a branch and gave her his hand to help her out.

"It'll be fine," he said. "Trust me."

He led her by the hand to a small clearing, hidden completely from the rest of the park. A picnic blanket was laid out, with a bottle of champagne and a hamper beside it.

"Did you do all this?" Charlie said, turning to him in amazement.

He shrugged. "Come and sit down."

She sat on the blanket and he opened the bottle of champagne and poured them both a glass.

"I know you're leaving soon," he said. "But while you're here I want to make the most of our time together. As friends, if that's what you want."

"As friends?" Charlie said innocently.

"Sure," he said.

She sipped from the glass of champagne, and looked him directly in the eye. Then she spoke.

"It's just . . . being friends seems a waste of all this, don't you think?"

The corners of his mouth lifted. Charlie smiled, then touched his arm and kissed him gently. There in the clearing, with the warmth of his skin and the tenderness in his kiss, she gave in completely, her doubts fading away.

# 31

Sunday, September 28

Séraphine closed the textbooks she had been using to teach Zoe and slid them across the table toward her. "So, we're finished for today. Your pronunciation is coming along so well, Zoe. I'm impressed."

"*Merci*," Zoe said playfully. "Thank you."

These days, Séraphine looked forward to her time with Zoe. It wasn't always easy, and there were times when Zoe was reluctant to learn, but when that light went on and Zoe embraced the class it made everything worthwhile.

"One more thing," Séraphine said. "Do you have the homework I set you?"

Séraphine readied herself for the excuse, but instead Zoe produced a neatly typed printout. "Here you go."

Séraphine took it from her with a smile. "How did you find it? Easy?"

"I had to use a dictionary for some of the words, so I'm not sure they're right."

"That's fine, that's part of learning," Séraphine reassured her.

"I guess I didn't find it that easy, but not because of the French."

"Why then?" Séraphine asked.

"Because it's about something close to my heart."

⌒

That evening, Séraphine climbed into bed in her pajamas and Skyped Carla.

"*Salut!*" Carla said. Her dark hair was bundled into a top-knot and she wore a white T-shirt, her face makeup-free apart from a little mascara.

Séraphine brightened immediately. "Hello," she said. "How are things?"

"Good," Carla said. "Better for seeing you. It's been a long week. I'm still not used to the early mornings."

"What's new in the bakery this week?"

"I tried the scone recipe you sent me, and made some strawberry jam to go with them. They are going down well. One or two grumbles about us not having as many pains au chocolat as usual, but for the most part I think our English Week has been a success."

"I'll tell Letty," Séraphine said. "She'll be happy to hear that."

"It seems you have found some good friends over there," Carla said warmly.

"Yes, I have," Séraphine replied, reflecting on what it had meant to her to meet Charlie, Kat and Letty. "I've been lucky."

"And how are the plans for the party going?"

"It's coming together nicely. We've got most things organized—and plenty of cake."

"I wish I could be there," Carla sighed.

"I wish you could too. In fact I wish you could be here all the time." Séraphine smiled.

"Not long now," Carla said.

"Just over a month," Séraphine said. "So soon."

"You won't forget to come home?"

"Never."

They wished each other good night and Séraphine made herself end the call. She missed Carla even more now.

She switched off her computer and brought the duvet up around her.

Before she went to sleep, she took out Zoe's homework. It was a creative writing task that she'd set: "Imagine you are an animal. Which one are you? What do you usually do in a day?"

*I am a horse.*

*When I'm at home, my owner cares for me, brushes me gently with the horse brush and looks at me lovingly. She helps me if I have a stone in my hoof, or when the flies gather round my eyes. It's annoying when they do that. She strokes me gently.*

*Then we go out. I can feel the wind in my mane as I race through the countryside. It is just me and the fields, the grass under my hooves—I am completely free. I want to run and run. My owner is riding me. I trust her to guide me. We are a team.*

*This is where I have lived since I was a foal. Fields of green and lots of sunflowers. Little houses scattered around, other horses nearby. It's a beautiful country.*

Séraphine touched the page. "Oh, Zoe," she whispered to herself. She remembered the girl she'd met when she first arrived—the unhappy girl who hated France, swore she would never go there, and disliked Séraphine on sight. It had seemed that, for Zoe, everything about the country she'd grown up in was tied to the tragedy of her mother's death. At the time, Séraphine had wondered if that would ever change. Now, she had a glimmer of hope that it could.

# 32

Monday, September 29

*Still no sign of Jake,* Kat texted Charlie. *Three nights now. We've called the police, rung round his friends and the hospitals. Fingers crossed he'll come back today. Kx*

She put down her phone. Since Saturday she, Diane and Andy had been looking for Jake, trawling the local cafés and his friends' houses, pretending to Leo that it was all a game of hide-and-seek. That had been Andy's idea—it distracted Leo from asking questions, but sat uneasily with Kat. After all, what would they tell him if, in the end, his dad couldn't be found? She felt sick to the pit of her stomach thinking about it.

She went into the kitchen, where Leo was having breakfast with his grandparents. Their smiles were in place, laughing and playing with him, but Kat could see the worry lines etched on their faces. Jake had never been the most reliable person— he'd come home late without warning, and forget meetings and appointments, even important ones. But this—going missing for three nights—he'd never done anything like this before.

"How about a banana?" Diane said, offering one to Leo. His eyes lit up and he reached for it. Andy smiled at his delight. In spite of the circumstances, Kat could see the joy that their grandson brought to Diane and Andy's lives, and was grateful for their support. She shouldn't have doubted them. Jake had always had a way of making her believe what he said, even when she should know better.

She nursed the cup of tea that she'd left on the table when she went to text Charlie. It was warm enough still to offer a little comfort. She looked at Leo, merrily eating and chattering. Something had to change today; they couldn't all go on waiting. The police knew about Jake, but nothing seemed to be moving very fast there.

Kat thought back to the days that she and Jake had spent in the city, when she was a student—she'd revisited most of their regular haunts on Saturday; some had changed, some stayed the same, but Jake hadn't been in any of them. His friends had agreed to keep a lookout and stay in touch with the staff in case things changed. Those places were where she had happy memories of being with Jake, and they'd come to her first. But what about the times when they'd argued? She realized she'd filtered those moments out, not wanting to revisit them. She forced herself to do it now. When she was upset, she'd gone to her room, lost herself in a book and tried to ease the pain that way. But Jake had always gone out. Always. It came back to her in a flash.

"You're OK to mind Leo, aren't you?" Kat said. "I need to go out for a while."

"Yes," Andy said. He had a trace of hope in his eyes, as if he understood. "Don't forget your coat, and there's a scarf on the coatrack you can borrow. It's chilly out today."

"Thanks."

Kat left the house, her pace speeding up as she neared Arthur's Seat, the hill that overlooked the city. The cold wind stung her cheeks. It didn't make sense that anyone would choose to sleep outside in the cold weather—but it had to be worth a try. She climbed the hill and saw the bench in the distance. How had she forgotten it? Time after time it was where she'd found him. Repentant, usually, but occasionally still angry. With the architecture of Edinburgh laid out in front of them, they'd talked, and kissed, and made up, found their way back together more than a dozen times.

Two days of searching and it hadn't crossed her mind until now. She neared it, and could make out a figure slumped forward, head in hands. It was Jake. Her breath caught. She had found him.

Kat approached the bench quietly and sat down next to him. He seemed to sense her presence. He didn't look up, but he looked across at her denim-clad legs, and down at her brown leather boots, familiar to him.

"Kat," he said, without looking up.

"Hi."

She saw that his shoulders were shaking and there was the sound of quiet sobbing. Instinctively, she put an arm around him.

He burrowed his head in her shoulder, just as his son did whenever he was in need of comfort. Kat held him. The anger and frustration that had been building in her since their phone call was still there, but at the same time she felt sorry for him.

"I've messed everything up," he said into her shoulder, the words coming out muffled.

She took a deep breath. She didn't have to be here, she didn't have to speak to Jake now—or ever again. But as she stroked his arm, she knew that she would.

"Yes, you have messed things up," Kat said, pulling away gently. "You've put me and your parents through hell."

"I'm sorry," he said weakly.

"Not good enough. We need to talk."

⌒

They walked through town and found a café. Kat ordered a cup of tea and toast and a fried breakfast for Jake.

"You're hungry," she said, as he devoured the food in front of him.

"I haven't been sleeping or eating much. Just walking around town, trying to get my head straight. It's been freezing. I got into a hostel on the first two nights, but last night I was out on the bench."

"Well, you should have come home," she said, her sympathy reaching its limit. "Believe me, none of us have been sleeping much either. I was worried, Jake. Really worried. The way you were talking, I thought you were going to do something drastic, hurt yourself, maybe even take off with Leo without telling me—and then this, you completely disappear."

"It was stupid," Jake said, shaking his head. "I don't blame you for being angry. I was an idiot. I was saying things just to hurt you. And then I needed some space to figure everything out."

"But why did you want to hurt me?" Kat said, feeling angry all over again.

"Because you're cutting me out."

"What, because I don't want to get back together?"

"Because you wouldn't even consider it. I suppose I realized for the first time just how much I threw away. When we had Leo, all I could think about was what we had lost . . . our freedom, the way we used to be able to be spontaneous. It's taken me three years to fully appreciate what we've gained— Leo. I want us to be a family—but then you gave me a no, flat out, because you reckon it's 'too late' for that."

Kat looked him in the eye. Remembered the moments they'd shared together, the laughter, the intimacy.

"It's been too late for a long time, Jake," she said firmly. "And the way you've been acting recently has only confirmed that. I've done everything I could to ensure you and Leo could have a relationship, that he could have a dad. But now . . . I mean, how do we go forward from here?"

"You're right," Jake said, putting his head in his hands.

"I'm sorry, Jake, but I don't know if I can trust you again."

Jake's back, Kat texted Charlie. Me and Leo are on our way home. See you soon, Kx

D iane and Andy had greeted Jake with hugs in front of Leo, but as Kat packed up her son's things she'd heard their raised voices behind the closed kitchen door. Leo was oblivious, unquestioningly happy to see his dad again, and sad to say good-bye. Kat had spent the train journey walking up and down the carriages with Leo, talking to other passengers and keeping him entertained. Now that they were home, though, and he was settled in bed, she found herself alone with her thoughts and doubts.

She'd called Diane and Andy, letting them know that they'd arrived back safely and asking them to tell Jake. She kept her message simple and to the point, the way all communication was going to be from here on. She had hoped she and Jake would be the kind of people who would coparent smoothly, politely negotiating handovers and things needed for school trips. But it had rarely been like that with them, and now she had to accept that it never would be.

Kat poured herself a cup of hot chocolate and walked over

to the window. It was dark outside and in the distance she could see fireworks going off, the bright lights reflected in the sea water.

She kept telling herself that Leo was home, and he was safe. That was all that mattered.

The last thing she'd wanted was to exclude Jake from his son's life. She'd tried to give him space to build his own relationship with Leo. But in doing so she'd put Leo at risk. She'd left her son in the care of someone who wasn't even able to care for himself. How did you move on from that?

# 33

Monday, September 29

Letty got the chicken casserole out of the oven and sat down to eat it at her kitchen table next to the window. The view was as familiar to her as anything else in the room—the ebb and flow of the tide, the couples strolling on the beach.

She looked at her phone, but there were no messages. Nothing from Kat. The last thing she'd heard from Charlie was that Jake was still missing—she didn't want to add to Kat's worry by checking up. It would be fine. Of course it would be. Kat was sensible, and she'd proven time and again that she could get herself out of difficult situations. It was one of the things that Letty admired most about her. But at the same time she wished there was a way of knowing for sure that everything was all right.

She put some music on—she didn't like to eat in silence. The radio played "Midnight Train to Georgia." One of John's favorites.

She put her fork down as a memory came back to her. The two of them had danced to that song on the dark-red rug in the middle of her living room floor. He'd held her, late in the evening, when Euan was fast asleep in his room and they had some precious time alone together. It was a lifetime ago, but she still remembered perfectly the feeling of John's arms around her, the way she'd felt safe. As if maybe, just maybe, it would all be OK.

The time before. That's how she thought of it now. The time when the secret she held was no more than a tiny fluttering thing, not a solid truth that would uproot everything they both held dear.

# 34

Tuesday, September 30

"To look at them now, you'd think they'd always been the best of friends," Charlie whispered to Kat.

She, Kat and Séraphine were standing in the doorway to Pippa's living room, watching as Leo, Jacob and Flo stood up in the pirate ship they'd constructed from sofa cushions. Leo was waving a paper flag with a marker-pen drawing of a skull and crossbones. "Arrrr!" he called out.

"No grown-ups allowed!" Flo said.

"Looks like Flo's in charge. Let's leave them to it," Charlie said, leading her friends through to the kitchen.

"Is Leo OK?" Séraphine asked. "Do you think he realized what happened?"

"He seems fine, thankfully, and no, I don't think he had a clue what was going on—which is a blessing," Kat said. "Luckily his grandparents covered for Jake while he was missing, and then he was so excited about going on a train that he didn't ask many questions."

"You must have really been going through it on that journey up to Edinburgh," Charlie said, as they sat down.

"Those were the longest hours of my life. I had no idea what I would find—and if Leo would be all right. Jake was acting so completely out of character that I started to question what he might be capable of."

Séraphine touched Kat lightly on the arm, and Kat brushed away a tear. "Anyway, Leo's fine, and that's what matters. I'm so angry with Jake, though. It was all bluster—all engineered to make me feel bad because he felt rejected. So childish."

"What have you arranged with him about seeing Leo in the future?"

"I've told his parents that they need to talk to him about getting counseling, and they've agreed to do that."

"Do you think he'll go along with it?"

"They seemed to think that now he's hit rock bottom he'll be open to it. All I know is I can't take responsibility for his problems anymore. He's going to have to earn back my trust. Until he does, I don't want him in Leo's life, or in mine."

"I don't blame you," Séraphine said. "What he did was very wrong."

"I know. But Jake is still Leo's father, so for my son's sake I have to try and make it work." Kat shrugged. "Anyway— enough of me. It's good to see you both again. Tell me about something more cheerful. What's been going on while I was away?"

"I've been talking with Carla," Séraphine said. "I miss her like crazy and can't wait to see her, but I'm still no closer to knowing how to handle it all when I get back home."

"That's something you'll just have to deal with when you come to it," Charlie said.

"That's what I keep telling myself," Séraphine said. "Carla's being incredibly patient about it, thankfully."

"It sounds as though you two have what it takes," Charlie said. "You'll work it out."

"I hope so," Séraphine said.

"I was so caught up with everything in Scotland, I never

got to ask you how your date with Euan went last week," Kat said to Charlie. "It seems ages ago now."

Charlie smiled. "Actually it turned into more than one date."

"You're kidding," Kat said, smiling. "This sounds interesting. So how's it all going?"

"The timing's terrible," Charlie said.

"You're into him," Kat teased. She nudged Charlie. "I can tell."

"Maybe," Charlie reluctantly admitted. "I feel good around him. He makes me laugh, and we get each other. With him, I never have to pretend to be someone I'm not."

"That's a good sign," Séraphine said. "And how are you finding it—trusting again?"

"You know what I said about barriers? I wouldn't say there's been a miracle, but it does feel as though they're starting to come down."

"That's great," Kat said.

"Don't go buying a hat," Charlie said, laughing. "It's only been a couple of weeks. I'm a relationship disaster area, and you said yourself that's not his forte either."

"A perfect match, then," Séraphine said, smiling.

"I have a good feeling about this," Kat said. "I can picture you two together."

"You know what, it is pretty exciting," Charlie said. "I haven't let myself say that until now—but I enjoy spending time with him."

"Good," Kat said. "Relax and make the most of it."

As she said it, Kat thought about how easy it was to wish happiness for her friends, yet how rarely she let herself live by the same advice. She'd allowed Jake's temper to dominate her life for too long—living in the shadow of it, even now, had kept her from moving forward in her own life. She couldn't change him, but she could do her best to break free of the control he still had over her.

"Talking of relaxing, and enjoying," Charlie said. "It's less than a week to the party. I know we've had other things to think about, but is everything set up?"

"Yes," Séraphine said. "I went through the list we made at Kat's and we've got most things lined up. You're still OK to do the decorations, are you, Kat? I can take that over from you if you've got too much on?"

"I'm fine with that," Kat said. "I've started on them already, and I'm not going to let what happened with Jake stand in the way of a good time." Kat looked at the others and smiled, staying focused. "This is about Letty, and the three of us are going to throw her a party she'll never forget."

# 35

Wednesday, October 1

Kat was running Leo's bath and he was playing with toys in the bathroom when her phone rang.

"Stay here for a second, sweetheart," she said to him. "I'm just going to answer that."

She ran for her mobile and stood in the doorway where she could keep an eye on Leo.

"Hello."

"Kat—it's me."

"Dad!" she said, lighting up at the sound of her father's voice. Leo looked up and smiled.

"Is that Grandpa?" he asked excitedly. She nodded.

"How the heck are you? Where are you calling from?"

"Guess," he said.

The line was clearer than usual, but that seemed to vary regardless of how far away he was.

"Where do you think Grandpa is?" she asked Leo.

"Zanzibar," he said. It was the country he'd last found on the map.

"Leo says Zanzibar. I have no idea. We were plotting your route on a map, but we ran out of pins somewhere around the Russian border."

"Well, I'm closer than you might think."

"Really?" Kat dared to hope. He wasn't . . . was he?

"I'm at the station. In Scarborough."

She bounced on the spot in excitement. "You're back! Grandpa's home, Leo!"

Leo jumped up and encircled her legs.

"How about one of your fine cups of tea for an old, well-traveled man?"

"I'll put the kettle on."

Kat hung up and hugged Leo in delight. "It's Grandpa! Bath time's postponed."

An hour later, Kat's father was sitting with her and Leo in their living room. They'd talked almost nonstop since he'd arrived, Leo asking questions and Kat's dad telling them about his adventures.

Now he sat calmly in her armchair, a canvas bag on his lap. Kat smiled at him, content to have him nearby once more. He'd always made her feel calm, as if everything was going to be fine—and now, after what had happened with Jake, it was exactly what she needed.

"I'm so glad you're home," she said quietly.

"It's good to be back. And I brought you a few little things," he said, passing Leo a package.

Leo unwrapped a set of Russian dolls. He looked at the large one in puzzlement, until his grandfather showed him how to open it.

"It's got tons of babies inside," he exclaimed happily, taking out the smaller dolls and lining them up.

"And, Kat, I got you this," he said, passing Kat a hand-embroidered tablecloth: yellows, reds and blues on white cotton.

"It's beautiful," she said, touching the stitching. "Really special. Thanks, Dad." She reached over to kiss him on the cheek.

"It sounds as if you had a wonderful time," she said.

"I did. It was everything I'd dreamed of and more. Friendly people, incredible sights—I've got so many photos to show you."

"Show me!" Leo said.

"Love, it's already way past your bedtime, I'm afraid. Grandpa can show you tomorrow. Go and get your pajamas on."

Reluctantly Leo toddled off to his room, clutching his Russian doll.

"So, what have I missed?" her father said.

"Leo's grown a shoe size, and I have become a food critic."

"A what?" he asked, curious.

"I've been trying my hand at food and drink reviewing—visiting tearooms with a journalist friend." It felt good to be able to tell her dad what she'd been doing, and how much she'd achieved by stepping out of her comfort zone. Thanks to Charlie and Séraphine, she had rediscovered the importance of pursuing her dreams instead of letting life pass her by.

"That's my girl!" He beamed proudly. "This is wonderful. You've always enjoyed writing, haven't you?"

"I love it. It's only a short-term thing, but it's reminded me what I want to be doing."

"And you're doing all right for money, are you?"

"Yes," she lied. She couldn't bring herself to tell him the truth—she'd never admitted to him that she was struggling, and she wasn't about to start now. He'd worked hard all his life to provide for her, and he was entitled to enjoy the money he had left and pursue his own dream of seeing the world. She didn't want him feeling guilty about doing that.

"Are you sure? You know I can help you, don't you?"

"I'll be fine. I'm still looking for a job, but something's bound to come along soon."

"I hope Jake's been doing his bit?"

"It's complicated," Kat said. "I'm afraid that side of things hasn't been good."

"What's he done?" Her father's expression, normally soft and kind, hardened a little.

"Jake announced he was going to push for custody of Leo." Her eyes welled up thinking of it—that awful time she'd spent, convinced that her future with her son was hanging in the balance. "It's OK now, but to be honest it's been a nightmare."

Her father furrowed his brow. "I wish you'd said something. I hate to think of you going through all that on your own."

"I didn't want to ruin your time away. In any case, I wasn't alone. Letty's been supportive, as always, and I've had some good friends here with me."

"I'm pleased to hear it. But still, no one should treat you that way. I've half a mind to—"

"Dad, let it go. It's the way I've chosen to make peace with it. Jake's said sorry, he knows he was in the wrong."

"You deserve better."

Hearing the words from her father—the same words Charlie and Séraphine had said to her—cemented the thought in her mind. It was true. She did deserve better. And that meant setting new boundaries for her relationship with Jake, rules that wouldn't be broken.

"I missed you, Dad," she said. "I might be a grown-up, but I don't always feel like one."

"Come here and have a hug," her dad said. She went over to where he was sitting and he took her into his arms, a warm comforting embrace. He kissed the top of her head. "I love you, Kat."

Leo came back into the room, toothbrush in hand. "I want to hug too," he said. They opened up their circle and brought him into it. Kat kissed his hair and they all held one another tightly. "And we love you," Kat said.

# 36

Friday, October 3

Charlie took out the outfit that she was planning to wear to the centenary party: a black halter-neck dress, with bronze hoop earrings and brown suede boots. It was her tried-and-tested party outfit, and she was glad she'd brought it with her. This would be her last night with Euan, and she wanted to look and feel her best. Her excitement about seeing him again was tinged with the regret that the two of them couldn't let things develop naturally, without the pressure of time and work commitments. Once she left, that would be it. She'd have the memories, but that would be all.

She put the dress and shoes to one side so that she wouldn't accidently pack them into her suitcase, then she dialed Jess's number.

"Hi, Jess." She held the mobile between her ear and shoulder, folding the rest of her clothes up, ready for packing, at the same time. "Just to say I'll be back in the office on Monday, as we agreed."

"Good. I have to say, I'm not sure how you've done it, but you seem to be on track for a strong issue of the magazine."

"Thank you," she said, feeling a wave of relief at her boss's words. She thought of Kat and Séraphine, and smiled. "I had a good team."

"You must have done."

"Are the cover designs through yet?"

"Yes, already on your desk for checking. In terms of the internal layout, there's still some content missing."

"I thought I'd write a piece myself—a feature telling the history of a particular tearoom, quite a special one. I think our readers will enjoy that context."

"Fine. Make sure it's done by Tuesday. And, Charlie . . ."

"Yes?"

"No dillydallying on the motorway, eh? We've waited long enough."

Charlie hung up and tossed her phone on the bed. Work aside, with Pippa and Luke building bridges, and Luke having agreed to come back to the house, it was the right time for her to go home—or so she kept telling herself.

She got up and started to pack away a few things from her dressing table. She paused for a moment and looked at her reflection in the mirror. The creases in her forehead had smoothed out, and there was a glow in her cheeks. Perhaps there was something to be said for sea air, she thought.

Pippa stuck her head around the door of the spare bedroom.

"Packing up already?" she asked.

"Why, will you be sorry to see me go?"

"I never thought I'd say this, but I will be sorry," Pippa said, slouching against the doorframe. "In all seriousness, you're not such a bad sister."

Charlie turned, waiting for the sarcastic smile, the sneering follow-up comment. Neither came.

"Really," Pippa said calmly.

Charlie looked at her sister and realized things had changed. There was a peace between them now; they were no longer competing.

"I've enjoyed being here," Charlie said. "It's been good to

spend time with the kids. And with you. But it feels right to be leaving too, because I get the sense things are going to work out OK for you."

"You do?" Pippa said. There was uncertainly in her eyes.

"It's over to you and Luke from here, isn't it."

"I'm nervous," Pippa said, tilting her head. "Is that weird? Being nervous about the man I'm married to coming back to our house, back to our bedroom. Because we have to make it work this time, Charlie."

"You will." Charlie put down her washbag and walked the few steps toward her sister. She put out her arms and welcomed her into a hug.

Pippa laid her head gently on Charlie's shoulder, and stayed like that for a moment. Charlie stroked her soft hair. Pippa spoke softly: "God, I really hope so."

# 37

Saturday, October 4

On Saturday evening, the night of the party, Kat approached the Seafront with a sense of anticipation. Her dad was at home with Leo, and she'd taken the opportunity to go all out—taking time over her makeup and putting on the dress that Séraphine had given her. She thought of her last conversation with Adam, and of how he would be there. It felt like a lifetime ago—she'd been so caught up in worrying about Jake and Leo—but now she found herself wondering what it would be like to see him again.

"Hello there!" Séraphine called out. She was standing by the front door of the tearoom, her blond hair up in a ponytail.

"Hi," Kat replied, waving back.

"Wow, look at you!" Séraphine said as they hugged hello.

"Thanks," Kat said. "Thought it was the perfect opportunity to wear this," she said, pointing at the dress.

"It looks fabulous," Séraphine said with a smile.

"Is it all clear?" Kat said, peeking over her friend's shoulder and into the tearoom.

"Yes. Letty's out with her friend Sue, and we've got the place to ourselves, ready for setting up."

"Excellent," Kat said.

"Look," Séraphine said, excitedly lifting a large box out of her bag and giving Kat a peek inside. "I made a Victoria sponge.

A proper English cake. And some drop scones and tea cakes to go with it. What do you think?"

"Smells incredible. You've done us proud." Kat smiled. "I brought strawberry tarts too."

The interior of the Seafront Tearoom twinkled with white fairy lights strung up from the rafters and along the counter.

"Hi, you two," Euan said. He was tinkering with the stereo in the far corner of the room. "Just getting the music sorted. Charlie's out the back putting some muffins in the oven. She's gone into baking overdrive."

"That makes three of us," Séraphine said.

"What have you got there, Kat?" Euan was eyeing the large bag she was carrying.

"Are you ready?" Kat said. She took the banner out of the bag, and unfurled it, holding one end as Séraphine held the other.

In quilted blue, silver and red letters were the words:

## 100 Years of the Seafront!

On one side was an appliqué teacup, complete with a flower pattern, and on the other a slice of cake.

"You made that?" Euan said. "That's amazing."

"It's beautiful," Séraphine said.

"Charlie," Euan yelled. "Come and take a look at this!"

Charlie popped her head out of the kitchen to see.

"Wow!" she said, brushing flour off her forehead. "That's stunning, Kat."

"I'm quite nerdy with quilting," Kat said, embarrassed. "Any excuse." She brought out the flowers and small vases that would go on the individual tables.

At six o'clock, when the cake stands were filled, the plates piled high and all the decorations finished, Euan poured out Prosecco for Séraphine, Kat and Charlie.

"Cheers," Séraphine said. "A moment of calm."

"Enjoy it," Charlie said. "It's not going to last long."

"Finally!" Euan called out, looking over at the door to the tearoom. "I thought you'd never get here."

Kat turned to see Adam coming in, wearing a white shirt, with his car keys still in his hand. As their eyes met she felt a surge of adrenaline run through her.

"There are two crates out the back that need shifting," Euan said to his friend. "Could you give me a hand?"

"Sure, I'll be with you in a minute," he replied, glancing at Kat.

"Hi," Kat said. "Let me guess: Dad taxi?"

"Right first time. Zoe's got her first slumber party tonight."

"I remember that," Kat said to Adam. "It's a rite of passage. Chatting till all hours, sneaking downstairs for midnight feasts. I bet she was excited."

"She was pretending not to be, but I could hear her on the phone in her room earlier, whooping and giggling." Adam smiled. He lit up when he was talking about his daughter, and Kat enjoyed seeing it. It was clear they were a real team—the way she hoped she and Leo would always be.

"So you have the night off?" she asked.

"Yes, I do. You?"

"Me too, yes. My dad's with Leo."

"Shame your dad couldn't come himself."

"It is. He loves a party. But what can I say . . . He's a saint," Kat said.

Euan walked over to where they were standing. "We haven't got that long," he said. "Come on."

"Sure, sorry." Adam looked at Kat again. "Catch you later."

"See you then," Kat said.

As she laid the table with cakes, Adam's laughter drifted over from the back room, where he was shifting crates with Euan. Charlie appeared beside her.

"You look miles away," Charlie said, over her shoulder.

"Do I?" Kat said, returning to reality. "I suppose I was for a moment."

An hour later, a crowd of Letty's friends and the Seafront regulars had gathered, and everyone had hidden themselves out of view at various places in the tearoom—Charlie, Séraphine and Kat were ducking behind the counter, while the men had taken the nook under the stairs.

Kat rose her head a fraction and peered out through the window. She spotted Letty in the distance approaching the Seafront with her friend.

"Everybody ready?" she said in a loud whisper. "She's nearly here."

As Letty opened the front door, they all leaped out.

"Surprise!" they shouted.

Letty stood with her hand on her heart, her face pale, and looked up at the banner that Kat had made, tears coming to her eyes.

"My gosh," she said. "Is this all for me?"

"Yes," Euan said, stepping forward. "These three suggested that it was about time we celebrated." He motioned to Kat, Charlie and Séraphine. "So everyone here has come together to say thank you."

"How wonderful. It looks beautiful. I'll forgive you all for nearly giving me a heart attack."

A laugh went up from the crowd.

Charlie passed her a glass of champagne. "Here you go, Letty. This should help ease the shock. Now come and join the party."

Over the course of the evening, friends milled around, chatting and eating the homemade cakes, exchanging memories of the tearoom over the years. Charlie and Letty had gone into the kitchen to fetch the next batch of muffins, and they took the opportunity to talk in the relative peace.

"You three were so kind to arrange this," Letty said to Charlie. "It's been a fantastic evening."

"It was our pleasure," Charlie said. "The Seafront is a very special place."

"You know, it's the customers who make it that way," Letty told her. "There are days when it feels as though I'll never get through everything that needs doing, and the cakes come out flat, and I have a mountain of paperwork . . ." She shook her head. "But then there are days when people like you come in, and I know I have the very best job in the world."

"It's good to be able to celebrate with you tonight," Charlie said.

"I didn't see this one coming at all," Letty laughed. "I felt quite overwhelmed when I came in. I'm not used to this kind of attention. But now, well, I'm having a very lovely evening."

"I'm glad. That was the plan." Charlie smiled.

"Before I forget, Charlie," Letty said. "I know you're back at work on Monday, and I wanted to talk to you about something before you go. You seemed interested in the scrapbook and the other things, and you mentioned you wanted to research a bit more. Do you want to borrow a few bits and pieces from our archives? By which I mean the folders of junk

I've never got round to sorting through?" She smiled. "You could post them back when you're finished?"

"Sure," Charlie said. "That would be great—if you're certain you don't mind? I was thinking of writing a piece based on them. Completely anonymous, and with your approval, obviously."

"Of course. I'm only pleased someone else is interested. If you find something you can use for your writing, then please go ahead."

"Thank you," Charlie said.

Letty wove her way through the crowd, went into the kitchen and returned with a red folder and small cardboard box. "I'm not sure if you'll be able to piece it all together, but there's some notes from customers over the years, that kind of thing. Recipes my grandparents used to use."

Charlie took them from her. "I'll take good care of it," she said.

K at," Séraphine said, as they stood by the cake table, filling their plates with the sweet offerings. "Have you seen anyone since Jake?"

"No, no one," she said. "Why do you ask?"

Séraphine lowered her voice to a whisper. "Because I think my boss might have a crush on you."

"Adam?" Kat could feel herself blushing.

"Yes. I'm afraid I let it slip that you were single. Since you first came round, I've lost count of the times he's said 'Your friend Kat . . .'"

"That's sweet," she said, a smile coming to her lips. She hoped that it wasn't too obvious that her cheeks were burning up. "I mean sweet of you to say it. Adam's lovely but I'm sure he doesn't see me in that way."

Séraphine raised an eyebrow.

"And I don't see him like that either," Kat added quickly.

"You wouldn't consider it?"

"I don't think so, no," she fibbed. "All I'm interested in now is a bit of stability." It was true—and yet Kat couldn't deny that what Séraphine had said sent a tingle of excitement through her.

"Oh well," Séraphine said. "I can understand, I suppose. With everything that has been going on in your life. It seems a shame, though. Are you sure you wouldn't like to at least get to know him better . . . ?" She gave an encouraging smile.

Charlie approached them, and Kat quickly took hold of her arm. "Charlie, come and change the subject," she said playfully.

Charlie smiled, confused, glancing at both women, then opting to go along with Kat. "OK, if you really want a new topic of conversation, there is something I've been wanting to ask you two. What are you up to in a fortnight's time?"

Kat shrugged, relieved that Charlie was the center of attention now. "I don't have any plans."

"Me neither," Séraphine replied.

"Well, how about a trip to London? My treat. I want to take you out to say thank you for all the hard work you put into the reviews."

"You don't need to do that," Kat said, shaking her head. "We enjoyed it."

"I know . . . but I'd like to. Plus I'm not ready to say goodbye to the two of you yet. I'll get your train tickets, and take us out somewhere lovely—all you need to do is come."

"I'd love to," Séraphine said. "It sounds perfect."

Kat hesitated. "I don't know. I mean, it's very tempting, but things have been so crazy lately . . ."

"Which is exactly why you could do with a break. Could

your dad look after Leo for the day?" Charlie suggested. "You said how excited he was to be spending time with him again."

"I'll ask him," Kat said, with a smile. "Maybe we could work something out."

Charlie and Euan stood outside the Seafront, the night air crisp and cool, and the sky full of bright white stars. The music and the sounds of guests chatting drifted out of the café, but where they were standing felt hidden, as if no one would find them there.

"I wish you didn't have to go," Euan said, taking Charlie's hands in his.

"Me too," Charlie said. The wind swept a lock of hair into her eyes and Euan brushed it away. "But I think my boss would have something to say about it if I extended my stay *again*. I've put off reality for long enough."

"It's been great spending time with you," Euan said, his voice husky and quiet.

"Likewise. Thank you."

"You're thanking me?" he said, with a slight smile on his lips.

"Yes," she blundered. "You showed me around, took me out."

"You make it sound as if I'm a tour guide," he said, bringing his brows together, confused. "Charlie, I took you out because I like you. I thought that was obvious."

"It is. But . . . you know I'm going back to London. We'll be miles away from each other."

"So you don't even want to try?" Euan asked, subdued.

"I don't see how we could make this work," she said. For a moment it felt better, taking control of the situation, cutting things off before she got hurt again.

He let go of her hands. The closeness that they had nurtured over the past few days, the togetherness they'd built out of laughter and shared stories, started to disappear.

"This is the end of the line, then. If that's what you want," he said.

Her stomach tightened. This wasn't what she wanted. Not at all. To have it be over. To never share another moment with Euan. But she didn't know how to fix it, what solution to suggest. She nodded. "Yes, it is what I want. I think it's easier if we just say good-bye, don't you?"

"Good-bye it is, then," Euan said flatly. "I wish it wasn't, but you've made yourself clear." Reluctantly, he walked away.

Charlie watched him go back into the party, and then turned toward the sea, covering her face with her hands. "You're an idiot, Charlie," she muttered to herself. She wished desperately that she could take back every word she'd just said.

At a quarter to midnight, with the room still full of people, the lights and music cut out completely.

"Oh no!" Kat heard Séraphine's voice call out into the darkness.

"Must be the fuse box," Charlie said from the other side of the room. "Can anyone see Letty?"

"I can barely see anyone," came a male voice.

"I think she went out to the car park with a friend," someone else said.

Kat vaguely recalled a previous power cut, when she'd been in the Seafront with Letty. The fuse box was on the wall near the stairs up to Letty's flat. "Don't worry, I think I know how to fix it," she said.

"Here," Adam said, passing her his phone, with the torch function on. "This should help."

They walked together through the crowded room to the back of the shop. Adam fumbled for the door handle, then opened it, leading Kat to the stairway up to Letty's flat. The hallway there was also in darkness, save for the beam of light coming from the phone she was holding.

She turned the torch to face the wall and found the fuse box, then struggled to open it with one hand still holding the light.

"Here, let me," Adam said. He leaned close to her and pulled the box open.

She stood on tiptoes and peered inside.

"Hurry up, will you!" came a call from the tearoom.

"It must be one of these," Kat muttered. She flicked one.

"That one, I think," Adam said. As he pointed to the switch, their faces were almost touching. Séraphine's words rang through Kat's mind. She was sure of it now. He felt something for her too.

In the darkness, she could hear the sound of both of them breathing and was aware of the closeness of their bodies. She moved toward him and her mouth found his. They kissed, their hands joined, lips moving together naturally. Kat's heart began to race. This felt so right.

Then, in an instant, doubts cut in. She couldn't let this happen, not now. There had been enough upheaval in her life, and she owed it to herself, and to Leo, not to introduce any more.

She broke away from Adam, then located the switch Adam had previously pointed to and flicked it.

The music started up again and the lights in the hallway flickered on.

She saw his expression then, startled, confused at the way she'd distanced herself from him.

"You were right," she said quietly. "That was the one."

# PART THREE

Water is the mother of tea,
a teapot its father,
and fire the teacher.

—CHINESE PROVERB

# 38

Monday, October 6

"Here's one that will fit you," Kat said, passing a small white apron from the back of Letty's kitchen door over to Zoe. She, Zoe, Letty and Séraphine were gathered in the kitchen at the Seafront for an evening baking session. Kat helped Zoe tie the straps behind her.

"So, I wanted to show three of my favorite women how to make madeleines," Séraphine said. She unpacked the ingredients onto the kitchen counter. "I managed to find some proper tins," she said. "You can use muffin tins, but they come out much more prettily with these shell-shaped ones."

"Perfect," Letty said, putting the oven on to heat. "Euan tells me his dog's addicted to these. Seems an awful waste of good cake, if you ask me."

Séraphine and Zoe looked at each other and laughed.

Kat was grateful that her dad had offered to babysit Leo again. Baking, and being with friends, was exactly what she needed at the moment. Her mind had been on Adam ever since the party. What had happened with Jake had obviously thrown her off course—why else would she have done something so foolish? Now she just wanted to forget about it.

"OK, Zoe—do you think you could grate the rind of this lemon for us?" Séraphine asked the question in French, and Zoe took the lemon from her and got to work.

Letty raised her eyebrows at Séraphine and Kat discreetly, to show she was impressed, and Séraphine smiled proudly.

They worked together in the kitchen, preparing the madeleines, and then when they were in the oven cooking, sat down on the kitchen stools.

"Baking's kind of cool, actually," Zoe said, watching the cakes rise in the oven. "I wouldn't mind learning how to make a few more things."

"You should come to my village one day," Séraphine said. "There's a fantastic patisserie course that runs in the summer—you could take it."

"Sounds fun," Zoe said, with a smile.

Kat imagined it—the pleasure of a holiday in France with nothing to do but bake and learn and taste. It sounded like complete heaven. But it was another world, that kind of thing. For someone else, not for her.

"I might join you," Letty said. "I've always dreamed of doing something like that."

Kat nodded in encouragement. "You should go," she said.

"You should, Letty," Zoe said. "You're not that old."

"Zoe!" Séraphine exclaimed, tapping her on the arm.

"What?" Zoe retorted.

Letty laughed. "Don't worry, Zoe. And well, perhaps you've got a point."

Kat collected her things together at the end of the evening, and pulled on her coat.

"Here," Séraphine said, passing her a silver card box filled with the cakes she'd made. "Don't forget these!"

"Thanks," Kat said, shaking her head. "How silly of me."

"Are you OK, Kat?" Séraphine asked her quietly. "It seems like you've got something on your mind."

"It's nothing," Kat said.

"The same nothing that got Adam stirring salt into my tea this morning?" Séraphine asked.

Kat smiled. "The very same one."

# 39

Tuesday, October 7

Charlie breezed past Ben's desk and settled down on her swivel chair with a cup of hot coffee. She'd caught a glimpse of him and looked away quickly. It was only her second day back at the office, and work was what she was going to focus on; there was no time for distractions.

She switched on her computer. She noted, as she had the day before, how everything on her desk was exactly as she'd left it—down to the Post-its with scribbled one-word notes that framed her monitor. It was as if she'd never been away.

On Sunday night, she'd gotten back to her flat late and had a bath before settling into bed. She'd expected to feel good about being home, being in her own space again, with no complications—but instead the flat had felt empty and cold—her neglected plants were the only ones who'd missed her. As she'd lain in bed in her Egyptian cotton sheets, she hadn't been able to shake the feeling that no one aside from her boss would have cared if she hadn't come back. The temptation to call Euan, to tell him that she hadn't been honest with him, almost overwhelmed her. She'd switched off her phone—something she never did—and put it away in her handbag.

"It really is good to have you back, Charlie," Jess said, coming over and perching on the edge of her desk.

"Thanks. It's good to be back." She smiled but the words

didn't ring true. In the gray office with its familiar frosted glass–dividing walls and her colleagues hurrying by in suits, she felt adrift.

She missed the calmness of the seafront, Letty's scones, talking to her friends—and the warmth of Euan's arms.

"The content's looking great, by the way," Jess said. "You've pulled it off. Listen—I'm late for a meeting. Let's catch up later."

The feature Charlie was planning to write—a late addition to the November issue—began to take shape in her mind. It would be an anonymous insight into what the Seafront had seen through the century, the history of a secret tearoom. She wished she'd had time to look through the box that Letty had given her—but the deadline was too tight. She'd just have to work with what she'd already found out.

She put her notes to one side and started to type.

*In the Second World War, Scarborough experienced tragedies, including a raid on the town. During those difficult times, the community rallied together and the traditional tearoom was converted into an RAF training center. The tables were pulled back and the trainees were fueled with Julia Brown's vanilla sponge cake . . .*

She sent the article over to Jess at lunchtime. Changing Letty's name, she'd written the story of the tearoom through the sixties and seventies, how Letty and John had overcome everything from financial hardships to vandalism and managed to keep the place going. She hoped that she'd done the complex story of the tearoom justice.

She opened her ready-made salad. The sugar-snap peas and

cherry tomatoes tasted bland and disappointing after the cakes she'd just been revisiting in her mind.

Her desk phone rang with an internal call, and she picked up.

"Charlie, it's Louis." The managing director's voice was brisk and businesslike, as usual. "Have you got a minute?"

"Sure," Charlie said, straightening in her seat. You didn't tell the managing director you were having lunch, did you? "Your office?"

"Yep. Thanks."

She got up, checking her outfit was uncreased, and made her way to Louis's corner office. He was bent over his laptop with his reading glasses on, draft cover printouts of the Secret Tearoom edition of the magazine cluttering his desk.

He glanced up and smiled when she knocked on the door.

"Hi, Charlie. Take a seat."

She sat in the chair facing him, the large windows giving a clear view out over the Thames. The Millennium Bridge had a steady stream of pedestrians passing over it, tiny specks with colorful umbrellas to shield them against the heavy rain. She wondered if it was raining in Scarborough too.

"I wanted to update you," Louis said, his eyes bright. "We're all delighted with how this edition's shaping up—and how the orders are looking. You've done a great job."

Charlie smiled. "Thank you."

"I'll be honest—I'm impressed. Despite the fact you weren't here in the office for meetings—which I wasn't too happy about at first—you've come up with a sharp concept, and delivered the kind of enjoyable and honest content that readers expect from *Indulge*. You've found fresh new writers, and brought them on board. Qualities that make you a very strong editor. As you know, Jess is leaving. I see no need to look outside the company for a replacement."

Charlie's chest was tight. This was it. The news she'd been waiting and hoping for the last few months. This was what she'd been working toward ever since she started work at the magazine.

"How would you feel about being editor? It's a promotion we all believe you're ready for. Over the last eight years you've built up your skills here at *Indulge*, and proven yourself time and again. On a personal level, I've always enjoyed working with you. I'm very much hoping you'll say yes."

Charlie smiled and bit her lip, excited. Editor! She'd done it. With Kat and Séraphine's help—she'd done it.

"Yes," she said, her enthusiasm bubbling out.

"Well, that's agreed, then," said Louis, reaching out to shake her hand. "I'm thrilled."

"Thank you, Louis. I look forward to getting started."

She walked back to her desk in a daze, unable to keep the smile from her face. The magazine would be hers to run; she'd have free rein with ideas and be able to build up her own stable of writers. She'd be involved in the business side, building sales. Instead of following someone else's orders, she'd be the one calling the shots.

The journey to this point had started years ago, but she knew she would never have made it through the final stage alone. Kat and Séraphine had supported her when she needed it most—practically and emotionally. Back at her desk, she clicked the icon to compose a new e-mail message.

To: Séraphine and Kat

Hi you two,

I just got the most exciting news. I've been made editor of *Indulge*! I can't quite believe it. I owe you both a

huge THANK YOU. I simply could not have done this
without you. Your research, ideas and writing were a
huge part of what sealed the deal.

Looking forward to celebrating with you when you
come to London.

Thanks again,
Charlie x

She pressed Send, and sat back in her seat.

There was one more person she wanted to tell. If they were
still together, she knew Euan would have shared her excitement. She could picture his face, the warm smile crinkling
his eyes, his delight at her achieving something she'd been
working toward for so long. What she wanted now, more than
anything, was to be with him, to celebrate together.

"I hear congratulations are in order."

Charlie looked up on hearing the familiar voice—husky
with the trace of a London accent. There he was—the same
tanned skin and dark hair, easy confidence and dressed-down
look. The man she'd once imagined spending her future with,
only for him to leave her brokenhearted.

"Ben," she said. She'd played out this moment in her mind a
dozen times. When she was up in Scarborough, feeling confident
and strong, she'd thought through what she would say when she
came back to the office and saw him again. The cool reaction,
the witty, sarcastic put-downs. But now he was here, leaning over
the divider on her desk into Charlie's workspace, so close they
were almost touching—her heart raced. She felt small, as she had
in the days after she heard the news that he had cheated on her.
Her smart, considered reactions deserted her.

"Editor, eh." He smiled, showing perfect white teeth. "Well done, Charlie."

"Thanks," she answered, grateful that it had come out sounding controlled and calm, even though that wasn't at all how she felt.

"Seriously, Charlie. You deserve it."

The words were there, just out of reach. *Yes, I do deserve it. And it has sod all to do with you. I've managed this in spite of you. You've got no right to be here, trying to share my success.*

"Thanks," she said again.

"How was the time off?" he asked brightly. "Jess said something about your sister. Everything OK with Pippa?"

The familiarity in his tone grated on her—he had no right to ask about her life. He'd lost that when they broke up. He wasn't her friend. He wasn't anything to her now. The way he made her feel, the way he'd always made her feel, was the opposite of how she'd felt with Euan. She wished Ben would just disappear.

"It was fine," she said. "Pippa's fine."

"Great, glad to hear it." He straightened. "Well, it's nice to see you again, Charlie. You look much better—the break must have done you good."

# 40

Wednesday, October 8

"A letter," Leo said, running to the mat that the small package had just plopped down onto. He picked it up and passed it to Kat. It was addressed to the two of them. "It might be a present for us." She smiled. Since her dad had come back from his travels, letters with handwriting on the front were few and far between, and she was curious about who this one might be from.

"Open it, open it!" Leo said, hopping up and down on the spot.

"OK, hold your horses," she said, ruffling his hair. She still hadn't quite gotten used to having him around again—she loved it so much that she even forgave him the six o'clock in the morning bouncing on the end of her bed. With him there, her flat was a home again.

"What horses?" He screwed up his eyes, confused.

"It means wait a minute, hold up, be patient." She laughed, ripping open the envelope, full of curiosity. "All those things you never do."

"What is it?"

"Let's see." Inside the package was a smaller envelope holding two tickets. She pulled them out and smiled broadly when she saw what it was—entry to the Sealife Centre. Who would have sent her these? Her puzzlement turned to delight. It must have been Jake, trying to make amends. Leo would be thrilled.

She scanned the letter. Apparently admission to the Sealife Centre wasn't the only treat in store. They were both invited to a VIP meeting with dolphins.

She looked at Leo, his brown eyes dancing with excitement. "Mum! Tell me."

"It's a surprise," Kat said. "You'll have to wait until the weekend to find out."

That afternoon, Kat and Leo walked around Morrisons, and Kat took groceries off the shelves and loaded them into the trolley in a daze. Packets of oats and multipacks of juice. She sifted through the vouchers in her wallet to make sure she would be able to make use of some of them.

She'd make the phone call when she got home. She wouldn't allow herself to be swayed by Jake's gesture—of course not. Leo's welfare was too important for that. But the thought behind it, the fact that Jake had taken the trouble to find out what Leo dreamed of doing, and had saved to be able to provide it—that meant something, didn't it?

Back at the flat, Leo played on his xylophone and Kat took her phone into the kitchen, pressing Speed Dial 1.

"Hi, Jake."

"Hi there," he said, sounding pleased to hear from her. "Everything OK?"

"Yes." She turned to face the window. The late afternoon sunshine was glinting off the small windows at the top of the lighthouse. "I'm calling to say thank you. We got the package this afternoon."

"The package?" Jake said, sounding confused.

"Yes," Kat said. "The tickets. To the Sealife Centre?"

"Is this a dig?" Jake said, his voice taking on an edge. "I

mean, I'm sorry that I can't afford things like that, but I thought we said basics have to come first. I'm starting to save up—"

"Oh," Kat said, her heart sinking. "Jake—sorry. It's a misunderstanding. It wasn't a dig at you. You're right that we should be focusing on the bills and things first."

"Right. OK." His voice was brusque, distant. "Well, that was weird," he said.

"Yes—sorry, I got confused. Let's speak in the week."

"Sure. Give my love to the little man, won't you?"

"Of course."

Kat hung up, feeling a little bruised from the interaction with Jake, as fraught as when they'd talked in Edinburgh.

So nothing had changed, after all.

In the living room, she looked at the tickets on the mantelpiece. If Jake hadn't sent them, who had?

# 41

Saturday, October 11

The seahorses glided about the tank, bouncing and gracefully entwining their tails around the fronds of seaweed.

"Do you know what's special about them?" Kat said, playing idly with her son's hair.

"They have magical tails?"

"Yes. There is that. But there's something else too . . ."

"Horse faces?"

"And that. It's also that the daddy seahorses are the ones who carry the babies."

"Really?" Leo said, his eyes widening. He peered closer, pressing his face up against the glass. "They all have fat tummies. Are they all having babies?"

"I don't think so," Kat laughed. "I think that's just the way they look."

"Hi, Kat."

Kat looked up and saw Adam standing beside them. Their eyes met. Her heart was racing, and she hoped desperately that it wasn't obvious. She hadn't seen him since the night they'd kissed, but as he smiled any awkwardness between them disappeared. It was good to see him again. His presence was calm and steady.

"Hello there," she said.

"How are you enjoying the visit?" Adam asked them both.

"We're having a brilliant time, aren't we, Leo?"

"It's the best day ever," he said.

Kat turned back to Adam. "It's nice to see you. What brings you here?"

"I had to see a man about a penguin. And I thought I'd come and say hi."

Then the realization dawned on Kat, and she wondered how she'd ever missed it. "It was you, wasn't it?" Kat said, narrowing her eyes playfully. "You were the one who sent us the tickets, weren't you?"

"Yes," Adam said. "I remembered you saying that Leo was into this kind of thing, and well—I do get the odd perk in my line of work."

"Thank you, Adam. It was very thoughtful of you. Leo's been wanting to come for ages."

"You're welcome." Their eyes met, and Kat felt drawn to him, just as she had the night of the party.

"Have you got time to stop by the café afterward?" he asked.

She opened her mouth to make an excuse, but none came. Instead, she nodded.

"Yes," Kat said, smiling. "Why not?"


An hour later, Kat and Adam were in the café, Leo off chatting to the woman at the counter about how he had met the dolphins in their pool.

"We've had a very special day," Kat said to Adam. "Thank you again. The dolphin meet was just brilliant."

"I'm glad you enjoyed it," Adam said. "It's fun to meet a boy like Leo who's interested in the same things as me. I'm not sure quite what that says about my mental age . . ." He laughed.

"I spend so much time talking to Leo I sometimes forget

how to have an adult conversation," Kat said. "And you know what—I rarely miss it."

He nodded. "I know exactly what you mean. Zoe's far more grown up than me these days, though."

"How is she?"

"Good," Adam said. "We've been talking about secondary schools. I can't really get my head round where the time's gone, but she's going next year."

"Is there somewhere in particular she's keen on?"

"Up until quite recently she had her heart set on going to a boarding school."

Kat raised an eyebrow. "I'm not judging, but . . ."

"I know. I was surprised too. And that's before we even go into how on earth I'd afford it. I told myself she was reading too much Mallory Towers, but I don't know. Anyway, she's gone off the idea all of a sudden. Which makes me wonder if what she was really interested in was escaping."

"And now?"

"She's so much more settled at home. I can't explain it. It's the little things. Séraphine makes sure we always sit down and eat meals together. Before she came, I'd grab a coffee in the mornings and Zoe would be eating her cereal. Even with the best of intentions we'd only say a few words to each other some days. We make time for one another now."

"That's good. So, now that she's gone off the idea of boarding school, where are you thinking of?"

"You know—and this is funny—she wants to go to Parkview Comp."

Kat smiled at the memory of the school she, Adam and Euan had all gone to. "That is funny."

"Yes. Some of her friends are going there, which is really all she cares about."

"You're pleased, aren't you?"

"I had some good times there. Didn't you?"

Kat nodded. "I have some good memories."

"I know you were younger, but you always seemed the cool one." Adam smiled at the memory. "You had this aura. As if you didn't need to follow what everyone else was doing."

"Ha!" Kat laughed. "Well, I suppose I wasn't in any of the cliques, but it wasn't because I was cool. In fact, I spent most of my time feeling like an outsider. I spent all my time reading books. Still do."

"Well, you seem to have plenty of friends these days. I know Séraphine feels she's found soul mates in you and Charlie."

Kat smiled. "Yes. I feel the same. We're going to see Charlie in London next weekend. It'll be nice to catch up."

"That sounds fun."

Kat turned to see Leo was skidding on the floor on his knees. "Leo, come on. Up." She hurried over to him and got him on his feet again.

"We've lost a lot of trousers this way," she explained to Adam. "I think it's time for us to go."

"Shop!" Leo chimed in.

"Yes, we can go to the shop first," she said, before turning back to Adam. "Thanks again."

She leaned in to kiss him on the cheek, closing her eyes for a moment as her cheek touched his, the trace of stubble, the faint smell of aftershave. It felt good, being close to him. She remembered how it had felt to kiss him, that night at the party, and she realized how much she wanted that to happen again.

As she pulled away, their eyes met.

"See you soon . . . Maybe somewhere with more wine and less marine life," he said with a smile.

# 42

Thursday, October 16

In her living room, Charlie opened the box Letty had given her back at the tearoom. It was too late to use anything in the feature—finished copies of the magazine were already in—but she was still curious. She wanted to have a look before sending it back, with a note of thanks. She took out a 1970s map of the town and smiled as she saw the locations that had become so familiar to her. The street with the old cinema on it, and Rosa's, where she and Euan had drunk coffee together.

She delved back into the box and sifted through cards from customers thanking Letty's parents, Julia and Leon, for their hospitality and the fine scones, as well as personal correspondence, invoices from suppliers, photocopies of the deeds.

She was distracted by a ping on her iPad as a new e-mail appeared.

Her heart thudded in her chest as she saw Euan's name, for the first time since they'd said good-bye to each other almost two weeks ago. She clicked to open it.

Hey Charlie,

I've been trying to forget what happened between the two of us—as you made it clear you wanted us to.

But the thing is—I can't.

I can't stop thinking about you. I know I felt a connection between us. That's not something that happens
often—at least not to me.

I don't want to give up. I want to give this, us—
whatever that is—a chance. Yes, there are a few miles
(OK, quite a few miles) on a motorway between us. But
that doesn't mean we have to let this slip away.

I want to see you laugh again.

Euan x

Closing the message, she sat back on her sofa and let his words slowly sink in. He'd seen through her. He'd felt the same connection she had, and he hadn't bought her attempt to brush their encounter off as nothing serious. He was brave, where she'd been cowardly. And she couldn't help thinking that he was the one in the right.

The next day at work, Charlie dressed for her new role in a smart gray suit with an ivory-colored blouse under-neath. She spoke up in the meetings she'd often kept quiet in, and talked her new assistant through what she'd need help with. Jess was still in the editor's office until the new year, but she'd already started to hand over to Charlie, and as far as the *Indulge* team was concerned, the switch had already happened. After lunch Charlie sat down at her desk and began brain-storming ideas for the next edition. As she worked, her thoughts about Euan could be pushed to one side. His e-mail was still unanswered.

Ben tapped her on the shoulder and passed her a coffee. "Peace offering," he said, with a smile.

She took it reluctantly, feeling the same uncomfortable mix of irritation and anxiety she'd experienced the last time they'd talked. But she reasoned that if they were going to work in the same office it was easier to be civil.

"How about I take you out for a drink to celebrate your promotion?" he said.

Charlie shook her head, putting the coffee to one side. "No. No way." She felt a rush of power as she realized the words had come out just the way she'd wanted them to—clear and assertive.

Ben's face fell. "Why not?"

Charlie looked back at him. "Do you really have to ask?"

"What happened—well, it's all water under the bridge now, isn't it?" he said. "Don't you want to move on, be friends? We work together, after all."

He looked so pathetic, standing there on his own, failing to comprehend her rejection of his friendship. His shirt was cheap and synthetic, fitting too tightly over his chest. Charlie wondered what she'd ever seen in him.

"I want to move on, yes," Charlie said calmly. "But I don't want to be friends. My life is infinitely better without you in it."

She noticed that people working at the desks around her had fallen silent, and their eyes were all on her and Ben.

"Come on," Ben said, lowering his voice. "Be reasonable, Charlie. Don't be a cow."

"No, you're the one who needs to be reasonable, Ben. You took me for a fool. You lied to me, you cheated on me, and you humiliated me. I'm lucky enough to know what true friendship is—respect, support, kindness. I don't think you're even capable of those things."

Ben's mouth was agape.

"You're being harsh," he said, almost under his breath.

Jess was watching from her doorway, a huge smile on her face—and a couple of Charlie's other colleagues were discreetly giving her the thumbs-up.

As she looked at Ben, a small, floundering man, trying to find a way to erase his wrongdoing through forgiveness, she felt a wave of relief. She'd escaped marriage with him. The hurt she'd felt hadn't been a broken heart but a deep sense of humiliation and wounded pride. At last she could see him for what he was—pathetic, needy and shallow. She no longer felt tied to him in any way whatsoever.

"No, Ben. Trust me, you don't want to see me when I'm being harsh."

# 43

From: Séraphine
To: Kat and Charlie

Re: LONDON. Can't wait to see you!

Hello you two,

It's tomorrow!

I wanted to say how much I'm looking forward to seeing you again in London before I leave—it will be the perfect farewell to England, and to you, my good friends.

Séraphine x

_____

From: Kat

Hey you two,

Can't wait to see you both. Charlie—hope it's going
well back at the office. We have so much to catch
up on! See you at the station at eight tomorrow,
Séraphine.

Kx

# 44

Saturday, October 18

Charlie, Séraphine and Kat walked across Green Park in the crisp winter sunshine, chatting happily as they made their way toward the Strand.

"London's exactly how I pictured it," Séraphine said, passing the queues outside the Royal Academy of Art. "I've wanted to come here since I was a teenager, hooked on watching *Love, Actually*."

"Oh, it's every bit as romantic as that," Charlie said. "That's exactly what my life is like!" She smiled.

There was a spring in Séraphine's step as she passed the Ritz and snapped a photo. "I've only got a fortnight left of being a tourist and I need to take advantage of it."

"So where is it you're taking us, Charlie? You've been very mysterious about it all," Kat said.

"Here we are." Charlie pointed to the sumptuous displays in Fortnum and Mason's windows. "One of the finest afternoon teas in the city."

They walked inside and Séraphine looked eagerly at the hand-crafted chocolates and tables laden with fine treats and boxes of tea.

"My parents would love some things from here," she said.

"We'll have time to shop later," Charlie said. "Right now we've got a lot of catching up to do."

The lift climbed to the top of the building, opening onto a spectacularly elegant high-ceilinged reception area of the Diamond Jubilee Tea Salon. After giving Charlie's name, they were seated by the window with a view overlooking the tall buildings of central London, and Charlie gave the waitress their order.

"I've got a surprise for you both," she said. She bent down to rummage in her bag. She took out copies of *Indulge* magazine, glossy and bright, with a picture of a teacup on the front. "Ta-da! It's hot off the presses."

"It's out!" Kat said delightedly.

"These are early copies. I practically snatched them out of the hands of our production manager so that I could bring them to you. It'll be in the shops next week."

Kat flicked through the pages, seeing her and Charlie's words in type next to photos of the places they had visited. "It looks gorgeous."

"Here, see—both of your names are in print."

"And this is the feature you wrote? The history of the Seafront?" Kat asked.

"Yes—I had to get it in somehow, it wouldn't have been right to leave it out. But don't worry—I haven't given away too much, and I ran it all past Letty first. Here, I've got another copy for you to give to her."

"It's so . . . *real* now," Kat said, holding it in her hands.

"And there's something else, Kat. *Indulge* was delighted with your writing and they're very keen to use you again. It would be on a freelance basis, so I can't guarantee a regular income, but it should be interesting work when it happens. Would you be up for that?"

Kat could hardly believe what she was hearing. Here was an opportunity to earn money doing what she loved—it was no longer a distant dream, it was something that was actually happening to her.

"Yes," she said, a smile spreading across her face. "You're serious about this?"

"Of course," Charlie said. "You've certainly proved yourself."

"This is amazing." Kat was almost numb with the surprise of it.

"You deserve it," Charlie said. "We'd be lucky to have you."

"Congratulations," Séraphine said, giving her friend a squeeze.

"Thank you," Kat said, beaming. "So, is everything going well at the magazine?"

"Yes, I've settled right back into London life," Charlie said. "It's busy, since I got the promotion, but that's how I like it."

"No regrets about coming back, then?" Kat asked innocently.

"What do you mean?"

"Just a hunch." Kat shrugged.

Charlie's voice took on a cooler tone. "If you're talking about Euan—and I know you are—then I'm completely committed to my decision. I've been working toward this promotion for years."

"If you say so," Kat said, and she and Séraphine exchanged glances.

"Don't look at each other like that. I'm not about to throw it all away."

"Has he been in touch?" asked Kat.

"Yes," Charlie said, toying with her spoon. "He sent an e-mail."

"And what did you say?" Séraphine asked, her eyes lighting up.

"I haven't replied yet."

"It seems a shame to let it all go," said Kat. "I could have sworn there was something special happening between you two."

"I haven't replied to him because I don't know what to say," Charlie told them, letting her guard down a little. "It feels easier to just say nothing at all."

W ho's having the last macaroon?" Kat asked an hour later. "Everyone's being far too polite."

"You have it," Charlie said. "I couldn't eat another thing."

"Macaroons are one of the few things I'll be able to get back home. I'm happy to let it go," Séraphine said.

"How's Letty doing?" Charlie asked.

"Good," Kat said. "She's helping my dad out with Leo later—she wanted to be sure I'd come down and see you. It's so nice to have a day off and relax with you two. It's a real escape."

"How have things been since I left?"

"OK. Leo and I are getting on well, in our own little way—it's brilliant having him back, and to have Dad home too."

"Adam mentioned that he saw you the other day," Séraphine said.

"Don't start—"

"You see, you dish it out, but you can't take it!" Charlie laughed.

"Ha, perhaps you're right. It was nice to see him, actually. Really nice. I have a feeling we might be seeing a bit more of each other too."

⁓

Charlie walked Séraphine and Kat back to the train station, the sun low in the winter sky. They were surrounded by people carrying bags of shopping, and commuters bustling past.

"What a wonderful day," Séraphine said.

"It's been fantastic," Kat agreed. "Thanks, Charlie."

"No—thank *you*," Charlie said, touching both women gently on the arms. "You helped me out when I needed it most. I couldn't have been there for Pippa if I hadn't been lucky enough to have the two of you being there for me. It's been brilliant getting to know you both. I feel blessed to have met such good friends."

"Same here," Séraphine said. "I was lost at first. I thought I'd made a huge mistake—but instead it's turned out to be one of the best things I've ever done."

"Aw, you two," Kat said, bringing them into a hug. She pulled away and spoke despite the lump in her throat. "Where do I even start? I feel much stronger knowing that I have you both on my side."

"We'll always be there," Séraphine said. "Even if we're not living in the same place. Because I guess this is good-bye, Charlie. Well, let's call it *au revoir*. I'm hoping you'll come out to France. Both of you."

"That's very tempting," Charlie said.

"You'll always be welcome," Séraphine said.

They hugged each other close.

# 45

Saturday, October 18

Séraphine climbed the stairs to her room. The house was quiet. Adam and Zoe must still be at the cinema. She and Kat had mostly dozed on the train journey home, both tired from the day, comfortable with the silence in each other's company.

She took the items out of her handbag and laid them on her small desk:

A model of a red London bus

A tube map

Serviette and packet of sugar from Fortnum and Mason

A pink and yellow flowered vintage teacup, wrapped in white tissue paper

A worn paperback of *84 Charing Cross Road*

A black-and-white postcard of the Beatles on the zebra crossing outside Abbey Road Studios

She turned the postcard over and wrote on the back:

*Dear Carla,*

*A few souvenirs from London—one day let's go back together?*

*Love, Séraphine x*

"Do you *have* to go?" Zoe asked at breakfast the next day. "Can't you stay longer, maybe until Christmas?"

Séraphine laughed. "I'd love to. But I think my family might have something to say about that."

She looked over the kitchen table at Zoe and felt grateful that in the short time they'd known each other Zoe had come to trust her. In Zoe, Séraphine had seen true resilience, and the suffering the young girl had endured in her life had helped her to put own experiences in perspective. And then there was Adam. She thought of what Kat had said the day before. She really hoped that the two of them might get together.

"You'll be missed," Adam said. "It feels as though you've become part of our family."

"It's true," Zoe said. "It'll be strange without you."

"You've been so kind to welcome me the way you have," Séraphine said. "You've made me feel completely at home."

"It'll be boring when you're gone," Zoe said.

"I'm sure your dad will bring home some enormous dog or other soon," Séraphine said. "Then you'll forget all about me."

"I won't," Zoe said. "For starters, dogs aren't nearly as good at baking."

"I hope you'll keep up your French studies," Séraphine said. "I left you those books, and I'll be expecting full reviews. I'll e-mail you in French too."

"OK," Zoe said, with a playful sigh. "I can't believe you're leaving the country and you're still going to be bossing me about."

Séraphine laughed. "I only bother bossing around my most able pupils," she said.

"You must be looking forward to getting back to your own life," Adam said. "I imagine there are a lot of people who will have missed you."

"One or two," she replied, with a smile.

Séraphine thought of Carla, and how soon their long wait would be rewarded. More than anything she wanted them to be together again.

Dear Carla,

I'll be home a week on Friday. Maybe we could meet and talk on Saturday afternoon—shall I see you outside the bakery at two? I have been craving one of your blueberry brioches the whole time I've been here. Perhaps you could save some from the Saturday batch and we could have them with coffee in the square? I've missed you so much, and can't wait to hear how you have been. I don't know what's next for us, all I know is that I have so much I want to say to you, and when I am by your side again, I know I will feel complete.

Sx

_____

Dear Séraphine,

Of course I want to meet you. I'm so excited about you coming home that I've barely been able to think of anything else. Apart from making brioches for us. I don't want us to hide who we are anymore, though. I don't want to live a lie when we have nothing to be ashamed of.

Cx


Dear C,

You're right. I've been doing a lot of thinking about it while I've been away. When I get home I'm going to tell my parents about us, about you. And I'm going to tell them how happy I am.

Sx

# 46

Tuesday, October 28

Kat looked through the photos on her phone of the day she'd spent in London with Charlie and Séraphine. Raising cups of tea in a toast, the elegant high ceilings of the Fortnum and Mason tearoom in the background.

Ten days on, it seemed like a dream. She'd been in touch with *Indulge* about writing more for them, and Charlie had promised there would be work in the new year, but payments for her heating couldn't wait until then. That morning she'd accepted a job at a call center on the outskirts of town—it would give her enough to cover the bills that were due.

"Mummy, I can't sleep," Leo said, standing in the living room doorway in his pajamas.

"It's late, darling," she said, walking over to him. "Back to bed."

She led Leo quietly to his room and tucked him in under the covers. Then she gave him his stegosaurus to hold and kissed him on the cheek. "Go to sleep now."

"I can't. I'm not sleepy." He looked up at her. "When will I see Daddy again?"

Kat took a deep breath. She'd known the question would come. "We'll call him tomorrow and you can talk to him then."

"OK," Leo said, turning on his side and playing with the cuddly toy. "It's not the same though, as seeing him."

"I know." She felt a stab of guilt. "We'll work something out, I promise."

He nodded and pulled his duvet up under his chin.

"Sleep tight, darling, sweet dreams."

She went back into the living room and dialed Jake's number on her mobile.

"Hi, Kat," he said. "How are you?"

"All right. I got a job today." She tried to sound excited, even though the prospect of starting work at the characterless concrete offices left her feeling numb with dread.

"Really? That's good news."

"Thanks. I start on Monday. I got your payment this month, by the way."

"Glad it came through. Listen, I know I've got some catching up to do. I'll send the money when I can. Work's coming in more regularly now."

"I understand."

"I've started the counseling," he said. "And it's going OK."

"I'm glad to hear that," Kat said.

She wavered. She thought of how it had seemed, for a brief moment, as if she could have a life aside from all of this. Adam had called her to arrange to go out, but she kept putting him off. In her heart she knew what mattered most was getting Leo and his dad's relationship back.

"Leo's been asking about you," she said at last.

"He has?" Jake's voice lifted.

"I said we'd call you tomorrow, have a chat."

"Sure."

"But what he really wants is to see you. So I was wondering, would you like to come and visit us?"

"Are you serious? You wouldn't have a problem with that?"

"It's fine. But I'd want to be there. The whole time—and

I'm not sure when that'll change, when I'll be happy to let go again. We'll have to see how things go."

"I know. I understand."

"I don't want to cut you out of his life, Jake. No matter what's happened or what happens between us. You're Leo's dad, nothing can change that."

"I won't mess up again, Kat. I won't hurt you. Either of you. Promise."

# 47

Tuesday, October 28

Charlie turned off the taps and climbed into her bath. She let the warm water soothe her tired body. It was after midnight. She'd gotten home after a long evening in the office and had almost fallen asleep listening to music on the tube. As she sank down into the foam, a memory drifted into her mind. An early morning by the sea, the fresh air, the exhilaration of running. Of laughing.

Was any job worth missing out on life for?

Kat and Séraphine's words echoed in her head, and what she had feared losing didn't seem so important anymore. Maybe it was time to be open again, even if that meant the risk of falling flat on her face. Ben's betrayal might have tripped her up, but what she did with that experience was in her hands. Her past was written in stone. But her future wasn't. She was in charge of that.

The next day, Charlie called in sick.

It's been a few weeks, I know. So I hope nothing's changed . . . Charlie tapped out on her phone to Euan. Because I'm coming up to see you. Cx

It seemed as if she'd held her breath for a full half hour, until Euan's reply came through. Nothing's changed. I can't wait to see you x

⁓

Hey," Euan said, when she arrived on his doorstep later that same day. "You're here."

"I'm here."

He closed the front door behind her and they stood for a moment in his hallway, close but not touching. "I missed you."

"Me too," Charlie said. A smile spread across her face. Euan's expression mirrored hers and he put his arms around her, drawing her in toward him. He pulled back slightly, so that he could see her face. "It's been quiet without you."

He kissed her on the mouth, one hand tracing the sensitive nape of her neck. With the touch of his lips she felt grounded, more sure than she'd ever been that she was finally in the right place.

So what happened?" Euan asked, handing her a glass of wine. "When you didn't reply to my e-mail I thought maybe I was making an idiot of myself."

"You weren't," she said quickly. "You were braver than me, that's all." She took a sip of wine while she composed herself. She'd tried all the other ways out: the only one left was the truth. "Euan, you're a nice guy . . ."

"Oh no, I've heard this one—" he said, shaking his head.

"I don't mean *nice* nice . . . I mean gorgeous. Hot. A bit of everything I like."

He smiled. "Better."

"But I don't find this easy. It wasn't long ago I was planning to get married to someone else."

"Really? God. Well, I'm glad you're not still doing that."

"So am I," she said, "It would have been a huge mistake.

But what I'm trying to say is that, while I thought I was over it, perhaps I'm not yet. I'm a little . . ."

"Emotionally backward?" Euan said.

"Not quite how I would have put it, but yes . . ."

"Well, you're not the only one."

"You seem so chilled out."

"I'm not. I find it hard to trust, to commit, all of those things. I'm rubbish at relationships."

"So, what . . . what are you saying?"

"When I met you I realized I wanted to change, to try and find a way to be better at this stuff. And it was so obvious I couldn't ignore it. When you care about someone enough, your whole outlook on life gets turned upside down."

"And now you want us to blunder together into the unknown, as clueless as each other?"

"That's exactly what I want." His eyes crinkled at the edges as he smiled.

She reached across and touched his cheek, ran her hand over his stubble. He tilted his jaw toward her hand and kissed it gently. She moved closer and kissed him on the mouth.

"OK," she said, pulling back. "We can do that."

He stroked her hair and brought her close to him, kissing her again.

"Stay with me here tonight?" he said.


You're back!" Flo said, clambering onto Charlie's lap the next day. She put her arms around her aunt's neck and nuzzled her head into the crook of her neck.

"I missed you too, sweetie," Charlie said. "It's good to see you all again."

Charlie looked across the room to where Pippa was sitting

on the playmat with Gracie and Jacob, who was dangling a toy over his baby sister's face.

"Mum told me you've landed a brilliant promotion," Flo said. "She's so proud of you."

Charlie's eyes met Pippa's. "That's nice of her. Yes, I'm very excited about it."

"We've got something new too," Flo said. "Shall I show you?"

"Don't say it," Pippa said. "I know I must be mad."

Intrigued, Charlie followed Flo, who pulled her by the hand into the kitchen.

In the corner of the kitchen, prowling by the door, was a scruffy black cat with hair sticking up and a chunk missing from his right ear. Venus, the Prussian blue, was cowering in her plush cat basket.

"His name is Roger," Flo announced proudly. "Roger the Punk Cat."

Luke came into the kitchen dressed in jeans and a polo shirt. "It's all Adam's fault," he said, smiling. "Last thing we need, as you can see—the other cat's petrified."

"You love him really," Pippa said, snaking an arm around her husband's waist. "I caught him chatting to Roger the other night."

"This is what working less has driven me to," Luke said. "Instead of yakking in a boardroom all hours, I'm in here talking to an ex–street cat."

"I've made the bed up for you in the spare room." Pippa turned back to her sister. "Do you want a hand taking your things up? Is your bag still in the car?"

"No, thanks. It's fine. I'm staying somewhere else tonight."

Pippa raised an eyebrow.

"OK, OK. Put the kettle on and I'll tell you all about it."

⌒

"Here you go," Euan said, passing Charlie a cup of tea in bed.

"Thanks." She pulled the duvet up around her and kissed him. His lips were warm and soft. She felt content and secure there—as if the two of them existed in a bubble where nothing could touch them.

"Are you sure you have to go to work today?"

"Afraid so," he said, sitting down next to her on the bed. "As much as I'd love to stay in bed with you all day, I have a feeling the buyers won't accept that as a reason for not meeting their deadline."

"Good luck," she said, running a hand over his arm, feeling the warmth of his skin. "Do you think you'll have time for lunch?"

"Of course. I'll call you. What are you going to do today?"

"I have a few things to return to your mum at the tearoom, then I'll give Kat a ring and see what she's up to."

"Cool. I'm sure you guys will have a lot to catch up on."

"I hope you're not suggesting we'll be gossiping."

"Never. Listen, I'd better run." He kissed her and stroked her hair gently. "See you later."

Charlie showered and dressed, then got the folders Letty had given her out of her bag to make sure she had everything.

The past two nights with Euan had left her feeling calm, complete. Even the dozen missed calls on her mobile from work couldn't take that away. Charlie had no idea how she was going to explain her three days off when she got back. With

Euan she didn't have to try and be anyone else but herself. It had been natural and easy. She felt at home in his flat, as if waking up in his bed was where she was always meant to be.

Bagel barged into the room and bounded up to her, jumping and licking her face. He knocked the stack of folders off the bedside table, and a card fell out of one of them onto her carpet. *Thank You*—the words were in silver script, and there was an image of a bouquet of flowers on the front. She opened it and saw a handwritten note.

"Shh, Bagel, sit," she said, pushing him down and away from her.

She read the note.

*August 1988*

*Dear Leticia,*

*I can't thank you enough for what you did for us. You have made our lives complete. I know it wasn't easy for you—but we will always be grateful for the sacrifice you made. I have always dreamed of being a mother . . .*

Charlie read the card to the end. Then she sat back down on Euan's bed, steadying herself, the card still clutched in her hand and her head spinning.

# 48

Friday, October 31

Séraphine stepped off the plane and out onto the tarmac at Bordeaux airport. She put on sunglasses to shade her eyes from the bright winter sun. Her parents and the twins were waiting for her at Arrivals holding a sign with her name on it; she smiled when she saw it.

"Séraphine!" Mathilde called out. She and Benjamin ran up and encircled her waist, nearly knocking her off balance as they did so. She kissed her mother and father hello on the cheeks.

"We have the car just outside," Patrick said. "Here, let me get your suitcases." He took them from her and led the way across the car park.

Hélène hung back with her daughter and looped her arm through hers.

"So, your English must be fantastic by now," she said playfully.

"I suppose it is better," Séraphine said.

"And you taught them how to bake, I hope? You hear such terrible things about English food . . ."

"I taught them a few things, but I think they taught me more."

"Everyone in," Patrick called out. The twins piled into the car and Séraphine squeezed in with them.

They drove back toward the village and parked up under

the apple tree beside their home. Séraphine got out and inhaled the fresh air and sweet scents of their garden. It was as if time had stood still here. Apart from the seasonal changes to the landscape, as predictable as the sun rising and setting, the house seemed the same as ever. She could almost pretend that nothing had changed within her—but not quite.

That evening they sat down to a meal of steak and vegetables prepared by Hélène. Séraphine chewed without tasting, too preoccupied to join in with the conversation going on around her. She was desperate to tell her parents what she needed to say, what she'd been building up to saying, but the prospect terrified her. It had to be done, though—she owed it to herself, and she owed it to Carla.

She took a sip of wine and opened her mouth to speak.

"I have some news," she said, readying herself.

"We have some for you, too," Patrick told her.

"You do?" Séraphine said, startled.

"You first," Hélène said.

Séraphine's courage deserted her. "No—you go ahead."

"A few things happened when you were away," Hélène said. "We didn't want to worry you but—"

"What is it?" Séraphine's heart raced. "Is it to do with the twins?"

"No, no. It's not that."

"What is it?"

"It's your brother."

"Guillaume," she said, her voice coming out in a whisper.

"Yes. We heard from him a week ago."

"How is he? What did he say?"

"He says he got in trouble," Hélène said, furrowing her brow, anxious.

"We don't care what he did," Patrick said, taking his wife's hand. "All we care about is that he's safe."

"He said he wants to change. He didn't tell us everything . . ." Hélène took a breath. "Only that he wants to come home."

# 49

Friday, October 31

Letty put on a light inside the tearoom and unlocked the door to Charlie.

"Hello," she said. "What a nice surprise. Come in, it's freezing out this evening."

"Have you got time for a chat?"

"Of course."

Charlie had been waiting anxiously all day to talk to Letty alone. She'd canceled her lunch with Euan, knowing that there was no way she could sit and talk to him as if nothing had changed, when in reality she had found out something that would turn his world upside down.

Letty's eyes traveled down to the folder that Charlie was holding.

"Shall we go up to the flat and talk there?"

"Yes, sure."

Letty switched off the till, then led Charlie through a door at the back of the café to a set of stairs. They walked up them together and entered into a hallway lined with photographs.

"I'll put the kettle on. You sit down."

Charlie sat down on a maroon-and-gold-patterned armchair and looked around the room while Letty made tea in the kitchen. A fringed standard lamp stood next to the mantelpiece, and on a side table there were more photos—mainly of Euan as a young boy, one or two black-and-white ones of people who Charlie now knew to be Letty's parents. The lovebirds were up in a cage hanging by the kitchen, chattering to each other.

The small arched window looked out over the sea, and from the higher vantage point Charlie could see the lighthouse in the distance. As she'd been driving up from London, it hadn't felt like leaving home—instead, she realized now, it had felt as if she was returning there.

Letty placed a gold-trimmed tea set on the table. "You'll have had your fill of tea these past few weeks, I expect. But you see I always have a cup this time in the evening. Once the customers have gone, it's my turn." She smiled. Those china-blue eyes, so pale they were almost translucent—and yet, Charlie knew now, they didn't give a thing away.

Charlie poured a cup and added milk. She took a moment to think about how to phrase what she'd come to say.

"I know why you're here," Letty told her.

"You do?"

"Oh yes. A smart girl like you, I wondered if you'd figure it out. Then when I realized I'd left a few personal things in those folders, I was certain you would."

"You've kept it a secret all these years," Charlie said.

"How could I not?"

"But all this time, you've kept the truth from Kat?"

"I didn't have a choice," Letty said. "Kat had a mother who wanted and loved her more than anything in the world—and I made her a promise before she died, that I would never tell Kat what happened. That once, for a brief, precious time, she was my daughter."

"But why—"

"Why did I give her up? Is that what you're going to ask?" Letty said.

Charlie nodded.

"I gave her to the people I knew could make her happiest, and who I knew she would bring light into the life of, and I've never regretted it."

"It wasn't . . . Her dad wasn't John, was it?"

"Can you imagine it?" Letty said, pushing away her tea, which was untouched. "How terrible a person I was?"

Tears came to Letty's eyes.

"Euan was young still, and John was traveling with his work all the time." She brushed the tears from her eyes. "All the other mothers around here seemed to find it easy, but the truth was I found it hard to cope on my own. I was lonely back then."

She took a sip of tea, then replaced the cup in its saucer.

"My parents had recently left the tearoom to us, and I was trying my best to run things here. John loved Euan—of course he did—but he also loved his work. There are no excuses. I hurt John, and I started a lie that has lasted—well, until now."

"What happened, with Kat's dad?"

"A man came back into my life when John was away on one of his trips—someone I'd loved when I was younger, and I was foolish enough to think still loved me. He offered comfort, I suppose." She shook her head. "But then John came back, and I found out I was carrying a child. I knew that it wasn't John's.

"Not having the baby wasn't an option. With Euan I'd seen what an honor it is to bring a child into the world. I wouldn't judge anyone else for their choices, but for me . . . I knew I wanted to have her. But I wasn't prepared to lie to John about it. I told him from the start what had happened."

"How did he react?"

"Life's a funny thing. He didn't react the way I'd expected, not at all. He said he wanted to raise the child as his own. He loved me, and he knew he'd let me down by not being there. It was me—I was the one who couldn't do it. It just didn't feel right. I knew her life would be a lie. She didn't deserve that."

"So you gave her away."

"I knew them well, the Murrays. They were regulars in here, always chatting and friendly. They used to play with Euan while I worked. We became close, and one day Kat's mother confided in me that they'd been trying for a baby for years, but they hadn't been able to have one. She was trying to be positive about it, but you could see it was eating her up inside."

Charlie tried to imagine what that must be like, longing for a child that you couldn't have. She felt a deep sympathy for Kat's mother, a woman she didn't even know.

"So I had something she wanted," Letty continued, "and she had something I did—a relationship that was honest, and uncomplicated. I knew mine and John's could never be that again. We loved each other so much—I loved the bones of him and, if I'm honest, I still do. But when I went away and had that baby—had Kat—away from prying eyes, and handed her over, I lost a part of me.

"As much as John tried to forgive me, I'm not sure he ever could, any more than I could forgive myself. Over the years we grew apart, and I threw myself into my work here, trying to forget about it. Kat—such a beautiful little girl she was— she'd come in from time to time, and we formed a friendship, the one we have to this day. Her mother died, but it still wouldn't have been right for me to step in and tell her the truth, no matter how badly I wanted to. When I handed her over, I did so with the promise to her parents that I wouldn't ever try to get her back."

"And so your ex-husband knows about her?"

"John? Yes, he always has. He knows her. In many ways it's a small place, this town."

"So he knows her, just like Euan does." The words came out sounding flat, an accusation. Charlie hadn't intended it—and yet she didn't take it back.

Letty nodded. "Yes, like Euan does."

"Didn't they live nearby?"

"Yes. I had to tell Euan something, so when he was old enough I explained that I'd had to give a child away. You know Euan, he's so laid-back he's set to fall over. He didn't even flinch—simply gave me a hug and said it must've been a difficult decision for me. I love that boy," she said, wiping away a tear. "But I couldn't tell him who it was, not when Kat was in the dark herself. It wouldn't have been fair."

"It could have been him who found the card," Charlie said. "That's what you were thinking might happen, isn't it?"

"Perhaps. But I didn't plan it."

"These things have a way of coming to the surface, don't they?"

"You'll tell her, won't you?" Letty said, looking concerned.

"I don't think it's my place to. If you want, I'll do what I can to forget I ever found out."

"No," Letty said, shaking her head. "You came to me today for a reason. This happened for a reason, you walking into my tearoom, just when life had fallen quiet." She took a deep breath. "It's time."

# 50

Saturday, November 1

"I'm going into the village," Séraphine said, looking in through the kitchen doorway.

"We're baking, look," said Mathilde excitedly, waving a lump of dough in the air. "Raspberry tarts."

"Delicious. Save some for me."

"OK, then," Hélène said. "Enjoy yourself. Could you pick up a bottle of wine for this evening? Anna and Ravi are stopping by."

"Sure. It would be nice to see them again. I've got some photos to show them. See you later." She kissed her mum on the cheek.

"See you," Benjamin called out. "Get us some sweets."

Hélène shook her head and looked back at her eldest daughter. "No more sweets for them."

The twins squabbled over the dough and Séraphine took the opportunity to have a quiet word with her mother.

"Are you OK?" Séraphine whispered.

"Yes, yes. Nervous. But OK. His bed is all made up. He said he's getting here at midday tomorrow."

"Good. It'll be all right. Maybe not immediately, but it will be. It'll just take time."

"I know," she said, biting her lip.

"And Dad?"

"He's gone out for a walk. He said he needed to clear his head."

Séraphine squeezed her mother's hand gently and saw that there were tears in her eyes.

"I thought he was never coming home. But he is. He's coming back to us."

Séraphine picked up her bike and cycled into the village. She passed the fields and vineyards, the thin wheels of her bike occasionally bumping along on the rougher bits of road. She cycled into the town square.

A whistle made her turn. There, by the bakery door, was Carla—in jeans and a white T-shirt, her long brown hair held back by the sunglasses perched on her head. "Hey, stranger," she called out.

Séraphine set down her bike and went to hug Carla. They held each other closely and Séraphine whispered into her ear, "I've missed you so much."

"You only want me for my brioche!" Carla said. "Come and sit down."

They sat at the outside table, and Carla took the freshly baked cakes out of a brown paper bag, and asked her friend in the bakery to bring out two Orlanginas.

"You look different," Carla said, considering Séraphine. "Your hair's longer, and . . . I don't know, I can't put my finger on it. It's something more than that."

"I feel different," Séraphine said. "It changed me, going away. It changed the way I think."

Carla raised an eyebrow, wary.

"In a good way," Séraphine said, smiling and reassuring

her with a touch of her hand. "When I left here I was so scared. Scared of being myself, scared of my feelings making my decisions for me—being out of control. But being away from here, away from you, brought home to me just how much I care about you. And it taught me that there are so many ways to live, so many ways to create a family where people love one another. I don't have to fit in some tiny box anymore."

Carla smiled. "I'm glad. It hurt a lot at first, your leaving. I knew that part of you wanted to escape—and that that meant being apart from me. You seemed so determined to deny what you were feeling that I thought you might just succeed. But once I'd decided to wait for you—first to change your mind, and then to come home—I realized it wasn't difficult at all, it was easy. There was nothing else I wanted to do other than be here for you when you finally came home."

"And here you are." Séraphine smiled. "Thank you." She squeezed Carla's hand.

"There was something sweet in it, toward the end, the waiting. Hearing from you and receiving these lovely little gifts. It made me crave you, like when a good cake is baking in the oven and all you have is the scent of it."

Séraphine laughed. "Well, now you have the whole cake."

They looked at each other for a moment, a deep sense of intimacy between them, a secret that still wasn't ready to be shared.

"So what have I missed here in the village?" Séraphine said lightly.

"Oh, an awful lot," Carla replied, with a mischievous smile. "You know how quickly life moves around here. I mean, you have Madame Augustin—she has finished knitting that new hat for her grandson and it suits him perfectly. Jeanne, the librarian, was seen kissing that *younger man* who lives by the bridge . . . Oh, and little Samuel has got a new puppy. A brown one. I think that covers it."

Séraphine laughed. "I knew I could trust you to keep me informed."

"But most importantly, I hear your family have had some good news."

"The grapevine got there before me?" Séraphine said.

"Yes, I'm afraid so."

"Guillaume's coming home tomorrow. I still can't quite believe it."

"Your parents must be happy."

"They are. Anxious, but happy. It feels as if a weight has been lifted."

"You can start to talk again, build bridges."

"Exactly." Séraphine stared down at her brioche, unable to meet Carla's gaze. "You know, with all this going on, I haven't said anything—about us."

"I thought as much." Carla took a sip from her bottle of Orangina.

"It didn't seem right, telling them then."

"Don't worry, I understand. They have enough to think about right now. They need to focus on Guillaume coming home. And that really is good news."

"It's going to be a long journey, but he has started. He's taken the first steps."

Carla looked at Séraphine, her gaze steady, then spoke. "And so have you."

# 51

Saturday, November 1

"Dad, would you be able to look after Leo for an hour or two?"

"Sure, love. You going out?"

"Yes, just down to the tearoom, I had a call from Letty. She wants to talk to me about something."

"Of course, you go. Enjoy yourself. I'll get Leo bathed and put to bed."

Leo pushed his trains around the track on the living room floor, lost in his own world.

Kat kissed her son on the head. "Thank you, Dad. It's great to have you back."

"It's good to be back."

"The traveling's out of your system?"

"I think so. For a while, at least." He smiled. "Although I did get another guidebook out of the library. Apparently Brazil is the place to travel to these days."

"You're unstoppable."

He started humming "The Girl from Ipanema" to himself.

"Stop winding me up!" She nudged him playfully.

"What's that you've got?" He pointed to her Thermos flask.

"Hot spiced apple with cinnamon," she said. "There's yours." She pointed to a mug on the kitchen table. "Can't have you feeling left out."

⌐

Letty and Kat sat out on the terrace, the Closed sign hanging in the door of the tearoom behind them. Letty was wearing a red woolen coat, and Kat was wearing her parka, with the hood up. They held mugs of the apple drink Kat had brought.

"This is good," Letty said, taking a sip. "The cinnamon comes through nicely."

"Thanks. You sure you're warm enough out here?"

"Yes." Letty looked distracted. "Nothing like fresh air after a long day."

"Are you OK?"

"Kat, this isn't easy. And there's no right way to do it. I have something I need to tell you."

"You're sounding very serious all of a sudden." Kat laughed. She'd expected Letty to smile, but her expression didn't change. She was calm and composed, but Kat saw a shadow of something else there, an uncertainty in her eyes.

"What is it?"

"I haven't always been straight with you over the years." Letty spoke slowly, with her hands crossed in her lap. "I haven't been honest with you at all, in fact."

"What do you mean?" Kat asked, confused.

"I had my reasons, and it seemed right at the time not to tell you the truth."

"And now something's changed."

"Yes."

"Don't leave me in suspense," Kat laughed nervously.

"You know how much your parents wanted you in their lives."

"Aha."

"Well, in order for that to happen, someone else had to let you go."

"Right."

"But that doesn't mean the other person didn't love you too."

Kat looked at Letty questioningly, and she continued.

". . . Doesn't love you too."

"Wait," Kat said. "What are you getting at?"

She looked at Letty again—her pale blue eyes honest and open, her expression earnest.

"I'm your mother. I gave you away."

The words hit Kat like a blow to her stomach.

"What?" she said, reeling. "No, you're not." She shook her head.

Fragments of conversations, memories in snapshots, came back to Kat. But nothing fit together.

"I wish things had happened differently," Letty said. "You're my daughter—or at least you were once, for a short while."

"Don't say that," Kat said. "I don't know why you're saying this, but I don't believe you."

Letty stared at her calmly.

Kat got to her feet silently, unable to process what she'd heard, then turned and walked away without saying good-bye.


Kat walked through the backstreets to her house, Letty's words playing on a loop in her mind. What reason could she possibly have for lying to her?

The evening already felt like a blur. Kat struggled to remember how the conversation had even started. All she could recall was the final exchange, those words, the way they had taken the wind out of her.

She climbed the stairs to her flat, putting one foot in front of the other on autopilot. She wasn't going to be drawn into this. Letty was confused. It happened to people. They got older, and memories twisted and turned. It pained her to think of Letty being unwell, losing the sharpness of mind Kat had always admired—but that had to be what was happening. It was the only explanation.

Kat settled on that thought. Devastating as it was to comprehend—it was the only thing that made sense. She had to stay strong. She'd find a way to support Letty, work through this. Nausea nagged at her, making the short walk home seem arduous.

Her dad met her at the front door. "You're home early," he said brightly. "I've only just got the young chap off to bed."

Kat came in and took her coat off in silence, hanging it up in the hall.

"He wanted a book after his bath, and then begged me for another, then another." He laughed. "In the end, we got through nearly a whole library's worth."

Kat stood, rooted to the spot. She felt powerless to move.

"Are you OK, love? You don't look well. You're very pale."

She looked up at her father—his kind, crinkled eyes. The welcoming arms that had comforted her the other day, and so many times. He could make this better.

"I think I need to sit down." He held her hand and walked with her through to the living room, where they both sat down.

"Letty was behaving very strangely," Kat said. She could hear the words come out of her own mouth, but felt detached, as if someone else was saying them.

"Was she?" her father said gently.

"I think there's something wrong," Kat said. "She's not herself."

"Oh dear. What makes you think that, love?"

Kat had a lump in her throat, and found it difficult to form the words. "She said something that didn't make any sense."

"She did?"

A flicker of unease passed across his face.

"It seems silly even repeating it," Kat said. "Which is what I mean—she's normally so sensible. Then she comes out with something weird like this."

"I think perhaps you should tell me."

"She . . ." Kat stalled. The words slipped away from her, superstitious thoughts creeping in. Perhaps if she said it she would make it real. She brushed the thoughts aside. It was ridiculous to think that way.

She spoke quickly, and was matter-of-fact. "She thinks she's my mother."

"OK," Kat's dad said slowly. "I wondered when this would happen."

"When what would happen?" Kat said, confused. "Has she said the same to you?"

He put his hand on hers.

"I'm sorry," he said, his voice soft.

"This isn't real—" She shook her head.

"What Letty told you is true. I would rather have been the one to tell you, but she must have her reasons."

"It can't be," Kat said. But her certainty was fast evaporating. The denial was now nothing more than a weak attempt to shore up her fragile sense of reality.

"Your mother wanted you to think of us as your parents," her father explained. "If you'd wanted to trace your birth mother, this might have come out sooner. But you always insisted you didn't want to know."

"I didn't want to meet a stranger trying to take my mother's place, no," Kat said firmly. "I might not have known her for long, but I still feel loyalty toward her."

She hesitated, what her father had said slowly lodging in her mind. "But Letty? *Letty?*"

She thought of her friend's high cheekbones, the shape of her eyes, her chin. Flashes of her own features came to her. The similarities were undeniable. They must always have been, and yet only now were they becoming clear. How had she never noticed before?

"It's an awful lot to take in, I know," her father said. "We didn't want to deny Letty the chance to be part of your life. We didn't bring the two of you together, you found each other naturally. It would have been wrong to stand in the way of your friendship."

"All my life she's been there," Kat said, dazed.

"How did you leave things with her?"

"I told her it wasn't true. Then I walked out. I just left." She rubbed her brow. "I didn't even say good-bye. I should have at least said that."

"Don't worry about Letty. She'll be OK."

"I think I need to sleep," Kat said. "I feel dizzy."

"Let's get you to bed."

She walked into her bedroom and her dad put the bedside lamp on, giving her a hug and a kiss good night. In the dim light, alone, she felt safer. She wanted to stay in here. Not talk to anyone. She wanted to stay in her room, in bed, until the whole thing went away.

The next day, Kat forced herself to get out of bed and get dressed, then she took Leo to the park. The ground was wet from the rain overnight. Kat's dreams had been vivid, full of the storm, and flashes of her childhood, distant memories of her mother. She'd woken up in a cold sweat. There was a fleeting period of grace before memories from the previous evening had come back to her. The truth—concrete now—in the room with her. Letty was her mother. She was Letty's daughter. They were tied together and always would be in a way she'd never imagined. Even now she didn't want to imagine it.

That morning she was grateful for Leo's constant questions about the movement of the moon and sun, his dreams of space travel distracting her from the unsettling question of who she was. In the playground Leo went straight for the swings, and Kat pushed him. The rhythmic action lulled her.

"Higher!" Leo called out, his Wellington boots kicked forward in excitement. "I want to get right up to the sun."

"I'll push him," came a voice. "I can do it super high."

Kat turned and saw Zoe by her side, smiling.

"Hi, Zoe," she said, making herself smile back.

"Can I?" Zoe asked again.

"Of course." She stepped away. "Leo, this is Zoe. She's going to push you for a while. She'll get you to the sun."

Leo whooped in excitement.

"You'll be careful, won't you?" she whispered to Zoe.

"Yes," she whispered back. "Don't worry."

Kat looked over and saw Adam on a bench nearby. He waved. In spite of everything, her heart lifted to see his warm smile. "I'll be on the bench over there," she explained to Leo.

She sat down next to Adam. "Morning," she said.

"Hi," he said. There was a silence between them, and a gentleness in his expression that told Kat all she needed to know.

"You've heard, haven't you?" she said, pulling her coat more tightly around her.

He nodded. "Euan told me last night."

"So he didn't know either," Kat said flatly. "I suppose he wouldn't have."

"He knew he had a sister. But he had no idea it was you. I think he's still in shock."

"Well, that makes two of us." Kat managed a weak smile.

"How are you feeling?" Adam asked.

"Strange."

"Strange how?"

"Do you really want to know?" Kat asked.

"Yes." His answer was so simple. Kat's urgent longing for resolution, to know every part of the truth seemed to slip away when she looked into his eyes. Maybe it was too early to know everything. Maybe what she was feeling right then was the truth—the one that mattered.

Kat thought of the way she'd felt when Letty had delivered the news—it hadn't been one statement, but two. *I'm your mother. I gave you away.* It was the second one that had stayed with Kat, that had echoed in her dreams. Letty was someone she loved and admired—someone she believed had chosen her as a friend. But now, things were different—she knew the truth, that Letty had found her wanting. Not good enough. Letty had chosen to give her away. Her father, the man who'd always told her to tell the truth, no matter what—had lied to her for years. For her entire life. He might not have said the words, but he'd lied by omission, again and again.

"You want to know how I feel?" Kat said again. "I'm angry," she said. She bit the inside of her lip, but couldn't stop hot tears spilling onto her cheeks. "I'm angry, Adam. The people I trusted most in this world aren't who I thought they were. I don't know what it is I should be feeling, but the truth is I'm furious with them: Letty, my dad—even my mum, who's not here to defend herself."

Adam put his hand over hers and held it. She looked up at him, her heart beating harder in her chest. It felt natural, him being there.

"Be angry," Adam said. "I would be."

Her tears came faster. Here with Adam, she didn't feel that she had to be strong.

"It's going to be OK, Kat," he said. "You're going to be all right."

# 52

Sunday, November 2

Charlie was sitting with Euan in his living room, his eyes glazed over, a cup of coffee in his hand that must have been cold by now. The night before, the two of them had been ready to leave the house to go out for a meal when Letty had called. She wanted to talk to him, and no, it couldn't wait.

Euan had questioned what could be that important. The restaurant booking would have to be canceled, he'd muttered, disappointed. He and Charlie had so little time together as it was, and now, because of this, they would lose an evening. It had been difficult for Charlie to keep quiet, knowing what she knew. She'd simply encouraged him to take his mother's request seriously, and to go and see her.

This—the news about Letty, and Kat, and Euan—was one of those revelations that come from nowhere, she thought. You start the day thinking that it matters which cereal you choose for breakfast, what the headlines are, or whether you're five minutes late for work. She'd been there once, when she'd heard about Ben. That hadn't been as serious, of course, but all the same, it had taken only a handful of words for the elements of her everyday life to be rendered mere trivialities.

Now, for Euan and for Kat, two of the people Charlie cared about most, the cereal, the clock, the headlines, wouldn't matter anymore. And they probably wouldn't matter again for a long time.

"I knew there was someone," Euan said, his words coming slowly. "I knew I had a sister out there somewhere. But I never for one moment imagined it would be Kat."

When Euan had gotten home the night before he hadn't wanted to talk. He must have known that Charlie knew. Letty would have explained, Charlie was sure of that. But when he came to bed, he'd simply asked Charlie to hold him. They'd lain in his bed, limbs intertwined, while the rain lashed against the window. Both of them had remained silent, their breathing steady, waiting for sleep to come. Charlie had resisted the urge to ask, taming her natural inclination to draw out all of the details of a scenario as quickly and fully as possible. She could sense that what he needed most was space to take it in. In the morning, however, he'd been ready to tell her.

"Mum told me half of the story when she and Dad separated. She said she'd given away a baby girl, because she wasn't my father's child and she couldn't face living a lie. I assumed the girl had grown up somewhere else, not here in Scarborough. Kat lived so close to me. We weren't friends, but we could have been."

Charlie put her hand on his arm, looked at him to show she was still listening.

"I feel such an idiot," Euan said. "I look at the two of them and I don't know how I missed it. You said you saw Mum in me—but the two of them are far more similar, aren't they? The shape of their faces. Their eyebrows, the way they light up when they're about to say something they think is funny." The flicker of a smile came to his lips.

"I know what you mean," Charlie said. "I can see it too

now. But of course you're not an idiot. How could you have noticed something when you had no idea that it was even a possibility?"

"I'm glad you're here," Euan said, stroking her arm.

"I'm glad I'm here too," Charlie said. "I'm sorry I . . ." She searched for the words. "Well, sorry I made this all happen."

"My mum made it happen, not you," he said, shaking his head. "It was her choice. It was then and it is now."

"Kat must be a mess," Charlie said, frowning.

"You should go and see her."

"I know. I will. I don't want to leave it too long. I'll head round there now."

Charlie and Kat were in the kitchen of her flat that afternoon, while Leo watched cartoons in the front room.

"So you've been out today," Charlie said, looking at the wet anoraks in the hallway.

"Yes, I took Leo to the park." Kat's voice was quiet and flat, as if she were only half there. It pained Charlie to see the spirit gone out of her. "I needed to clear my head. I'm guessing Euan's told you everything."

"He's told me about what he and Letty discussed, yes. In terms of you . . . Kat, there's something I need to explain," Charlie said. "I want you to know that I'm on your side, completely. But I'm part of the reason Letty spoke to you, why everything came out the way it did last night."

"You?" Kat's eyes were wide, but the expression was blank rather than annoyed, as if she was too drained of emotion to respond. "You're in on this too?"

"I'm not in on it—"

"You know what, Charlie, I don't think anything you say

would even shock me anymore. First Jake, then this with Letty and my dad."

Charlie took a deep breath. Even if it went down badly, she had to at least explain.

"I found a note, from your mother to Letty. Thanking her, saying she'd always dreamed of being a mother, and now she was—to you. It didn't spell everything out, but it was clear enough for me to put two and two together."

"Where did you find the note?"

"It was mixed up with some other documents from the café. I wasn't snooping—you may not believe that, but in this case it's true. Perhaps deep down Letty wanted someone to find out the truth. Who knows."

Kat nodded for her to carry on talking.

"I was torn—I wasn't sure whether to come to you first. It felt wrong that I'd found out while you and Euan still didn't know. But I didn't want to give you, or both of you, a fragment of the story, with the risk that you wouldn't want to find out the rest. Letty's a good person—I felt certain she would have done what she did for a reason, and she deserved a chance to explain that to you both."

She waited for Kat to say something, but she sat in silence, picking at the worn Formica on the kitchen counter with her nail. Minutes went by before she looked up and said, "What about me and Euan?" The tone of her voice hardened: "What about what *we* deserved?"

"Letty wants so much to make things right," Charlie said.

Kat shook her head. "I have no idea who I am anymore," she said. "I feel like Letty tricked me. Lied to me. My dad too. And now I find out you knew . . ."

Charlie felt a tug at her heart. "Kat—please believe me. It was never my intention to keep anything from you. I suppose it must seem as if I went behind your back, but I only did it to make sure that, when you did find out, you found out the whole truth. I never wanted to hide anything from you."

Kat bit her lip. "I'm sorry. I'm taking this out on you. Classic shooting the messenger, isn't it?"

"It's understandable," Charlie said. "I'd probably shoot me."

"The thing is, even if I was annoyed—and I'm not, not really—I need a friend more than ever right now."

Charlie took a chance, knowing she might be pushed away. She stepped toward Kat and held out her arms. After a moment's hesitation Kat came toward her, leaning her head on her shoulder, and Charlie held her close in a hug.

On Monday morning, Charlie and Euan were sitting in his kitchen over a breakfast of French toast and strawberries, winter sunshine coming in through his large windows.

"Are you trying to persuade me to stay with all this?" Charlie said, pointing to the food.

"Shamelessly. Is it that obvious?" Euan smiled.

"It's very tempting."

"What a weekend, eh," Euan said, putting a hand through his hair. "I bet you came up here expecting a big romantic reunion . . ."

"Which we had," Charlie said.

"Yes, which we had. But then you end up in the middle of all this."

"It was my choice. I could have put away that card and made myself forget about it."

Euan rolled his eyes playfully. "As if you could ever have done that."

"You're right."

She went around to his side of the table and put her arms around him from behind, kissing the side of his face. "It might not have been the weekend either of us expected, but it's still been perfect."

He turned and kissed her.

"I wish this wasn't another good-bye," she said. "So soon after the last time."

"There are other options, you know," he said.

"Like what, you coming to live in London? I can't see that somehow."

"I could. I will," Euan said. "If that's what it takes."

"No," Charlie said. "Anyway, you have to see your project through here. But my job isn't moving."

"We can still see each other at weekends," Euan said. "Maybe not every weekend, but . . ."

"This situation sucks." Charlie wrinkled her nose.

"Yes. It does."

"Because I like you. I like you a lot," she said, looking down.

"I made you say it," Euan said, taking her hand and smiling.

"You didn't make me." She laughed. "I wanted to say it."

"I don't care why you said it," Euan said, beaming. "Just that you did."

# 53

Monday, November 3

Séraphine was sitting in the library at the chateau, putting the books she'd bought in England, and the ones Kat had given her, away tidily on the shelves. Today was a day for settling back in at home, she'd decided. It weighed on her mind a little that she needed to start looking for a teaching job—and that she couldn't live with her parents forever—but all of that could wait another day.

Her thoughts were interrupted by her mobile ringing in her pocket: Kat.

"Hello!" she said, delighted.

"Hi, Séraphine," Kat said.

"Hey, so lovely to hear your voice." Séraphine took her phone over to the window seat and curled her jean-clad legs up under her. "I was just thinking of you, funnily enough. I was putting those Agatha Christie books you gave me away on the shelves in our library."

"You have a library?" Kat marveled. "I really must get one of those."

Séraphine laughed. "We have a little more space here."

"So how is everything?"

"It's good to be back." Since she'd been home, Séraphine had felt more settled, complete. Her outlook had shifted.

"Did it all go OK with Carla? How was it, seeing her again?"

Séraphine shut the library door and lowered her voice to a whisper. "It was fantastic. We just clicked back—the two of us, as if we hadn't been away from each other at all. And yet we've grown in the time we were apart, we've been through it together. You know, Kat, in some ways going to England was a good test—you know? I've never been more sure that I want to be with her."

"I'm pleased to hear that," Kat said. "I hope to meet Carla one day soon. And how are things with your family?"

"Busy." Séraphine thought of the excitement and upheaval in the household with her brother's return the day before. "And interesting."

"Oh yeah?"

"You know I told you about Guillaume? My brother who disappeared? Well he's back living with us again."

"Wow. And that's good, I hope?"

"It's good, yes. Not entirely straightforward—he still has some things to sort out—but it's good."

"Is he settling back in OK?"

"Yes. The twins are delighted, and I think playing with them is a good distraction for him too. We haven't talked much about what happened yet."

"And what about you—have you told anyone about you and Carla yet?"

"No," Séraphine said. She paused for a moment. "It's not that I don't want to. I do. But it never seems to be the right time."

"Is Carla OK with that?"

"Yes. No. She wants us to be out in the open. So do I. But now I'm here—it's harder than I thought it would be. I have a lot to lose."

Every time Séraphine tried to imagine telling her parents,

the scene would end in one of them—usually her mother—storming out. She couldn't picture them understanding or accepting it. What would they say at church? That was what her mother would be worried about. Last night, in bed, she'd wondered if her parents would go so far as to cut her out of the family.

"But what will happen if you don't tell them?" Kat said.

"My life will keep on being a lie," Séraphine said. "Not so brilliant, I suppose, when you look at it that way."

The line fell silent for a moment.

"Enough about me," Séraphine said. "How are you?"

"Ugh," Kat said.

"Ugh, what?"

"Ugh—everything's a mess."

"What's happened?"

"How long have you got?"

"There's no hurry."

"I have no idea where to start, Séraphine. The last couple of days have been so insane. I feel as if I want to laugh and cry all at once."

"Start at the beginning. Take your time. BREATHE."

Séraphine heard Kat take a deep breath, then she started to talk. She told Séraphine everything—what had happened with Letty, and the new relationship she had to Euan. How she'd nearly fallen out with Charlie, until they managed to talk things through . . .

"So, let me get this straight," Séraphine said, her mind reeling with all the information. "Since I saw you last, you've gained a mother—and a brother?"

Kat laughed. "I told you it was insane. Yes, Euan's my half brother."

"You weren't exaggerating. That is crazy."

"I know. It's been pretty awful."

"Awful?" Séraphine said, slowly processing what she'd heard. "I mean, I can understand that it would be a huge shock. I'm not trying to say otherwise. But does it have to be a bad thing?"

"I don't know. I'm not sure I can get past feeling betrayed about it all. Letty lying to me, my dad lying to me . . ."

"That will take time, sure," Séraphine said. "But look at it this way. You've gained someone new in your life—two people, in fact. You haven't lost anyone."

"I don't know. I feel as if I have."

"Do you think talking to Letty again would help?"

"I'm not sure I'm ready. I passed the Seafront on my walk home. It was the strangest thing, walking by and not going inside to say hi. I don't think I've ever done that."

"Letty doesn't have to be a mother to you, you know," Séraphine said. "You don't have to accept her as anyone other than who you want her to be."

"I know it sounds strange, but Letty's the one I feel I've lost."


Séraphine walked upstairs to her room, thinking about Kat and wishing she could be with her, if only for an evening, to help her feel stronger again. She felt sure that Letty would be suffering too, possibly regretting the decisions she'd made.

She looked into Guillaume's room. He was sitting on his bed, dark-blond hair covering one eye, his acoustic guitar on his lap, strumming it quietly.

"I've missed that sound," she said.

He looked up at her and smiled. "Come in."

She closed the door behind her and sat on his beanbag. "So here you are again," she said.

"Here I am again," he said distantly.

"Are you feeling OK?"

He nodded. "Better than I thought I would. I think the hardest part has been realizing what I put Mum and Dad through."

She raised an eyebrow.

"What I put you all through."

"Do you want to talk about it?" she said. "What happened?"

"I guess I had to hit rock bottom before I realized that something needed to change. That rock bottom was a police cell, and knowing I had no home to go back to."

"Were you staying with friends, before that?"

"I thought they were friends," Guillaume said, brushing his hair out of his eyes. "But they weren't, not real friends. Acquaintances that disappeared when I needed them."

"We thought about you all the time," Séraphine said. "Mum and Dad never gave up hope that you'd get in touch."

"I should have," he said. "But I couldn't face dealing with what was happening. I couldn't lie to them."

"Have you told them what happened to you?"

"Some of it. They were OK, you know. They took it better than I thought they would."

"That's good."

"You've got something you need to tell them too, don't you?" he said.

Séraphine felt the wind go out of her. "What do you mean?"

He couldn't know. She and Carla had always been so careful.

"That you're in love. And that it's not with whatever farmer's boy they'd pictured you marrying."

"How did you find out?" Séraphine said, her chest tight with anxiety.

He smiled kindly. "I've always suspected you wouldn't follow Mum and Dad's plan—but wasn't sure. Until now, that is."

She waited for something—him to reject her, disgusted. Or to laugh at her for thinking she was in love. One of the many things she'd prepared herself for.

"She must be someone special," Guillaume said. "You seem much happier these days."

"She is." Séraphine felt relief flooding through her. "And yes, I am happier."

"They'll cope, you know. Mum and Dad," he reassured her. "It might take time, but they love you. They'll have to get used to it."

"You think?"

"Yes. You should tell them."

Guillaume's laid-back acceptance and understanding lifted a weight from Séraphine's shoulders. He loved and cared about her for who she was—not who she loved. Perhaps he was right, and her parents would do the same.

# 54

Tuesday, November 4

Kat held Leo's hand and they approached the doors of the nursery. She smiled at the other mums with their pushchairs, and took Leo's scooter from him.

"You be good today," Kat said, bending down to kiss Leo bye. "Have fun. Grandpa is going to collect you this noon."

"Bye, Mummy," he said. She ruffled his hair and he sped off through the doors, his trainers flashing tiny red lights. At the bus stop, she rooted through her bag for something to read while she waited for the bus to the call center. Inside was a copy of *Indulge*—the one that Charlie had given her to pass on to Letty. She opened it—flicking past the photos of the places she, Charlie and Séraphine had visited together.

She came to Charlie's piece, the secret history—she'd been waiting for a quiet moment to read it. She read it, picturing Letty.

*. . . the tearoom came to its current owner when she had a young son, and with her husband working abroad, it was down to her to keep them going in financially challenging times. When the Seafront was broken into and vandalized, she had to repair the interior herself, and find furniture to replace the pieces that had been stolen . . .*

She pictured Letty finding chairs and tables, just as she'd had to do for her own flat when they'd run out of money. They'd both had their challenges in life, making decisions that seemed best at the time, and finding a way to be at peace with the consequences. Perhaps that was why Letty had always been able to understand how Kat was feeling, why she'd always instinctively known what kind of support Kat needed, been there for her whenever she'd needed it. Perhaps it was time for her to be there for Letty now.

The day at the call center had been long and tiring, but at least her second day in the job had been easier than the first. She'd begun to master the technique, there'd been fewer hang-ups when she called, and at the end of the day her boss had called her into his office to commend her on a good start. But everything about the office made her feel empty. After lunch she'd poured herself a cup of tea from the office machine, stale and flavorless with shelf-stable milk, and made a resolution to stick it out and make whatever money she could there while searching for alternative employment.

On her way home, she passed the Seafront. She thought of the way a warm teapot arriving at her table had turned around a bad day for her so many times. Letty would be in there now, Kat thought—doing the accounts or cleaning the tables.

She thought again of what Séraphine had said. Letty didn't have to be her mother.

She knocked on the window, and Letty let her in.

"Hi," Kat said. She felt a surge of mixed emotions. It was impossible to look at Letty's face now without comparing her features with her own, searching for some clue in each feature or mannerism as to who she truly was, and why Letty had given her away.

"It's so good to see you," Letty said. "Come in."

"I brought you something." She passed Letty the magazine. "Charlie wanted you to see it. I'm afraid I forgot I had it until now."

Letty looked through it and smiled. "So this is what you three were working away on. It turned out quite nicely, didn't it?"

"Yes." Kat sat down. "I read the feature, about this place."

"Oh yes."

"It's quite a story, isn't it, how you and John set it up. There was a lot I didn't know."

"Everyone has bad times and better times," Letty said. "That's life for you, isn't it?"

Their eyes met, and Kat felt a lump form in her throat.

"I've got so many questions," Kat said.

"Of course you do," Letty said, nodding. "And I'll do my best to answer them."

"I don't need to know about my father. Dad's all I need in that department," Kat said firmly. "But other things. A lot of other things."

Letty nodded earnestly.

"The only thing is, I don't think I'm ready for the answers yet," Kat said.

"Then let's just chat today, shall we?"

Kat smiled and nodded.

"We'll have time for the rest. Plenty of time," Letty said.

# 55

Christmas Day

"Séraphine, it's Christmas!" Benjamin said, bounding into her room and jumping onto her bed. Mathilde followed close behind. "You can't sleep through it, it's too exciting."

Séraphine pulled the duvet up over her head, groaning playfully. But even at six in the morning, she welcomed the intrusion. She'd missed the twins so much.

She and her mother had spent the day before making the final preparations for the Christmas meal. When Guillaume had come home at the start of November, all Hélène had talked about was how wonderful it would be to have Christmas as a family. But then things had changed.

For Séraphine the prospect of Christmas at home didn't seem wonderful at all. The atmosphere in the kitchen had been tense and frosty, and she couldn't help feeling her mother would have been more comfortable if she'd left her to cook alone, or, perhaps, disappeared altogether. Sometimes Séraphine was tempted to do just that, leave and be with Carla rather than making do with secret meetings and brief moments on the phone.

Things had been awkward in the house for a month, ever since Séraphine had told her mother and father about Carla. Hélène had been unable to accept what Séraphine said. She refused to hear the words, even going as far as covering her ears.

Patrick had taken the news slightly better. He seemed at

first not to quite understand, and had spent the day silently working in the frost-covered garden. He'd come back inside shortly before dinner and laid a hand calmly on Séraphine's shoulder, kissing her head. No words had been necessary.

But with her mother it had been a different matter. Since that day, she and Hélène had avoided talking, immersing themselves in entertaining the twins or preparing food.

Guillaume reassured Séraphine that Hélène would come round, that she just needed to get used to the idea. One evening Séraphine had even heard him trying to reason with his mother about it. She'd always imagined she'd be the one helping him settle back in at home—and yet instead he was the one trying to help her, in what seemed like an increasingly desperate cause.

In Bristol, Flo passed Charlie a carefully wrapped present from under the tree—a package sparkling with silver paper and ribbon. Charlie and Pippa's parents were in the kitchen making coffee and the room was relatively quiet for the first time that morning.

"Thank you," Charlie said, reading Pippa's handwriting on the tag and smiling over at her.

She unwrapped the package and took out a charcoal-gray silk dress from her favorite shop. "It's beautiful," she said.

"I wanted to get you something special. After all, if it wasn't for you, we might not all be here today."

She cast a glance over at Luke, who was on the sofa with Jacob on his lap.

"Pippa told me how much you helped when I was away," Luke said. "We're both very grateful."

"There was a point when I thought *I* might not make it

here," Charlie said. "That perhaps our last family Christmas had already happened."

"No way—there's no separating you two," Luke said.

"He's right," Pippa said. "I think we're all stuck with each other. And him—" She tilted her head in the direction of the kitchen.

"Are you talking about Grandpa?" Flo said, looking up from the present she'd been opening.

"No," Pippa said hurriedly. "Roger. I meant Roger the cat."

Flo narrowed her eyes suspiciously. "It didn't sound like that."

"Why don't we go and check on him?" Luke said. "I think Roger and Venus are quite confused about being here in Grandpa and Grandma's house. We don't want them getting lost."

"Sure." Flo hopped to her feet, and Jacob tagged along behind.

Pippa passed her sister a box of chocolate mints and unwrapped one for herself. "How's everything going back in London?" she asked.

"OK," Charlie said. That about summed it up—she was managing. She had time for her early morning runs, and that cleared her mind for the day ahead. The editions of the magazine that she'd edited had sold well, and Louis seemed pleased with her progress. The hours were long but that was what she'd signed up for. "You know how much I wanted this promotion. I'm lucky to have the job." It was all true, just not the whole truth.

"That's good, then."

"What about you?"

"Things are better, thanks. I'm thinking of doing some part-time study. I'll wait till Gracie's older, but there's a law degree I've been looking into and Luke's said he'll support me if I want to do it."

"That's terrific."

"I hope it's going to be a happier new year," Pippa said.

Charlie took hold of her sister's hand and squeezed it. "I'm sure it will be."


When Christmas lunch was over, Charlie climbed the stairs to her childhood room, a cup of tea in her hand. Sitting on the bed, she texted Euan.

> Merry Christmas! We've had a brilliant day. Perhaps our best one yet. The kids loved their presents. It feels as if I've spent the day with someone else's family, not mine! Even Dad's behaving himself. How are things with you? Cx

She sat down in her armchair and put her phone on the bedside table, waiting for his reply. She never had to wait that long.

It was seeing him that was the problem. Weeks would pass when they were both too caught up in their work to make the journey in either direction. She missed him—the warm, safe feel of his arms around her in bed, the tenderness of his kiss. The way he made her laugh after a long day. The prospect of coming home to him rather than her cold, empty flat, was something she yearned for constantly.


Séraphine went into the kitchen and found her mother arranging potatoes on a roasting tray. Her hair was up in a ponytail, and she wore a floral apron. Everything about the scene was familiar, apart from the blank look in Hélène's eye when she saw her daughter enter the room.

Séraphine couldn't wait until she could get away and spend

some time at Carla's, talking through with her how hard it was to have her mother push her away. The moments she and Carla spent together—even when they had something so serious hanging over them—were precious. Snatches of time in which Séraphine had the space to be herself, and be with someone she loved more deeply with each day that passed.

"I'm sorry, Mama," Séraphine said quietly.

Her mother's eyes were shiny, wet with tears. Séraphine felt crushed at the thought she was causing her mother—who had always done everything she could for her—pain. Hélène shook her head, silent.

"I wish this didn't hurt you so much."

Her mother turned to her, her blue eyes wide, her vulnerability suddenly so visible. "You're sure? Absolutely sure?"

Séraphine nodded.

"This isn't a phase? There's no chance you'll change your mind?"

"I've never been more certain about anything."

Hélène looked down.

Séraphine bit the inside of her lip—knowing that she couldn't ever undo what she'd said, and even if she could, the fact that it was true would always remain.

"Well," Hélène said, brushing her hands off on her apron. "I'd better start getting used to the idea, then."

She looked over at her daughter and the faintest of smiles appeared on her lips.

So, a pretty different sort of Christmas this year," Euan said, as he and Kat watched Leo playing with a friend on the South Sands on Boxing Day, dipping in and out of the waves in his Wellington boots.

"Yes. You didn't mind us being there, did you?"

"Of course not. It made the day. It was so much more special with Leo around. I've always wanted a nephew."

"And then you gained one overnight," Kat said, smiling.

"He's great, isn't he?" Euan said, as Leo waved a stick he'd found in the air.

"You can babysit whenever you want. Honestly, don't hold back." Kat grinned.

"It seems real now, finally," Euan said. "How have you been finding it with Mum?"

"We're talking more. We're getting there. It's taken time, but I feel lucky."

"You've not done badly with her. It could have been worse," Euan joked.

"Hopefully she feels the same."

"She adores you, Kat. She always has. I think it hurt her a lot not to be able to be honest with you. But when Mum makes a promise to someone, she sticks to it. One of the best things about her—though, in this case, it's the thing that's made her most unhappy. Until now."

As Kat's dad cleared the table of their feast of turkey and stuffing leftovers, Letty and Kat sat on the sofa, Leo playing with his new toy sharks by their feet.

"I think I prefer turkey sandwiches to Christmas dinner," Letty said.

"Probably because you're not rushing round after us all like you were yesterday."

"It's been a pleasure, having you all here," Letty said. "It means a lot—you know that, I hope."

Kat nodded.

"I didn't expect it. But yesterday was the happiest Christmas I've had in years," Letty said.

"I'm glad," said Kat. "We really enjoyed it. Dad did too."

"Good." Letty picked up the *Radio Times* and opened it. "Now, let's see what's on this evening, shall we?"

Kat put her hand on Letty's. "Actually there's something I've been wanting to ask you."

"Yes?"

"You know we talked about spending more time together? Well, I've managed to save some money over the past month, so for the first time in ages I have a little extra."

"That's good," Letty said. "What were you thinking of?"

"What about going abroad?"

"That's a lovely idea. Where?"

"To stay with Séraphine. You remember that patisserie course near her she talked about? I know you're as keen as I am to try that out."

Letty's face brightened.

"She's right by a budget airport, and she said she could get us onto the course at a discounted rate. Dad's offered to mind Leo."

"I could shut this place for a few days," Letty said, looking around.

"I'm sure the customers won't mind the tearoom being shut for a little while if you let them know there'll be an even better range of cakes when you get back." Kat smiled.

"Exactly," Letty said, with a broad smile. "You're on."

That'll be Adam," Euan said, when Letty's doorbell rang. Adam. His face came back into Kat's mind. She remembered how for one fleeting moment it had seemed as if everything was coming together for them—just before her life was turned upside down by the news about Letty.

"Hi, everyone," Adam said, stepping into the living room. His eyes met Kat's and he smiled warmly. "Good Christmas?"

"Yes," Kat said. His gaze rested on her, and her attraction to him flooded back. "How was yours?"

"Great, thanks. My parents are staying with us, and Zoe's grandparents have come over from France, so it's been a full house. She's had a brilliant Christmas—with a ridiculous amount of presents. Séraphine sent her a beautiful dress she'd made. Anyway, with all those live-in babysitters, I thought I should take advantage and go out for a drink for once. Do you want to join us, Kat?" Adam said.

Kat thought about it for a moment, but then shook her head. "I fancy a night in tonight, but thanks for the invite."

"Are you sure, love?" her dad said. "Letty and me can mind Leo."

"It's fine," she said, shaking her head. "Another time maybe."

Euan put on his coat. "OK, you guys, see you later." Adam nodded good-bye to Kat and the two men left.

Once he and Adam were out of the front door, Kat felt as if she'd made the wrong decision. She'd promised she'd start to be more open, grab life with both hands—and yet here, at the first opportunity, she'd let it slip away.

Annoyed with herself, she walked through to the kitchen and stared out the window. She wanted the coming year to be different, but it was clear her life wasn't just going to change by itself. She looked out at the sea and someone came into her mind.

She took out her phone and pressed her third speed dial. There was one person who she was sure would know what she should do.

"Charlie, hi," Kat said.

"Hello!" Charlie said cheerily. "Merry Christmas to you."

"Thank you, you too."

"How's it been?" Charlie asked.

"You know what, it's felt surprisingly normal."

"That's good. Same deal here. Must be something in the water." Charlie laughed. "Is Euan behaving himself?"

"He's been on top from—Leo's loved playing with him. He's so delighted to have a new uncle. Seems to have taken it all in his stride."

"I'm looking forward to joining you all up there in a couple of days."

"I can't wait to see you again. Euan's popped out for a drink. Adam came around and . . ."

"Oh?" Charlie said.

"God, Charlie. I'm so hopeless at this stuff," Kat said, biting her lip. "Can I ask your advice?"

"Of course," Charlie said. "Oh dear, am I really the closest you've got to a relationship expert?"

"Afraid so," Kat said, smiling. Speaking with Charlie made her feel instantly more relaxed, as if she wasn't on her own.

"You've realized that you've got feelings for Adam. And that in a way you've known it all along," Charlie said.

Kat laughed.

"But now you think you might have missed your chance. And anyway, how do you go about asking someone out when you've both been out of the game so long—and you have children to think about."

"That's pretty much it," Kat said. "Am I that transparent?"

"You're an open book," Charlie said. "Besides, it's impossible to see you and Adam together and not realize that you're both smitten with each other."

"I feel as if I'm fifteen again, Charlie. Where do I even start?"

"Why don't you go out for a drink?" Charlie said matter-of-factly.

"He just asked me. I'm an idiot, I said no—he and Euan were going out and . . ."

"Oh no, I don't mean like that. Last thing you want is to end up in the friendship box. Thank God you said no."

"Oh, right," Kat said, relieved she'd made the right decision.

"What about New Year's Eve? Have you got plans?"

"No," Kat said.

"Why don't you see what he's up to?"

"Just ask him?" Kat said, her heart pounding at the thought.

"Yes," Charlie said.

"What if he says no?"

"He won't say no, Kat. Trust me."

On New Year's Eve, Kat busied herself tidying the flat before Adam came round. She still couldn't quite believe that he'd said yes—that any minute now he'd be here at her flat. After speaking to Charlie she'd gotten up the guts to text and invite him around, and he'd said yes as if it were the most natural thing in the world. He made it seem easy. Perhaps it was—she'd just put her energy into sorting out Jake's problems for so long that it felt strange to be putting herself first.

She had lasagna on the side, ready to cook, and melting-middle chocolate pots in the fridge for later. Leo was at her dad's for the night, and the flat was quiet. In a good way, this time. She put some music on and straightened her dress.

The doorbell went, and she ran to the window to check.

"It's me," Adam said, looking up. He was holding a bottle of champagne in one hand and flowers in the other.

"Hi," she called down. She pressed the buzzer. She'd never felt surer that she was letting the right man in.

# 56

*Please join us to celebrate our wedding*

*The Spa Hotel, Scarborough*
*3 July at 3 P.M.*

*Dinner will follow the ceremony,*
*with a live band till midnight*

*Wear your best dancing shoes*

---

Charlie got into her car and put the top down. The sun was out in Scarborough and it warmed her bare shoulders, exposed in a strapless dress.

It was a perfect day for it, she thought, with a sweet sense of anticipation. The light was glinting on the water, the air fresh. You couldn't ask for a better day to get married.

Kat put on a knee-length silk dress and tied her dark hair, longer now, with a delicate cream ribbon. Warm air drifted in through the open window.

"You look pretty, Mum," Leo said, watching her from his place on the sofa in their living room. He was dressed in a suit with a white shirt, his secondhand shoes buffed to a shine.

"Thank you," Kat replied. She felt different. Yes, she felt pretty.

"It's a special day, isn't it?" Leo said, kicking up his heels.

"It is, yes."

"Why's that?"

She came and sat down beside him. "A wedding is a way for two people to show their friends and family that they love each other, and they always will."

"Like you love me?"

"No, different." Kat considered how best to explain it. "It's when you meet someone who's not family, but is just as important to you, and you decide you want to go through life with them. For some people it's a big, romantic red-heart kind of love, for others it's a calm, peaceful thing. Some feel they've found the other half of themselves, and that being with that other person makes their life more complete."

As she talked to her son, Kat realized how well the last words captured the way she felt about Adam—that sense of completeness. It was different from how things had been with Jake—where once there had been friction, there was now openness, and patience, and laughter. They still trod gently with each other and in the new relationship between their two families. They didn't take for granted Leo and Zoe's tentative acceptance of what was happening, they worked every day to try and build security for the two of them, in the hope that one day their unit might feel more solid.

"So it's a happy thing?" Leo said.

"Yes. It's a very happy thing, and it's going to be a happy day. And I'm proud I'll have the most handsome date there."

She tickled Leo, and he collapsed in giggles.

She picked up the invitation on the mantelpiece. "Come on then, shorty. Let's go."

Y ou have everything?" Carla called out to Séraphine from the hallway. Séraphine gave her handbag a final check—wallet, camera, keys, lipstick.

"*Oui*," she called back.

"You're sure you're ready?"

"No," Séraphine said, nipping back into the kitchen. "I forgot this." She held up a bottle of water and drank from it. "Do you want some? It's hot today."

"I'm fine, thanks. Now?"

Séraphine took a deep breath. "All set. I think."

A taxi tooted outside. "Come on, *ma belle*." Carla smiled. "Let's go."

W hich one?" Letty asked Euan, holding two flowers up for him to look at.

"The cornflowers," he replied. "Blue's always suited you."

She pinned the cornflower in her hair, behind her ear.

"Perfect," he said.

"Are you sure this dress looks OK?" she asked, smoothing down the fabric.

"It's very elegant," he said. "Works well with your tan."

"All that fresh air in France did me the world of good, you know."

"It shows, Mum. You seem way more relaxed."

"I had such a wonderful time with Kat. And Séraphine's family couldn't have been more welcoming."

"You deserved a good holiday," Euan said. "I see Kat's looking very happy too. Although I think there's more than one reason for that these days."

"She and Adam make a good pair, don't they?"

"They seem very much in love. In fact, I barely get a look in these days," Euan joked.

"You have your own life to be getting on with," Letty said, giving him a nudge.

"I suppose I do." Euan smiled. "Happens to the best of us."

"So, do I look OK?" Letty said again. "Only . . . it's been a while."

"You look lovely. Come on, Mum. Let's go."


Charlie arrived at the hotel and stepped out onto the terrace. Sunlight glinted off the black-and-white checkered floor where deck chairs were laid out. Between them, the aisle was strewn with red and white rose petals. She spotted Euan, in a pale gray suit, standing with friends. He caught her eye and smiled and she made her way over to him.

"Hello there," she said, kissing him on the lips. He squeezed her hand.

"You look beautiful, Charlie."


The guests all took their seats, sitting back in the deck chairs, chatting to one another. The band played the opening of "Here Comes the Sun," and a hush gradually fell over the crowd. This was it—the wedding was starting. Kat clutched Charlie's hand.

As one, they turned around.

As she saw the couple walking down the aisle, Kat's breath caught.

"They look stunning," she whispered in Charlie's ear.

Séraphine's hair was swept up, with red roses pinned into it, strands falling loose around her face. Her warm smile was highlighted with scarlet lipstick. In an ivory dress that hung to just below her knee, and high-heeled satin sandals, she held hands with Carla—a red strapless dress setting off her tanned skin, chestnut hair falling loosely to her shoulders. Séraphine walked up the aisle, glancing around and smiling at friends, while Carla's gaze was focused straight ahead.

The brides reached the top of the aisle, and the celebrant greeted them warmly. "We are gathered today to celebrate the wedding of Séraphine and Carla . . ."

Kat felt the tears build up in her eyes, and bit her lip. Charlie turned to her.

"You're crying already," Charlie said, with a smile.

"I can't help it," Kat whispered back. "Look at them. So happy."

After the ceremony, Charlie and Kat went up to congratulate the couple and Séraphine's family. In Séraphine's calls and e-mails since the start of the year, they'd heard about everything that had led up to that day—Séraphine's long, at times fraught, conversations with her parents about how she felt. How she now realized she'd always felt. The first time she'd explained that Carla, who served her mother croissants each weekend in the local patisserie, was the woman she was in love with. There had been false starts and disagreements along the way, but with time they'd managed to smooth everything out. In spring came her mother's full acknowledgment that her daughter had taken a different path to her own—with the welcoming of Carla into their family and a long lunch in the shade of the apple tree.

"A beautiful wedding," Kat said to Hélène and Patrick, kissing them both on the cheek.

"This is Guillaume," Séraphine said, introducing her brother to Kat. Dressed in a beige linen suit with sun-lightened hair, he smiled warmly. From everything that Séraphine had told her, Kat felt as if she already knew him, and she got the sense he felt the same way.

"It's lovely here, isn't it?" Hélène said, interrupting Kat's thoughts. "They had the choice of the Dordogne, or Barcelona—but no, they definitely wanted to get married here, in Scarborough. They said it had to be here." She smiled.

"We wanted to come to the place that brought us together, even while we were apart," Carla said. "For Séraphine, there was no question."

Charlie held out her champagne glass, and the waiter dutifully filled it. "It's brilliant to see you," she said to Kat.

"You too. And from the sounds of things I'm going to be seeing a lot more of you from now on," Kat said brightly.

"It's looking that way." Charlie smiled. "I can't decide if what I'm doing is insane or not. Last month I had a steady job and a flat, now I'm moving cities and starting from scratch again."

"It's fate," Kat said. "The buyers pulling out of Euan's development—you inheriting that money from your great-aunt. It was all meant to be."

"I still can't believe I'm doing it. Starting up my own restaurant."

"It's brilliant. I'm a bit envious, actually."

"You are? Well I have a sneaky suspicion we might find a way to get you on board, one way or another."

Kat smiled.

"Let's stay in touch on that. I'm not going anywhere, that's for sure. I'm pretty settled round here these days."

"You seem it," Charlie said warmly, glancing pointedly in Adam's direction.

"He's part of that, yes," Kat said. "But there's Leo and my dad and . . . well, I've got more family here than I know what to do with."

Charlie laughed.

"But it's perfect that I can stay here and still write for *Indulge*. I'm really enjoying it. The feature I did about the patisserie course in France was a treat to write. They've asked me to do a similar piece on a sorbet-making course for the next edition."

"Does that mean it's good-bye to the call center?" Charlie asked.

"Yes. Thank God," Kat said, laughing in relief. "I won't miss that place. I'm doing a couple of shifts at the tearoom to give us a steady income, then the writing as and when that happens. Jake's also doing a lot more to help these days."

"How are things with him?"

"Getting there," she said. "He's had some counseling, which has helped I think, and the business is going well. There'll always be a distance between us, but he's regained my trust. He's seeing Leo on his own now."

"That's good."

"Yes. With one thing and another this year, Leo's getting pretty spoiled," Kat said with a smile. "My flat looks like a toy shop."

⁓

The band started up, and Carla took Séraphine's hand, leading her to the dance floor for their first dance: Van Morrison's "Moondance."

They'd been practicing the dance in Carla's living room the past week, pulling back the rug and stepping barefoot on the flagstones, holding each other, sometimes serious, perfecting the movements, but usually laughing.

Here, surrounded by family and friends, it felt different. Magical. Something that only six months before, Séraphine could never have imagined. She drank in the cheers, the celebration of her new marriage, and then the sound seemed to fade. The only thing she was conscious of now was Carla. Her smile, the warm brown skin of her bare shoulders, the smell of her perfume. They held each other and danced, their bodies moving in harmony, effortlessly, to each note of the music. Together—the two of them. The way Séraphine hoped they would always be.

After the first dance had finished, and Séraphine and Carla had taken a playful bow to the crowd, the wedding band struck up a Supremes tune. Other guests joined the newlyweds on the dance floor, and it began to fill.

"Join me?" Euan asked Charlie, holding his hand out to her.

She smiled. "I think there's a spot on my card."

From the dinner table where they'd been seated, he led her onto the dance floor and brought her in close to him, running a hand over her hair.

"It's not too late to change your mind, you know," he said quietly.

Charlie pulled back and smiled.

"Euan—I've accepted an offer on my flat, given in my notice at work and I've taken on a new restaurant—that you're building. So I think it probably is too late."

"Well, yes, when you put it that way," Euan said. "Please don't back out."

She laughed. "I won't. I can't wait to get started. I've been dreaming up menus for days now."

"But, in all seriousness, what I meant was, it's not too late to change your mind about moving in with me." He looked her in the eye. "You said when I asked you the first time that you weren't ready. I want to be sure that this time you are."

"I don't know if I'll ever be completely ready," she said. Thoughts had drifted into her mind as she'd shown potential buyers around her London flat. She didn't want to lose her independence. She wasn't sure if she could ever trust a man, even Euan, one hundred percent. She'd settled into her own way of doing things. And yet, those doubts and worries had drifted out of her head as quickly as they'd come. "But I do know it's what I want. In fact there's nothing I want more."

"That's good enough for me," he said.

He leaned in and there, on the dance floor, with a dozen other couples around them, they kissed—and the uncertainties that had been there for both of them since the day they'd met didn't seem to matter anymore.

# Epilogue

*In the garden of the riverside chateau, surrounded by spring flowers, we tasted the raspberry and chocolate tarts that we'd made. After a week of studying at Madame Yvonne's patisserie school, we were now reaping the rewards.*

Adam smiled as he read the magazine on Kat's sofa. "The course sounds amazing. How come you didn't bring me anything back? I'm getting hungry reading about it."

"Those tarts would never have lasted the journey. Or any longer than five minutes with me and Letty, in fact. But don't worry, it's all in here—" She pointed to her head. "I'll make some for you and Zoe next weekend." She sat down next to him, curling her body in toward his. He put his arm around her and kissed her hair gently.

"I suppose I can wait," he joked.

"And as for where Séraphine lives, you'll see that for yourself soon enough."

They'd arranged to visit Séraphine and Carla in the early autumn, in their new house in Bordeaux. Zoe hadn't stopped talking about the trip, and Leo hadn't stopped talking about the airplane.

Séraphine had found a job at a language school in the city, and Carla was setting up a bakery nearby. Séraphine had told Kat at the wedding that she and Carla still went back to see her parents for Sunday lunch each week, but moving out of the village had given her some breathing space. Contrary to everyone's expectations, Guillaume had been the one who had stayed on in the village, working at a bike repair shop and rehearsing with a new band.

Charlie and Euan had been invited to Bordeaux as well, but for the time being they were much too busy. Charlie had her hands full getting ready for the opening of The Dome, her new restaurant, and praying that the food critics would be kind. She'd been making changes to Euan's flat, too, including—after finding her brand-new high heels in shreds—an outdoor kennel for Bagel.

Despite their schedules, Charlie and Kat made time to meet every Saturday afternoon at the Seafront—a sacred appointment that Euan and Adam knew to stay well away from. There, over scones, they'd talk, and that time was precious to both of them.

Kat got up and went to the kitchen to put the kettle on. As it boiled, she got milk from the fridge. Pinned to the fridge door, among recipes torn from magazines and Leo's paintings, was a card with a photograph of a lavender field on the front. She took off the magnet holding it, and flipped it over.

Inside, in pretty, curled handwriting, was a message:

Kat,

Whether here in France, or at home in the tearoom, you bring sunshine into my life. What you might not realize is that, one way or another, you always have. Thank you for finding a way to forgive me.

Letty x

Kat brushed away a happy tear, and put the postcard back.

Hello,

I hope you enjoyed meeting Kat, Charlie, Letty and Séraphine in *The Seafront Tearoom*. All the women are passionate about baking, and it's one of the things that brings them together. Here are some recipes for the cakes and treats that help shape their relationships, so that you can share them with your own friends and family.

Happy baking (and brewing)!

Love, Vanessa x

# Letty's Classic English Scones

## MAKES 12 SCONES

*8 oz self-raising flour, plus extra for dusting*
*1 tsp cream of tartar*
*½ tsp bicarbonate of soda*
*½ tsp salt*
*1½–2 oz butter*
*¼ pint of milk*

Oven: 425 °F for 12–15 minutes

You'll also need: a pastry cutter with a diameter of about 5 cm; plenty of jam and clotted cream—plus friends to share these with!

Lightly butter a baking sheet.

Sift the flour, cream of tartar, bicarbonate of soda or baking soda and salt into a bowl together. Rub or cut in the butter, rubbing the mixture until it forms large crumbs with a flaky texture.

Mix in the milk and stir to form a soft dough.

Roll out to a thickness of around 1 cm and cut into rounds with your pastry cutter.

Arrange the scones on the baking sheet fairly close together, and dust them with flour.

Bake until they rise and turn golden.

*Serve! These really are best when eaten warm from the oven with a good dollop of cream and jam.*

## *Séraphine's Magnificent Madeleines*

### MAKES 24 MADELEINES

*2 eggs, separated*
*4 oz caster sugar*
*4 oz unsalted butter, melted*
*Finely grated rind and juice of half a lemon*
*4 oz self-raising flour*

Oven: 375 °F. Bake in the center of the oven for 20 minutes.

You'll also need: two madeleine trays (or muffin tins/jam tart trays will work too)

Lightly butter the madeleine tins.

Beat the egg yolks and sugar until they are thoroughly mixed but still bright yellow.

Beat in the melted butter, lemon juice and rind.

Sift the flour over the surface and fold in.

Stir the egg whites with a fork, and then beat them well into the mixture.

Spoon a small amount of mixture into each mold and bake in the center of the oven.

Cool slightly in the molds before gently easing out onto wire racks to cool.

*Enjoy them with a hot drink while they are still warm.*

# Charlie's Deliciously Indulgent Florentines

## MAKES 12 FLORENTINES

2½ oz butter

4 oz caster sugar

4 oz flaked almonds, chopped

2 oz sultanas

6 glace cherries, chopped

1 oz cut mixed peel

1 tbsp single cream

6 oz plain chocolate

Oven: 350 °F for 10 minutes

You'll also need: three baking sheets, parchment paper, palette knife/spatula.

Line your baking sheets with parchment paper.

Melt the butter in a large pan and stir in the sugar. Boil them together for one minute, then remove the pan from the heat.

Stir in the rest of the ingredients, except for the chocolate.

Drop small rounded heaps of the mixture onto the baking sheet, keeping them far apart, one in each corner, as they will spread quite a lot.

Bake until they are golden.

Using your palette knife or spatula, nudge the Florentines into their classic circular shape, then leave them to harden for five minutes.

Transfer them to a wire rack, taking care not to break them.

Leave them to cool.

Melt the chocolate in a heatproof bowl over a saucepan of boiling water.

Coat the flat side of each Florentine with chocolate, then trace a fork over it to make the distinctive wavy pattern.

Leave them to set.

*Dive in!*

# Kat's Perfect Afternoon Tea

### YOUR BREW

Choose your equipment carefully—a glazed china or earthenware teapot is best—and your tea even more so. A classic black tea from India or Ceylon, a Darjeeling or Assam, is a nice place to start, unblended so you can appreciate the flavor. If you are already a tea aficionado and fancy trying something different, then jasmine is a refreshing alternative, and some people enjoy the smoky flavors of Lapsang souchong.

### SETTING THE SCENE

A tiered cake stand makes the perfect centerpiece. Otherwise, use your best crockery and make it a little more special with lace doilies, folded napkins or personalized nameplates—edible names piped onto gingerbread are a nice touch. Charity shops and car boot sales are great places to find reasonably priced chinaware—mismatched floral teacups and saucers are ideal. Silver cake slices for serving lend a real sense of ceremony.

Soundtrack—music is a must for a memorable afternoon tea. For a 1920s, Gatsby-esque atmosphere, opt for jazz; or for a wartime feel, choose Frank Sinatra and Ella Fitzgerald tracks.

Most important of all, invite the best of friends—afternoon tea should be served with fine company and plenty of laughter.

*Enjoy!*

*Readers Guide*

# THE
# SEAFRONT
# TEAROOM

# Discussion Questions

1) Which character do you most identify with and why? Which character do you find most compelling? Why do you think the author chose the setting that she did?

2) The women in this book quickly bond and support one another through tough times. How easy or difficult is it to make friends and maintain friendships as an adult?

3) The Seafront becomes "home away from home" for several folks, including those who live near it. Do you have a place that serves a similar purpose in your life?

4) One underlying theme of the book is that people can most change when they enter a different environment. Do you believe this to be possible? Have you ever had such an experience?

5) Early on we learn that Charlie and Pippa don't get along. Then we see the tension during Charlie's initial visit with Pippa and her young family. Who do you think is in the wrong, or is this classic sibling rivalry? Do you think Charlie's decision to stay at a hotel was the right one?

6) When Séraphine is teaching Letty how to bake a tarte tatin, she shares the story of how the beloved dessert accidentally came to be. Letty comments on how sometimes

the best things come from accidents. Upon reflection, who or what do you think Letty is thinking of? And do you feel that she is being honest with herself?

7) Charlie is given a high-priority writing assignment. While she's utterly excited about it and sees what an opportunity it is, she calls her boss, Jess, to tell her that a family emergency has come up. She tells Jess that she'll still be able to meet deadlines and can write from where she is, but Jess doesn't think the setup is ideal. What does Charlie's decision to stay by her sister's side actually say about her feelings toward Pippa, family and, ultimately, her career? And do you think her decision is independent of or a reflection of her breakup?

8) What do you think possesses Charlie to open up to Euan the first time they hang out together? She later says that when she's with him she doesn't have to pretend to be someone she's not. Is it him or the context in which they meet that makes her feel this way?

9) When Kat returns from Scotland with Leo, she beats herself up for leaving Leo in the care of Jake—someone who cannot take care of himself. Is she being too hard on herself or is she finally seeing Jake for who he is?

10) Letty decides to share a truth after a long-buried secret is unearthed. Her decision has serious implications on the lives of others, not to mention her relationships with these people. What do you think of her decision and the approach she took in both hiding and then revealing the truth?

11) At different times and in different ways, Charlie and Séraphine struggle with the expectations their families have
placed on them. Meanwhile, Kat struggles to accept a
family she didn't know existed. At first glance the author
illustrates that families can be complicated, but then we
see things shift once the women make a choice. What is
the author saying, or what is the takeaway here?

12) Both Charlie and Kat are forced to confront the men who
betrayed and disappointed them. What did you think of
the approach that each took?